Any Chance You Can Take

The Chances
Book 9

Emily E K Murdoch

Dragonblade Publishing, Inc. is an imprint of Kathryn Le Veque Novels, Inc.
P.O. Box 23
Moreno Valley, CA 92556
ceo@dragonbladepublishing.com

Produced in the United States of America

First Edition November 2025
Trade Paperback Edition

ARE YOU SIGNED UP FOR DRAGONBLADE'S BLOG?

You'll get the latest news and information on exclusive giveaways, exclusive excerpts, coming releases, sales, free books, cover reveals and more.

Check out our complete list of authors, too!

No spam, no junk. That's a promise!

Sign Up Here

www.dragonbladepublishing.com

Dearest Reader;

Thank you for your support of a small press. At Dragonblade Publishing, we strive to bring you the highest quality Historical Romance from some of the best authors in the business. Without your support, there is no 'us', so we sincerely hope you adore these stories and find some new favorite authors along the way.

Happy Reading!

CEO, Dragonblade Publishing

Additional Dragonblade books by
Author Emily E K Murdoch

The Chances Series
A Fighting Chance (Book 1)
A Second Chance (Book 2)
An Outside Chance (Book 3)
Half a Chance (Book 4)
A Chance in a Million (Book 5)
Not a Chance in Hell (Book 6)
An Eye for the Chance (Book 7)
A Sporting Chance (Book 8)
Any Chance You Can Take (Book 9)

Dukes in Danger Series
Don't Judge a Duke by His Cover (Book 1)
Strike While the Duke is Hot (Book 2)
The Duke is Mightier than the Sword (Book 3)
A Duke in Time Saves Nine (Book 4)
Every Duke Has His Price (Book 5)
Put Your Best Duke Forward (Book 6)
Where There's a Duke, There's a Way (Book 7)
Curiosity Killed the Duke (Book 8)
Play With Dukes, Get Burned (Book 9)
The Best Things in Life are Dukes (Book 10)
A Duke a Day Keeps the Doctor Away (Book 11)
All Good Dukes Come to an End (Book 12)

Twelve Days of Christmas
Twelve Drummers Drumming
Eleven Pipers Piping
Ten Lords a Leaping
Nine Ladies Dancing
Eight Maids a Milking

Seven Swans a Swimming
Six Geese a Laying
Five Gold Rings
Four Calling Birds
Three French Hens
Two Turtle Doves
A Partridge in a Pear Tree

The De Petras Saga
The Misplaced Husband (Book 1)
The Impoverished Dowry (Book 2)
The Contrary Debutante (Book 3)
The Determined Mistress (Book 4)
The Convenient Engagement (Book 5)

The Governess Bureau Series
A Governess of Great Talents (Book 1)
A Governess of Discretion (Book 2)
A Governess of Many Languages (Book 3)
A Governess of Prodigious Skill (Book 4)
A Governess of Unusual Experience (Book 5)
A Governess of Wise Years (Book 6)
A Governess of No Fear (Novella)

Never The Bride Series
Always the Bridesmaid (Book 1)
Always the Chaperone (Book 2)
Always the Courtesan (Book 3)
Always the Best Friend (Book 4)
Always the Wallflower (Book 5)
Always the Bluestocking (Book 6)
Always the Rival (Book 7)
Always the Matchmaker (Book 8)
Always the Widow (Book 9)
Always the Rebel (Book 10)
Always the Mistress (Book 11)
Always the Second Choice (Book 12)
Always the Mistletoe (Novella)

Always the Reverend (Novella)

The Lyon's Den Series
Always the Lyon Tamer

Pirates of Britannia Series
Always the High Seas

De Wolfe Pack: The Series
Whirlwind with a Wolfe

Noble titles throughout English history have, at times, been more fluid than one might think. Women have inherited, men have been gifted titles by family or gained them through marriage, and royals frequently lavished titles or withdrew them as reward and punishment.

The elder Chance brothers in this series agreed to split the four titles in their family line during the Regency era, rather than the eldest holding all four. It is a decision that defines their brotherhood, and their very different personalities.

Now with the next generation, one Chance father has allowed his son to inherit his title before his own demise, echoing kings and queens who have abdicated their titles throughout history. Perhaps his brothers, the uncles of this next generation, will follow suit...

Get ready to meet a family that is more than happy to scandalize Society...

Chapter One

September 1, 1840

IT WASN'T THAT Miss Jessica Chance would rather have been anywhere else than here. There were lots of places in the world. Surely, some of them, though it was difficult to believe, were worse.

And so she resigned herself to the most difficult challenge a wallflower could endure: a family party.

"Are you sure you don't want to—"

"No, thank you," Jessica said firmly—or at least, as firmly as she could manage.

She was not one to speak firmly. Her voice quavered, even as her mother looked at her down her aquiline nose, full of concern.

"It's only a conversation about the latest novel by—"

"I'm going for a walk," Jessica said, launching upright from the sofa as two of her cousins stared.

Did they know how painful it was, when they stared like that? Did they understand how mortifying it was, to be the only one not to enjoy attention, not to want noise, not to wish for all eyes to be upon her?

Every step across the library floor of Stanphrey Lacey appeared to take an age, but somehow, Jessica managed it. Leaning against the wall in the corridor and wishing to goodness that she had managed to persuade her mother to leave her in London, she attempted to consider her next move.

The place was heaving. Stanphrey Lacey, the ancestral home of the noble Chance family, was large, indeed, but with her four siblings, three sets of uncles and aunts, and eleven cousins—plus a few of their spouses—it was difficult to find peace and quiet.

The garden.

Yes, Jessica thought with rising hopes. The gardens were surely sufficiently large to avoid a great number of people.

Passing two maids and a footman on her way to the front door, servants at whom Jessica did not look and hoped to goodness would simply pretend she did not exist, she finally breathed in the cool air of approaching autumn and felt her tension start to melt from her shoulders.

This had been a most excellent idea. All she had to do was cross the drive—a majestic one, but that would surely only take five or ten minutes to accomplish—then she could lose herself in the rose garden, or the water garden, or the long drive to the fountain, or perhaps even into the grove of silver birch trees that crept around one side of Stanphrey Lacey Forest. There, she could be quiet alone.

If anyone had been watching from the windows of the impressive Jacobean manor house, and Jessica fervently hoped no one was, they would see a rather unremarkable individual.

Jessica was well aware of this and thanked her stars on a daily basis that she had none of the striking beauty of her cousin Lady Lilianna, or the memorable hair of her sister Irene, or the dramatic figure of her sister Teddy.

No, she was a pale imitation of her mother. Edith Chance, Viscountess Pernrith, had been a striking beauty of the *ton* in her day. In truth, her mother's beauty had not dimmed with age; it had merely grown into a different direction.

But that was all to the good. *The fact that I am plain, that is,* Jessica thought as she marched as swiftly as she could across the drive. No one would miss her. Her dull, brown curls were unremarkable, which was precisely how she wanted them, and no one would—

"Good morning!"

The greeting had come from nowhere, and Jessica was so

thrown by the sudden voice that she almost tipped over.

Turning and glaring before she could stop herself, Jessica snapped, "What?"

"I-I said, *good morning,*" said the woman who had somehow appeared to her left.

Jessica blinked. The woman was unfamiliar—no, not unfamiliar, just not family. Recognition slowly arrived…of course, it was Kathleen. Katherine? No, surely, Kathleen. The woman who had married her cousin Leopold so recently.

Oh, hell, more family to gawp at me.

"It is still morning, isn't it?" said the woman, who raised a brow at the man whose arm she was holding. But then her lips parted in a small smile.

Jessica swallowed, hating that her nerves were so potent, hating that she could not even return for a holiday to the family home without being accosted by a stranger. A stranger who seemed to think Jessica was too stupid to know the time of day.

"Yes," said Leopold, who was grinning foolishly like a maniac and went so far as to wink at his spouse.

'Yes'? Jessica blinked, unsure why he had pronounced such a word. Yes—what did he mean? Had he asked her something? Oh, right. The fact that it was still morning. Were they *both* laughing at her now, even her own flesh and blood?

His new wife appeared desperate to make conversation, something that Jessica wished she wouldn't do. "Such a pleasant day."

And before Jessica could tame her tongue or marshal her thoughts into any particular order—any order at all—a plethora of random sounds erupted from her mouth. "No, it isn't. No, I'm not—no!"

Oh, hell. Perhaps if she had managed to keep her voice down, her erratic nonsense would not have mattered. But nerves had tightened Jessica's throat, causing the noise to be more a shout than a whisper.

And she knew what was coming.

Yes, here was the blush. Jessica did not need to see it to know that her cheeks were turning a nice, rich crimson, not unlike the damask of the second drawing room here at Stanphrey Lacey, though her face would look less resplendent. More…ridiculous.

Well, that was enough embarrassment for one morning. Hopefully.

Not saying another word and hoping to goodness that neither her cousin nor his wife would ever mention this again, Jessica turned on her heel and started marching away from them.

They might have called after her. Jessica wasn't sure. There was too much blood pumping through her ears, her pulse a roar, to hear anything.

Stupid, stupid!

Why couldn't she just have a normal conversation? Why did her nerves always overcome her? It was bad enough that she was ignored by half the family and pitied by the rest because of her unfashionable looks and her chronic shyness—but now she had to go about shouting nonsense at them?

When Jessica turned into the rose garden, she dropped onto a stone bench, relieved by the feel of its cool surface through her skirts. Her whole body appeared to be on fire, which was most inconvenient.

And then she froze.

"—haven't seen much of her, to tell the truth," came a voice from the other side of the hedge. They must have been in the White Garden. "I suppose she is here?"

That was her cousin Lilianna; Jessica would recognize that imperious voice anywhere.

Not that she minded Lilianna's remarkable belief in herself. It was something that Jessica could only hope for—but it did mean that her cousin's opinions were often stated as fact. And that her voice carried.

"I've met her, then?"

The voice that responded was not one Jessica recognized, but that was starting to become an occupational hazard in this family. Why, there had been four Chance weddings in the last year!

They had all thought Thomas Chance, now the Duke of Cothrom, had been rather radical to get wed so swiftly, but it had become a veritable trend.

"You have met her, but you probably do not recall her," Lilianna's voice said kindly. "She's not really the memorable sort."

Jessica wrinkled her nose. Whomever they were talking about, she was not very memorable. Poor woman.

"Jessica…" mused the masculine voice, causing a shot of disappointment and confusion to rip through her as she sat on the stone bench. "No, I cannot say I could pick her out of a crowd."

"I'll point her out at dinner," came Lilianna's voice, quieter now as footsteps crunched on gravel. They were walking away. "But you may need to be introduced a third time."

Whatever else her cousin and her husband said, Jessica did not hear. She did not need to.

Shame, piping hot and burning, slid down her throat into her chest, twisting painfully in her stomach and making her legs feel weak.

It wasn't as though she did not know she was thought of in such a way by her family. Her three sisters and brother could forget she was sitting in a room if she was quiet for more than five minutes. Which she often was.

Miss Jessica Chance was not frequently invited to parties, despite being the eldest of her sisters. She was often accidentally missed off the invitation to card parties. When she arrived at dinners, forced there by her mother, an extra place often had to be added, the hostess with pink cheeks.

Her arrival at Almack's, a place that simply wasn't what it had been, had been ignored. It was only after her parents had actually put something in the newspapers—Jessica closed her eyes in horror at the mere memory—that people appeared to realize that she had been there.

So yes, Jessica was no fool. She was a wallflower, and a good one.

But to hear such a thing from her own cousin...

"You look a little dour."

Jessica smiled as she looked up to see her sister Irene approaching her, a gun resting over her shoulder in that nonchalant way that her sister had.

Oh, what I wouldn't give to have such...such presence.

No, it wasn't that. It was confidence. An innate knowledge within herself that anyone speaking with Irene was going to enjoy the experience.

Precisely how her sister had gained such a thing and Jessica herself had not, she did not know. It was most unfair.

"I do not look dour," Jessica said smartly.

Apparently, speaking smartly did not create confidence. Irene grinned kindly and sat beside her sister, ensuring that the gun—not loaded; they had all been shooting for so long they knew how to handle weapons—did not poke Jessica in the ribs.

"You do too," said Irene conversationally whilst tugging a shawl around her narrow frame, as though accusing one's older sister of looking dour was a perfectly natural thing to do. "Why? I thought you would have come hunting with us this morning."

Jessica had considered it. She had wanted to go. She had told both Irene and their cousin Lucy that she'd wished to go with them.

They had seemed to forget about her. When she had come downstairs eagerly in her riding habit, she'd been told that they had already gone.

"I decided not to," she lied quietly, twisting her hands in her lap.

"This house party is supposed to be an opportunity for us all to relax," said her sister, nudging her arm. "But you do not look relaxed."

The remark almost made Jessica laugh.

Relax? When her life appeared to be slipping past her in the dullest of parades, and she did not appear to be able to stop it?

She was four and twenty, for goodness's sake. Four of her

cousins were married, and she had never danced with a gentleman to whom she wasn't related. The Chances were pairing off, finding their perfect partners, and she was still struggling to catch the eye of a gentleman long enough at a ball to gain a single dance.

Not that she could say these things. These were not words you said.

She was a Chance. She was supposed to belong to one of the most powerful, the most prestigious house in the whole of England.

It was just... Well. Sometimes, she did not feel as though she belonged anywhere.

"I suppose you're here avoiding his lovesick nonsense," Irene said quietly, breaking through Jessica's thoughts.

Jessica blinked. "I am?"

Irene grinned. "I told him yesterday he should have come. It doesn't matter that he's not family."

Jessica blinked again. "He's not?"

Strange, she had always thought of all her cousins as family...because they were. Even if they were not siblings, they had seen each other so much as children, her cousins were almost like siblings. And every year, they all came to Stanphrey Lacey, the seat of the head of the family, the Duke of Cothrom, and they spent part of the summer together.

And they were most definitely family. Who Reeny could be talking about, she could not fathom.

But her sister was looking at her as though she were completely mad. "Of course he's not. How on earth would Wilfred be part of the family?"

Oh. "Oh," Jessica said aloud, cheeks pinking at her mistake. "No, of course not."

Somehow she had gotten lost in her own thoughts again and the conversation had moved on. They were no longer talking about a cousin—they were speaking of Irene's closest friend, His Grace Wilfred Zouch, Duke of Aynor.

"Yes, I told Wilfred, if I had been able to gain an invitation for him to accompany us at the family house party again this year, at least we'd have one person here who wasn't going to get married by the end of it." Irene chortled with a sparkle in her eyes.

Jessica smiled weakly.

It was kind of her sister not to include her in that category: people who were not going to get married anytime soon.

No one said it. The rest of the family was very kind, when they remembered that she was there. Which was not often.

And it was not as though Jessica had anyone particularly in mind. Her time in Society had not exactly been short. At her age, she had spent six Seasons out and had not received a single proposal. She'd not received any invitations, not purely for herself.

She was not the sort of woman, Jessica had realized when very young, who was likely to attract a man.

And perhaps that is fine, she thought as Irene chattered away about her best friend.

"—can't shoot to save his own life—"

Spinsters existed. Even older bachelors. Perhaps some of them were satisfied with that.

Perhaps not everyone could expect romance. Perhaps not every woman had the fairytale ending. Perhaps there were some people who could enjoy a great number of things in life, but matrimony was not one of them.

If there were such people, Jessica was certain she was one of them.

"—don't you think?" Irene finished, her eyebrow arched.

It was not panic, precisely, that filled Jessica's lungs, but it was not far off. What had her sister been saying—what was she supposed to be agreeing with?

"Erm," she said aloud, as though that would buy her some time.

Irene's expression was far too knowing. "You complain a great deal about being ignored for someone who frequently ignores me, you know."

It was all Jessica could do to prevent the prickling heat in her cheeks from burning her sister by proximity. Even though it was a fair remark.

"I am sorry," she said quietly, hating every syllable that she had to utter. "It's just...I... When I think about... about..."

Shame burned through her.

What was wrong with her? She wasn't truly anxious, not like their Aunt Florence, who sometimes slipped into a stammer thanks to her shyness, even with family. It wasn't that she did not wish to speak, or entertain, or say something witty as their sister Theodora often did to make the whole company laugh.

Laugh with her, that was. Not laugh at her.

But every time Jessica attempted to find the right words, they slipped through her fingers. Her sheer ability to embarrass herself or be ignored combined to make Jessica assume she was going to be disregarded completely, and then when she wasn't—on the rare occasion—she had absolutely no idea what to say.

It was maddening.

"Come on," said Irene brusquely, standing up, readjusting the gun over her shoulder, and offering out her hand.

Jessica, despite being the elder of the two sisters, obeyed without a sound. Well, what was the point in arguing? This was a house party; time to oneself was at a premium. To be honest, she was surprised she had managed so much time as this.

Irene slipped Jessica's hand into the crook of her arm, and they started walking through the rose garden back toward the house.

"I would imagine it will be luncheon soon," her sister said, "and Nicholls mentioned something about a picnic on the lawn— there, look!"

Jessica looked, and her spirits rose, despite herself.

It was a spectacular sight.

Oh, Stanphrey Lacey itself was a beautiful building, there was no doubt about that. A great number of architects had apparently written to Uncle William asking if they could come and study the great building, and it was remarkably fine, with its redbrick and its towers, the spiraling chimneys and the sheer amount of glass.

But it was the gardens that she most liked, and the lawn at the back. The splendidly planted borders still buzzing with bees and butterflies as the autumnal color roared through the gardens were simply spectacular.

What was even more spectacular was how the housekeeper had organized their outdoor luncheon.

Blankets, and rugs, and small tables, and even some of the comfortable chairs from the west drawing room had all been brought out. There were platters of sandwiches and heaps of cakes, fruit in punch bowls and little sausages, slices of sponge cake and gallons, it appeared, of the most wonderful lemonade. Parasols and umbrellas were dotted about the place to shield the ladies from the sun—not that Irene seemed that bothered, as she passed her gun off to a footman and then threw herself onto a rug that was devoid of shade—and footmen quietly moved about the place, refilling this person's glass and helping another to a sandwich.

Jessica grinned. Say what she would about the family, and she always thought a great deal about them, there was something wonderful about being a Chance.

As long as she could get through this luncheon without embarrassing herself. Easier said than done.

"Come, sit by me," said Irene cheerfully, "and have a glass of lemonade."

Well, that was a start. She could hardly embarrass herself by drinking a glass of lemonade.

More and more Chance cousins were drifting across the lawn from the house, the gardens, the forest where some of them had gone hunting that morning, and soon, a little breeze of elegant chatter mingled around them.

Jessica sighed, a smile still lilting on her lips. Perhaps she had been overly concerned about this year's house party. Perhaps it would be a gentle succession of good meals, light conversation she could listen in on, and peace and quiet. She would eventually find a nook no one else had remembered, and there she could—

Her thoughts were interrupted by the gasps of her large family.

Jessica started, almost spilling her lemonade in her hurry to ascertain whether or not it was her at whom her cousins, aunts, and uncles were gasping. But no—there was a man on horseback approaching.

A man, on horseback?

It was most irregular. For a start, visitors to Stanphrey Lacey were far and few between. Outsiders simply did not get invited to the Chance ancestral home.

Furthermore, this was the back of the house. Guests who were invited dismounted at the front and were welcomed by the butler guiding them through the house if they were deemed worthy. But this man—this man had simply ridden around the side of the house, refusing to dismount!

Jessica glanced at her sister, but Irene shrugged, her eyes wide in fascination.

Clearly, something had occurred: something dreadful. *What news did this man bring?*

A low murmur of speculation was now rippling through the lunching Chances, and Jessica could a few theories just out of hearing.

"Someone unwell—"

"Parliament collapsed—"

"News from France—"

Jessica did not heed the theories. She was too busy looking at the man.

He had dismounted by now and looked a mite puffed, though elegantly dressed and clearly of some means. Why a man of means had not taken a carriage, rather than ride all the way— presumably—from London, she could not think.

He was tall—tall, and broad, his shoulders impressive and his stature regal. He had dark hair, almost black, and he was attired in riding clothes that looked well-made and therefore expensive.

When he turned around to look at them all, there were some giggles from the younger of her cousins.

Jessica could not blame them. He was remarkably handsome. Those dark eyes, flashing with what had to have been intelligence and charm. That mouth, intensely kissable—not that she would ever do such a thing, of course!

But beyond the mere facts of his appearance, there was something…something very proud, something very determined about his air. It was intoxicating.

Jessica shook herself slightly, taking care not to spill her lemonade. Silliness, that was all her thoughts were. Silliness. The man would never notice her. That was the occupational hazard of being from such a large family of beauties. There were six other Chances, more if he found women her mother and aunts' age attractive, by whom he would be captivated before his eyes even glanced over her—and his gaze would continue on by.

Besides, the man could not have been perfect. There was surely some fault. Perhaps his voice was squeaky, or he was not as charming as he looked.

"I hope you do not mind," said the man in a low, melodious voice that thrummed deep within Jessica. "I thought I would invite myself, as I have an important errand to perform."

Jessica's lips parted in astonishment, and it appeared she was not the only one.

Invite himself! To the Chance family house party—it was ridiculous. The man was out of his wits!

Instinctively, she looked over to her father Frederick Chance, Viscount Pernrith, who was seated two rugs away and had her mother nestled up to him. Jessica could see from the arch of his brow, the pinch of his full lips, that he looked just as astonished.

Why on earth was the man here?

"'An errand'?" The cool and calm voice of her Uncle William, Duke of Cothrom, rang out across the murmurs and brought the picnic luncheon to quiet. "Well, man, I suggest you carry out your errand and get back on your horse. I am afraid unless your name ends in Chance, or you are married to a lady once known by that name, you ought not to be here."

"That is precisely what I wished to come here to discuss," said the gentleman calmly, as though interrupting dowager dukes were something he did regularly in his spare time.

Jessica stared, transfixed, though she remembered in time to take a sip of her lemonade. It would not do to be caught staring at him.

"Tell me, where is Miss Jessica Chance?" the stranger asked pleasantly.

Jessica choked, lemonade roaring up her nose and causing her eyes to water.

What on earth had he said her name for?

Spluttering incoherently and wondering if she was truly to drown in her own lemonade, Jessica was relieved when hands grabbed the glass from her. When she coughed twice and managed to clear her throat, it was to see three things.

Firstly, that Irene had taken her lemonade from her, thank goodness.

Secondly, that the entire family was staring. *Oh, wonderful.*

Thirdly, that the handsome stranger who had interrupted the private house party was looking calculatingly the same direction everyone else was.

Oh, Lord.

Attempting not to sink into the ground and bury herself, Jessica tried to hold her head up high, as befit a Chance. After all, this was undoubtedly a mistake. The moment he looked at her, he would realize he was here for someone else. Her sister Gwendoline, perhaps, or—

"Miss Jessica Chance?" the man said, stepping forward and raising a quizzical brow.

A quizzical brow that should absolutely not have made her hot all over.

Well, there was nothing for it. Jessica rose to her feet, hating that there were splatters of lemonade down her gown, and tried to ape her cousin Lilianna's imperious expression.

"Yes," she said, her voice only faintly quavering. "Yes, I am Miss Jessica Chance. You… You have a message for me?"

For that could be the only reason that this strange gentleman had barged into a family party, Jessica reasoned silently as the man looked her up and down. Precisely who could have sent a message to her, she did not know, but there could be no other explanation.

The gentleman grinned. "Excellent. Will you marry me?"

A strange sort of ringing was echoing in Jessica's ears and she almost laughed. "Y-You know, I thought—I thought for a moment that you said—"

"Jessica," Irene breathed below her.

"—but you couldn't—you wouldn't…" Jessica tried to laugh to show just how ridiculous the whole thing was.

Because he couldn't have—he wouldn't have—no, it was her mortification at being singled out at all which had caused her to mishear that particular sentence.

Trying to ignore the gaping jaws of the whole Chance family, Jessica said in as clear a voice as possible, "Would you repeat that? I believe I misheard you."

And the strange gentleman smiled, and her stomach lurched just as he said, in a clear, ringing voice that could absolutely not be mistaken, "Miss Jessica Chance, will you marry me?"

Chapter Two

Twenty minutes earlier…

REGINALD HAD RIDDEN hard. He had ridden fast. He had ridden for an hour in the wrong direction after getting lost and he was tired.

And now he was about to put his plan into action.

The manor was far grander than he had expected—though he had heard a great deal about the annual house party that the prestigious Chance family enjoyed every September. The house loomed above him, welcoming and intimidating in equal measure.

Right. So. I am here. Now to find the lady.

"May I help you?" creaked an old voice.

Reginald looked down from his horse and saw what could only be a butler looking up at him. The man was elderly, yes, but there was a sharpness in his eye buried beneath a bushy brow that suggested he was not to be treated as a fool.

Which was all to the good. Reginald hated the thought that the family he was about to marry into would hire fools for servants.

"You may," Reginald said, not bothering to dismount from his horse. "I seek Miss Jessica Chance."

Apparently, that was not the right answer. It was certainly not the answer that the butler had expected.

"Miss… Miss Jessica Chance?" the servant repeated.

Reginald nodded.

Well, he was hardly going to explain his plan to a servant. He wasn't going to explain his plan to anyone. It was far less likely to succeed that way, and the odds were already pretty long.

But he had no choice. He needed respectability; he needed the connections that the Chance name offered.

He had to become a part of this family.

"Miss Jessica Chance? You are sure?" The butler, his head tilted ever so slightly, looked entirely unconvinced.

It was not an auspicious beginning.

Reginald had been very careful in his plan. He needed respectability, he needed to prevent any more scandal attaching to the Llyne estate, and so that meant marriage. Ideally, he would marry a woman with an excellent name, with a pedigree that could not be faulted.

The obvious candidate? The Chance family.

Now, he was no fool. Reginald knew that he could not propose matrimony to any of the daughters of the primary branch of the family. As far as he had heard, the Duke of Cothrom, or the "Dowager Duke of Cothrom," as everyone had come to call him—the man had given the title to his eldest son in a move that had shocked Society last year—had one daughter, and she was confident and proud.

Not the right target.

No, the more Reginald had thought about it, the more he realized that he needed a Chance bride who would feel grateful, who would happily accept his proposal in relief.

He needed a woman for whom no other man would offer.

It had not taken him long. Listening to conversations at White's, overhearing gossip at Almack's, and realizing that he had never encountered this particular Chance daughter, the decision had been easily made. After writing out a list of the remaining eligible Chance ladies, of course. A man had to put some consideration into these things.

<u>Miss Gwendoline Chance</u>—not officially out, might be too young. Described by the few who know her as a wallflower just like her older sister, which of course is a downside.

Lady Maude Chance—too old, though she is part of the most senior branch and so may therefore have more sway when it comes to influencing Society.

Lady Francesca Chance—rumors conflict about this one. Perhaps there is also a cousin Frank Chance with whom people confuse her? Far too dominant—I need a wife I can control.

Miss Theodora Chance—almost no dowry, as far as I can tell, and therefore doesn't have much social standing. Could she be enough to help with Peter? Probably not.

Miss Irene Chance—far too beautiful, likely to have many other suitors. No point in attempting to win her over; probably far too stuck-up for her own good.

Lady Lucy Chance—passionate prisoner reformer, perhaps far too close to comfort to the problem. Though on the bright side, might be able to help Peter if he got into a real pickle?

Miss Jessica Chance—by all accounts, dull as ditchwater and very shy. Should be easy enough to win over, as a wallflower, as she's had no attention. Poor thing.

Yes, he would marry Miss Jessica Chance. Then all his problems would be over with.

"Miss Jessica Chance," Reginald said aloud with a curt nod. "Where is she, please?"

"You were invited, sir?" the butler asked with a harumph.

Not exactly. Not if you defined "being invited" as receiving an invitation. No.

Reginald attempted his best, haughtiest expression. "I would not think you would ask the Baron Llyne such a thing."

The haughtiness did not work.

"I must ask all visitors to Stanphrey Lacey whether they have actually been invited," said the butler, not a little sternly. "You would be surprised and astonished, my lord, to discover that quite a number of people drop in on us here in the hope of an invitation being extended."

Blast. "And… And I suppose an invitation is rarely extended," Reginald hazarded, trying to ignore the tiredness in his bones.

The butler snorted. "It *never* has been, my lord."

Double blast. Well, that left Reginald only one choice, and it was not the one he would have originally chosen, but there did not appear to be any other option.

"Then I wish you good day, sir," Reginald said aloud, inclining his head to the servant.

The butler bowed in return—and that was when Reginald kicked his ankles into the sides of his steed, forcing the gelding into a sudden canter in the direction of the side of the house.

"My lord!"

Blood pumping through his veins, excitement pouring through him, Reginald knew what he was doing was madness, but he could see no other option.

If the butler was not going to permit him into the house by the front door, he would merely go around the side and enter by the back.

Not that it would be necessary. Ignoring the butler's shouts behind him, Reginald felt his stomach drop in awe as a vista of splendor swiftly appeared before him once his horse had cantered around the side of the house. The creature slowed as they approached a lawn covered in people.

People, and a picnic.

The Chances. Even now, Reginald could hardly believe that he had done such a thing. It was one thing to concoct such a ridiculous plan; it was quite another to enact it.

And here he was, sitting on a horse before the entire Chance family. Rich, clever, powerful—there was no end to the pleasantries one could say about this family.

And soon he would be part of it.

Just a twinge of guilt managed to surface, but Reginald pushed it down swiftly. What he was doing, it was not wrong. He was not promising marriage with no intention on following through. He truly was going to marry Miss Chance, the wallflower that no one talked about.

That was the whole point.

They were all staring. Only after a few heartbeats did Reginald realize why.

Ah, yes. The horse. That isn't the done thing, was it?

Dismounting as elegantly as he could—as elegantly as a man who had ridden on bad roads all the way from London could—Reginald looked around at the staring faces.

Dear God, but they were an impressive family. Every man handsome, every woman he could see pretty in their own way. A few of them were already married, he knew, and he would just have to hope that that one there, with the impressive blonde hair, was his Miss Chance.

Well, he'd soon find out, and there was only one way to do it.

"I hope you do not mind," said Reginald as cheerfully as he could manage. "I thought I would invite myself, as I have an important errand to perform."

Gasps echoed around the picnic and just for a moment, he felt wonderful. *This will be a family tale that they will tell for generations to come,* he thought as warmth rushed through him. *"Do you remember the time Grandfather rode up on a horse at Stanphrey Lacey and found Grandmother?"*

His attention flickered across the seated ladies. One of them was looking over at a man who must have been her father. She was plain, simply dressed, and clutching a very large glass of what looked like lemonade.

Reginald smiled to himself. Poor woman. The plainest in the family; that could hardly have been fun. He and the future baroness would be kind to her, once he was part of the family.

"'An errand'?" a voice rang out, a man's, confident and unflapped. "Well, man, I suggest you carry out your errand then get back on your horse. I am afraid unless your name ends in Chance, or you are married to a lady once known by that name, you ought not to be here."

The perfect way to broach the topic. "That is precisely what I wished to come here to discuss," said Reginald, hoping his nerves were not showing.

All he had to do was stay calm. He was so close to success, so close—all he had to do was say her name, and the beauty would reveal herself, and they would be married.

So. "Tell me, where is Miss Jessica Chance?" Reginald asked pleasantly.

The plain woman choked, lemonade splattering all over her gown and the gown of the beautiful woman seated beside her. The coughing splutters became so great that her sister, or cousin, hastily retrieved the lemonade glass from her hands and thumped her in a rather ungainly manner on her back.

Poor thing. Undoubtedly, she had hoped it was her name that would be called.

Reginald looked out across the rest of the dumbfounded party, and repeated, "Miss Jessica Chance?"

He spoke blithely, as though he turned up uninvited at family house parties all the time, and raised a quizzical brow.

Well, he wanted to impress her, whichever one she was.

And the most odd thing happened. The spluttering, lemon-ade-soaked woman slowly began to rise to her feet.

Reginald ensured his smile did not waver. Ah, so she was a sister of Miss Jessica Chance, then. Clearly, Miss Jessica Chance was not here right now, and this plain woman would lead him to her location.

"Yes," she said, her voice shaking as though she were about to be led out to the lions. "Yes, I am Miss Jessica Chance. You... You have a message for me?"

It was all he could do not to gawp in dismay.

This—*This* was Miss Jessica Chance? This was Miss Chance, wallflower? Part of the illegitimate line of the Chance family, her father a by-blow of the late duke? The eldest daughter and so, Reginald had calculated, the most desperate to be wed?

Of all the women he could have picked...he had to have chosen the least attractive?

Well, she wasn't entirely *unattractive*. She had the dark-chestnut curls that he always liked in a woman, and there was intelligence there in those sparkling yet fearful eyes.

Yes, there was something there. Not outstanding beauty, perhaps. But something.

Well, he had come all this way—and it was not as though it truly mattered which one he married. Miss Chance had just seemed, from his understanding, the most likely to accept him. Perhaps her paling in comparison to the others would only be another mark in his favor.

So, on with the question. Reginald grinned, as though he could not have been happier that his future bride was covered in lemonade. "Excellent. Will you marry me?"

Perhaps he should have expected the surprise. Perhaps the shock of the family was to be predicted. After all, it was not the most usual approach to courting.

What Reginald hadn't expected was for Miss Chance to laugh.

But she was—she was most definitely laughing. "Y-You know, I thought—I thought for a moment that you said—"

"Jessica," the woman clutching her glass of lemonade murmured.

"—but you couldn't—you wouldn't…" Miss Chance fell into peals of laughter again.

It was all Reginald could do to hold his head high.

She was laughing at him. At him. Here he was, proposing matrimony to her, and she thought it was amusing?

Shame, piercing and shocking, roared through him. It was just like it had been before; his family name would never recover. *He* would never recover. There would never be a societal event he could step into without hearing laughter, hearing the muttered rumors, knowing that all were staring because of the shame his brother would soon bring on them.

Was he never to be free of it? The whole point of the plan had been to reduce the future laughter, remove the stain upon his family. And instead, she—

"Would you repeat that?" Miss Chance was smiling, and

Reginald's stomach jolted. She was a tad striking when she smiled. "I believe I misheard you."

Reginald swallowed and tried to maintain his expression, as though he had not been cut to the quick by her derisive laughter.

The plan, man. Keep to the plan.

Clearing his throat and ensuring that his voice was clear, Reginald said loudly, "Miss Jessica Chance, will you marry me?"

He had not expected to need to propose more than once, but he supposed twice was acceptable. The trouble was, it appeared that he may need to do so a third time because after his second pronouncement, absolute chaos reigned.

Some of the Chance family were squabbling.

"No, he could not have meant—"

"Did he perhaps mean Irene? They look so similar, after all—"

Two of the Chance family of the older generation, perhaps Miss Chance's parents, were also arguing.

"—going to give him a ding about the—"

"No, Frederick, wait!"

A few of them were happily chattering away about something else, as though he did not exist.

"—and I told Frank, if she were truly serious about engineering—"

"Don't be daft, you know Society isn't ready to accept a lady engineer!"

And amongst it all, staring with parted lips and wide eyes as though she had never seen a gentleman before in her life, was Miss Jessica Chance.

Reginald grinned.

Well, he would be a fool if he didn't know what an attractive prospect he offered. Ignoring the family scandal, which few had heard about yet, he was tall, handsome, and titled. Any woman would be fortunate to have him.

Any woman, and especially Miss Jessica Chance. Why, she had none of the sparkling brilliance of her sister beside her, nor the presence of Lady Lilianna, or the gravitas of—

But she could move quickly.

"What the…?"

Miss Chance had stepped forward faster than Reginald had thought possible, and the wind had been completely knocked out of his chest as she had grabbed his arm and propelled him like a siege engine away from the picnicking family.

It was fortunate indeed that he was able to get his legs moving quickly enough, or she would have borne him to the ground.

Though now he came to think about it, as Miss Chance pulled him relentlessly across the lawn to a pretty sort of grove of trees, perhaps Reginald should have allowed himself to fall. Then Miss Chance would have fallen upon him, and they would have had to get married.

There was still time to try that.

"*What*," hissed the somehow not-out-of-breath-at-all Miss Chance, "are you playing at?"

Reginald straightened himself as she let go of his arm, pulling on his riding coat and trying to grin.

Of course, he should have expected this. So overcome by his proposal, it was natural that Miss Chance would wish to speak to him privately to ascertain just how besotted he was with her.

Well, he was happy to allow flatter her, even if he did not know her from Eve. Whatever he had to do to secure her.

"Miss Chance," he said with what he knew was a winning smile. "How wonderful to meet you at last."

That certainly surprised her. The woman hesitated, biting the corner of her lip and still staring, wide-eyed. "Why?"

Why?

Reginald was thrown. Ladies were not supposed to ask questions like that. She was supposed to be flattered, then accept whatever compliments he had decided to throw at her, then accept his proposal of marriage.

Goodness, he'd had no idea this was going to be so much work.

"Because I wish to marry you. As soon as possible, actually,"

Reginald said truthfully, trying to listen to whatever conversations were still occurring back at the picnic.

Perhaps he should have done this differently. Her father, perhaps, should have been the one with whom he spoke first. Yes, that was it. She was undoubtedly concerned that she had not gained the permission of her father.

Well, that would only take five minutes.

"Do excuse me. I will go and speak to your father and gain his permission for your hand, and I shall return posthaste," Reginald said with a wink.

He had not stepped two feet before there was a hand on his arm again.

"Why?" repeated Miss Chance, her eyes full of suspicion. "Why do you want to marry me?"

Ah—right, what was the speech I practiced on the ride again?

"I am sure it has not escaped your notice that you are most beautiful, most radiant, and most charming," Reginald said, trying to inject this tone with what he supposed was what affection sounded like. "It would be the greatest honor of my life if you would agree to marry me, Miss Chance. As soon as possible."

"Yes, you said that before," she said, cheeks now blazing red and her gaze fixed not so much on his face, but on his footwear. "But you don't know me. We've... We've never met before. How can you think me charming?"

She did not even ask about her beauty and radiance, Reginald noticed. Well, the woman was not blind. She must have known that she was hardly the most beautiful of her family. It was not a pleasant thought, but it was not unkind. It was merely a fact.

"You are charming," Reginald repeated, lost for additional words.

After all, what woman did not want to hear that she was beautiful, and charming, and all the rest? Truth be told, he had not prepared any other compliments.

He had not thought he would need them.

But apparently, Miss Chance was not to be so easily won.

"You and I have never met. Why... Why me, of all my cousins? Why any one of us?"

Blast it all to hell.

Reginald should have known he would have to answer this question sooner rather than later, and there were two approaches he knew he could take.

He could lie, and tell her that he had heard tell of her majestic elegance and found himself so attracted to her when they had met—she had forgotten, he would not hold it against her—that he simply knew he had to have her. His pretense at not knowing which one she was had been only to heighten the experience.

Or he could tell the truth.

Reginald grinned. "Oh, we have met, Miss Chance. It was on a warm night last summer at Lady Romeril's party when—"

"I was not invited to that party," Miss Chance said curtly.

He stared. "Not... Not invited?"

But he had done his research; he had been most thorough. The entire Chance family, all of them, had been invited to Lady Romeril's party.

The pink in her cheeks was a deep red now. "I...I was forgotten. She forgot to invite me."

If it had been in any other scenario, Reginald would have laughed. It was ridiculous; how could Lady Romeril have forgotten the eldest daughter of Viscount Pernrith?

But she was so...so forgettable. Miss Chance did not catch his eye, or smile at him, or flirt back. She did not patter pleasantries, or wear a gown that showed off her presumably impressive bosom. Her gown was not designed to attract attention, but rather to forego it.

Reginald swallowed. This was getting out of hand, and he needed a Chance bride as soon as possible. Announcing himself for Miss Chance before the whole family had been a mistake. Now he couldn't go back and request a different one.

Blast it all to hell.

"Perhaps it was not Lady Romeril's party, then. Perhaps

another—"

"No, we have not met," Miss Chance said quietly, and her focus was piercing as she finally lifted it to his own. "I want the truth, sir, whoever you are. The truth. Please."

And there was something in the way she'd said it—something that tugged at Reginald's heartstrings in a way he had not expected.

Something else had tugged too. Her eyes, when they looked like that…the intelligence in them, the determination…

Well, it was devastatingly erotic.

Reginald swallowed, his mouth somehow dry. *Focus, man! Focus on the plan. You are here to marry a Chance, and Miss Jessica Chance seemed like your best option.*

Do not lose her.

Allowing his shoulders to sag, Reginald decided on the truth. Not all of it. But enough to give Miss Chance sufficient reason to consider him to be truthful.

"I am Blakley. Reginald Blakley. I wish to improve my family's reputation. The Chance family is a noble and respected one, as you well know, and I can think of no better connection," he said quietly, and he found much to his discomfort that the shame in his voice was not aped, but genuine. "I need a good match, a marriage with a prominent family. I don't want to waste time with a matchmaker and I… I thought you would accept my offer."

And all of that was true. It was not the whole truth—wild horses would not drag that from Reginald.

That his brother was a traitor to the Crown.

That his sister had gone into hiding because of the soon-to-be scandal.

That Miss Chance was supposed to be dull and dour, and he did not want a wife who could bring more gossip to the Llyne estate.

That he was starting to wonder whether Miss Chance had not been the foolproof choice at all…

He would not tell her he was Baron Llyne yet. If she did not recognize him as the baron by name or face alone, that was for the best. But if he brought up the Llyne estate, well…perhaps news of his brother had already spread this far. He had to secure her promise before he'd test the waters when it came to the Llyne name.

"So, will you marry me?" Reginald asked brightly.

She would say *no*. He knew she would, and perhaps he could play the whole thing off with the Chances as a jest, an attempt to entertain them. Perhaps he could stay and charm one of her sisters or cousins. He would just have to hope they wouldn't spread the story in London once the house party was—

"Yes," said Miss Chance simply, her cheeks still pink. "Yes, I will marry you."

Chapter Three

September 2, 1840

"RIGHT," SAID JESSICA'S father heavily. "I'm going to need you to go through it one more time."

The strangest thing was happening, and Jessica could hardly believe it. Her family was all seated around the breakfast table and they were all looking at her. Moreover, they were all waiting for her to speak.

Well, not the whole family. Her Uncle William had, after grudgingly inviting her newly betrothed to stay the night, suggested that his brother Frederick—her father—might like to have the small eastern breakfast room the next day to 'talk things over.'

Jessica had not been there for that part of the conversation. After Mr. Blakley, her new betrothed, had marched them back to the picnic and announced she had accepted him, she had fled to her bedchamber and refused to come down for dinner.

Which, in hindsight, had probably instigated more questions than it had answered.

And now here she was, having to face her mother, her father, her three sisters, and her brother.

All of whom looked...shocked.

It was a little insulting, to tell the truth.

"There's nothing to tell," Jessica said quietly, sipping her chamomile tea and wondering just how quickly she could escape. "Mr. Blakley has proposed. I have accepted."

Her father stared, tugging a hand through his hair as though that would help. Then he turned to his wife with a lost expression.

Jessica almost smiled as her mother patted her father gently on the arm then turned to her eldest daughter. Her mother always thought there was an easy way out.

"Jessica," the Viscountess Pernrith said calmly. "What your father means is, we did not know that you and Mr. Blakley had formed an attachment."

Ah. Yes. Right.

It was not in her nature to keep secrets. There had never been any secrets to keep, when you were the wallflower of the family and you were never invited anywhere interesting.

No one whispered secrets to Jessica. No one took her into their confidence. Her sister Irene might have been her closest friend, had not her acquaintanceship with young Lord Wilfred—now the Duke of Aynor—many years ago blossomed into a deep friendship. Her two other sisters, Theodora and Gwendoline, were close to each other, and their brother, Michael, was a law unto himself.

So Jessica had never kept secrets—had never had anything that anyone particularly wanted to know.

And now she had to explain why a gentleman none of the family had ever heard of had ridden up to Stanphrey Lacey, uninvited, asked for her as if he did not recognize her, proposed marriage to her...and been accepted.

Jessica took another sip of tea as the weight of her family's gazes rested heavily on her.

"What I mean to say," her mother continued into the awkward silence, "is that I was not aware that you had ever *met* this man, this Mr. Blakley, before."

Oh, this was not going to be pleasant. "I had not," Jessica said quietly.

Her family reacted precisely as she could have predicted. Gwen and Teddy immediately rolled their eyes and started talking at the other end of the table, their older sister's marital adventures clearly not interesting.

Her brother, gangly and still growing into those long legs, snorted and stood, adjusting his lapels. "Well, congratulations, sister. Now I must be going. Cousin Leopold and Cousin Lucy are going hunting again and I don't want to miss out on the fine weather."

"You sit here, son. You'll be the head of this family one day, so you need to be aware of how a viscount must act in situations like this—"

Jessica watched as her brother soundly ignored their father, striding out of the room as a footman scrambled to open and close the door behind the future viscount in question.

Her parents exchanged a look, and just for a moment, Jessica was given a reprieve.

A reprieve that gave her time to think about... Well. About Mr. Blakley. The man had proposed marriage and appeared to mean it. This family of his, she had never heard of them before. Why did he want to improve their fortunes? Why on earth would he have chosen her?

Said reprieve did not last long.

"Jessica," her mother said firmly, fixing her with that look that told Jessica she was not going to escape this conversation, much as she might wish it. "Gentlemen do not generally travel forty miles on horseback to propose matrimony to a woman they have never met."

And yet he had.

She could not understand it, either. The whole thing made no sense to her, and yet it did not appear that it needed to. Mr. Blakley wished to marry her. She wished to marry him.

Oh, it was foolish of her—Jessica knew it, but she had said *yes* now and there was no point in taking it back.

Besides, this would undoubtedly be the best offer she would ever receive.

She was under no illusions; as a wallflower, there was little she could offer a gentleman in way of entertainment or charm.

She was not beautiful. She had a dowry, yes, but as part of the lowest branch of the Chance family—her father's illegitimacy still a stain, even though no one in the family ever mentioned it—it was nothing compared to that of her cousins' wealth. Her cousins, who had beauty and wealth and charm aplenty. Even her sisters, with similar prospects, offered more than she did. Tradition held the eldest daughter ought to secure a match before her younger sisters, but the Chance family was known for not always following tradition. No one would have objected to her younger sisters marrying before her.

Mr. Blakley was the first person to ever even notice her. He had offered marriage. She may not receive another offer. She had accepted.

She swallowed. He was handsome, too… But it had been a practical decision regardless.

It was not acceptable in her mother's eyes. The viscountess was fixing her with a stern glare. "Jessica."

"Yes, Mama," she said quietly.

"Jessica, you have just agreed to marry a man whom, I believe, you have never met before."

It took all of Jessica's strength to lift her eyes to her mother, but she managed it. "Yes, Mama."

"Why?" asked her father quietly.

For some reason, Jessica found herself blinking back tears. *Because I am always forgotten in this family,* she wanted to say but could not bring herself to. *Because I am a wallflower. Because I'm shy. Because no man has ever spoken three words to me other than that great-nephew of Lady Romeril, and he only did so as a favor to his aunt. And he thought I was Irene.*

Because there is something about this Mr. Blakley, was another answer she could absolutely not give.

Because I am determined to make him fall in love with me.

"You know that your Uncle William has invited your Mr. Blakley to stay."

Her father's words cut through her thoughts and Jessica almost dropped her teacup.

"'Stay'?" she said, lungs tightening.

No. No, Mr. Blakley could stay overnight, to be sure—it would have been cruel and most unmannered to send the man back to London on his horse the same day he'd arrived.

But to invite him to stay…to allow him to become part of the Chance house party…to face that man every day while she was here at Stanphrey Lacey…

She intended to make him fall in love with her after they had been married. That way, if she was not successful… Well, he would not be able to do anything about it. If he stayed here, and he got to know her before the wedding, and he realized what a complete bore she was… True, it was the lady's prerogative, not the gentleman's, to end an engagement, but that was a *suggestion*, really, not a law.

And another thought struck her mind like a weight. If she thought seeing him here at Stanphrey Lacey every day was too much—what was she going to do when they were wed?

It appeared her mother might have been having the same thought. "If you do not want him to stay for the rest of the three weeks, then perhaps you should not marry him, dear."

"No, I think it is an excellent idea," Jessica said as calmly as she could manage. Which was not very. "I-I think I shall retire upstairs, however, find a book, terrible headache, good morning."

"Jessica!"

She did not heed her mother's call. Already making it to the door at a rapid pace, Jessica desperately attempted to think what she would do next.

Hide.

Yes, that was it. It was often the wallflower's first instinct, and there was no better reason than a surprise future husband. Besides, this was Stanphrey Lacey; there would be a great number of places where she could hide where no one would even think to look. She had found them over the years of coming here every summer, the sorts of places that not even a servant frequented.

A small smile had crept over Jessica's face by the time she'd stepped into the corridor and started toward the east wing. Yes, she would hide. Give herself some time, help her to think about—

"There you are," came a voice that was both unfamiliar, and all too recognizable.

Mr. Blakley.

It was all Jessica could do not to tip over, her knees shaking and her ankles somehow entirely useless.

Not just because he was handsome. And he was handsome; somehow in the intervening hours, Jessica had forgotten *quite* how handsome he was. That quizzical brow, those sparkling eyes, the sharp edge of his jaw…

No, it was because he was here. She hadn't dreamed him. He really did exist. He really had ridden up to her family's estate and asked her to marry him.

And she had said *yes*.

"Are you quite well, Miss Chance?" Mr. Blakley inquired, his eyebrows drawing together in a look of genuine concern. "Would you like to sit down?"

Sit down, fall down—not that she should be horizontal any-where near this man. He oozed charm in a way that Jessica could not describe and had never seen outside a novel before.

Real men do not look like that.

"Here, take my arm," said Mr. Blakley without hesitation.

Jessica's lips parted, but no sound came out as the man took her hand—her actual hand!—and placed it in the crook of his arm before starting to walk down the corridor.

What—what is he…? How can this be happening?

"I suppose there's a room somewhere we can—ah."

Ah, indeed. Jessica's whole body roared with heat as Mr. Blakley opened a door and smiled at three of her cousins who had married this year, along with their spouses.

"Come to find the marrieds, eh?" Cousin Thomas grinned, his

hand territorially resting on his wife's huge belly. "We were just talking about baby names. Do you have any you favor?"

Jessica slammed the door shut.

"You do not wish to discuss baby names?" Mr. Blakley asked with an arched eyebrow. "Or perhaps you would rather keep your excellent ideas for our children?"

It was a good thing she was leaning upon the man's arm because at that moment, Jessica was ready to either faint or flee, neither of which was particularly easy with her hand trapped in his.

This is madness—madness! It was ridiculous enough that she had somehow managed to gain a betrothed from one day to the next, but to hear her betrothed talk about baby names of their children.

Children!

"I need to sit down," Jessica managed to say, as calmly as she could.

"And presumably not in there," Mr. Blakley said with a grin, glancing at the closed door. "Let us attempt to find an empty room, then."

It did not take long. Stanphrey Lacey was vast—her Uncle William had once said that he should have had twelve children to even attempt to fill the place up, and Jessica had seen her Aunt Alice hit him hard on the shoulder at such a remark.

The second door Mr. Blakley tried was the music room and it was empty, which was a surprise. She supposed Lilianna could not be practicing the pianoforte all the time.

"Here," said her betrothed softly as he closed the door behind them and led her over to a large armchair. "Sit."

It was an order that Jessica could actually obey and she grasped at it with both hands.

Metaphorically. What she actually did was release the man with both her hands, dropping like a stone into the chair and wishing to goodness that she had half the elegance of Gwen or half the composure of Teddy.

As it was…

"So," said Mr. Blakley with a wry smile, "I suppose I should properly introduce myself."

It was not as though we engaged in a great deal of conversation yesterday, Jessica thought awkwardly as she folded her hands in her lap, then unfolded them, then folded them again.

No, there had been a plethora of cousins surrounding them and probably attempting to congratulate them on their engagement, but she had escaped before she'd even let a single one get a word out. In fact, she had probably spent almost as much time in Mr. Blakley's presence today as she had yesterday.

Not very much.

Mr. Blakley pulled an armchair closer to hers so he could sit opposite her and languidly sat back in it. Jessica could not help but be envious. How was it that some people were just…just so much more at home in their own bodies?

She did not understand it. After all, it was not as though her body were new to her; she had had it quite some time. And yet every movement she made appeared to be awkward, unpleasant, disjointed.

There was Mr. Blakley, on the other hand, lounging back and examining her with a not quite critical eye, one foot resting on his other leg and his hands steepled together, as though he were perfectly content.

Content. And her betrothed.

"My name is Reginald, and my sister calls me 'Reggie,' which I detest," the man said quietly, a slow grin on his face. "I have a small family. Not like yours."

Jessica tried to smile. No one had a family like hers. Wild, loud, numerous, overbearing, nosy, and bouncing from scandal to scandal.

Well, not scandal. They were too well-respected for that. Adventure to adventure, perhaps.

Speaking of, it suddenly occurred to her that she ought to have had a chaperone present, shouldn't she? Then again, she thought that was for *before* the proposal and one was allowed some private time with one's betrothed... But she wasn't sure. She'd never had the need for a chaperone—because no gentleman who wasn't a relation had ever deigned to spend time with her alone before.

"Right," Jessica said tensely, realizing Mr. Blakley seemed to be waiting for her to respond in some form. If the man thought she had planned to start calling him 'Reggie,' though, he was quite mistaken.

Call a man she didn't know by his first name! Not even a first name, but a nickname?

"Most people call me 'Lin.'"

"'Lin'?" Jessica repeated. At least, that was what it sounded like he had said.

For some reason, Mr. Blakley chuckled. "Pronounced *Lin*, yes, but spelled L-L-Y-N-E."

Llyne. She was not sure why it mattered, though she couldn't see the connection to his name. But after all, they called her sister Theodora 'Teddy.' Her cousin Frank had confused many people. Frank Chance had been invited to a gentleman's club once by an unsuspecting gentleman new to Town and had had quite the shock when Lady Francesca Chance had arrived.

"Yes, I am the eighth Baron Llyne," continued Mr. Blakley— or rather, not Mr. Blakley, as it turned out. "So I answer to 'Lord Llyne' as well."

Jessica's eyes widened.

So, that would explain part of it: why the man was so self-assured, why he felt he could just barge into a family house party like this. He was a titled gentleman, just like her father.

Well, not like her father, not really. Her father had been the by-blow of the late duke, and according to family legend—or at least, what the cousins gossiped about among themselves—it had been a good few years before the three legitimate Chance brothers had accepted their illegitimate connection.

Besides, even though her father was illegitimate, he was still a viscount. This man was only a baron.

'Only a baron,' Jessica thought darkly. What had she become?

"I see you are not impressed," said Lord Llyne quietly.

Heat splattered over her cheeks, red marks surely across her face. "It's… It's not that. I just…"

Jessica's voice trailed off. Usually, whomever she was conversing with was quick to interject when her words failed her. It was irritating at times, but sometimes, it was a blessed relief. It was always pleasant when the other person in a conversation took the weight of it.

But Lord Llyne… He just sat there, looking at her.

Listening.

It was unaccountable.

"You will no longer be the Honorable Jessica Chance, once we are married," said Lord Llyne quietly. "You will become Lady Llyne."

It was a good thing that Jessica was seated, for her legs would most certainly have given way at that point.

Lady…Lady Llyne?

It had never been much of a point of contention between the cousins. The daughters of Uncle William, Uncle George, and Uncle John were all titled as Ladies. That was because they were daughters of high rank.

She and her sisters, on the other hand… Well, they were mere daughters of a viscount. No one said it. She rather believed no one even thought it.

But they were lesser. Just Honorables on a first introduction, and after that, just plain Miss Chance.

Miss Chance. Lady Llyne.

Jessica had to admit, even if only in the privacy of her own mind…it had a certain ring to it.

"I suppose you have an unimpressive dowry."

Her eyes darted up and the words had slipped from her mouth before she could stop them. "I suppose you have an unimpressive income."

Painful shame curled around her heart and Jessica's gaze darted to the door in an effort to think about escape—but a strange noise was coming out of Lord Llyne and it transfixed her to the chair.

The man was…laughing?

"I suppose I deserved that," he said with a grin. "And do not concern yourself, or your parents, Miss Chance. I have an income of five thousand four hundred a year. More than enough, I would hope, to keep you in comfort."

It was a might more than her father, to be sure, Jessica could not help but think. But then, there were so many of them. Her parents, herself, her four siblings, all the servants that running two households required.

The baron hadn't spoken of debts, naturally, which had to have been the reason he was seeking out a rich bride. Perhaps she would never hear about them, but her dowry would help them to go away. Was that not how it worked, so often?

And when she was the Baroness Llyne—

Can I really go through with this?

Jessica swallowed down her fears. Of course she could. The man wasn't unpleasant. That was more than enough for many ladies of her age and rank. They would accept any man their parents put before them who did not spit, snort, and spew tobacco in their faces.

It was a low bar, and yet so many gentlemen did not overcome it.

And he was…attractive.

Dazzlingly so. The man had charisma as though it were going out of fashion, and Jessica knew he was the reason that her skin was tingling and that her breath was short.

It was all too easy to grow distracted by just how good-looking the man was and completely lose the fact that she was going to be his wife. His wife. And that meant—

Do not think about it, Jessica warned herself as her décolletage did not get the message and immediately started boiling. Thank goodness she had had the foresight to select a high-necked gown for today, despite the slightly warmer weather.

"Look, this is perhaps not the way you had envisioned securing a husband," said Lord Llyne, cutting through her thoughts.

Jessica tried to smile. "Not exactly."

She had thought she would become a spinster. It was not all bad, she had reasoned. Spinsters had a greater choice of attire and hours, they selected their own meals if not in the care of a married parent or sibling, and there were surely going to be enough nieces and nephews from her four siblings to take care of her in her old age.

In truth, she rather wondered why more wallflowers of means did not aim for such a state.

And yet in had walked a gentleman who made her blood fizz, and intrigued her, and he had offered her his hand, and she had said *yes*.

Only now did she start to wonder whether she should have asked more questions about the man attached to the hand in question.

"Lord Llyne," Jessica said slowly, wondering how on earth to phrase the question 'Tell me all about yourself, including the bad bits so I know what I am getting myself in for' without being rude. "Tell me—"

"I am sure you have a great number of questions for me," interrupted the man, glancing at his pocket watch in a move that made Jessica feel intensely small.

Was she already boring him? Within ten minutes?

"Yes, I do, and—"

"And I will be more than happy to answer them for the next five minutes," said Lord Llyne with a smile he obviously thought was pleasant and Jessica instantly believed was vague. "I will then have some business to attend to."

Jessica bit her lip, her hands immediately twisting into her lap.

So, this was how it would be.

She was not sure what else she had expected. This was hardly a love match—clearly, the man wished to marry her because of her reputation, which was impeccable. It was difficult to ruin a reputation when you were never invited anywhere, but still.

But despite the fact that this was far more a marriage of convenience than a love match, as all four of her wedded cousins' marriages had been, Jessica had hoped for... Well. Not romance.

Effort, maybe?

She looked up into his dark eyes and swiftly lost herself within them. It was quite unfair for a man to have such beautiful eyelashes. So long, and thick. And that mouth, why, it just invited the onlooker to imagine—

"Questions, Miss Chance?"

Jessica started. Lord Llyne appeared far too pleased with himself. Had he noticed how she was staring at him—dear God, *had* she been staring at him?

Shaking herself mentally and straightening up physically, Jessica nodded. "Y-Yes, I have many questions. You said you had family."

"A sister and a brother. Parents dead," came the immediate reply.

"Oh. I am sorry for your—"

"It was a long time ago," said Lord Llyne with a shrug. "Next question."

It felt too much like an interview for Jessica's taste. Not that she had ever been interviewed for anything, but she had once assisted her mother in the interview of a new housekeeper for their London home. Rapid questions, rapid answers, but neither party appeared to actually learn anything new about the other.

And he was so damned attractive. Jessica was tempted to tug a finger around her high-necked collar. *Is it just me, or is it mightily warm in here?*

"I am sorry, I have to go," said Lord Llyne, rising to his feet and inclining his head. It could not have been five minutes. And what business did he have at her uncle's house that did not involve her? "But I am here for the next three weeks, Miss

Chance, after which we shall return to London and immediately get married. I look forward to getting to know my bride."

And then he did the strangest thing.

He leaned forward, picked up her bare hand, for she had not yet had time to put on gloves this day after breakfast...and brought it to his lips.

He kissed her hand.

Jessica could not help the gasp that passed her lips. His mouth, hot and firm on her hand, her skin tingling, a sizzling heat in the air, a connection, his eyes fixed on hers, a moment of frisson—

Lord Llyne dropped her hand, turned, and strode out of the room. He did not even close the door behind him.

Jessica fell back into the chair and fanned herself ineffectually with the very hand that was still burning from his touch.

He looked forward to getting to know his bride?

She looked forward to being able to be in the same room as him—and not expire.

Chapter Four

September 3, 1840

WELL, *THIS ISN'T awkward at all…*
Reginald tried not to think about it too much. He tried not to think about the fact that around this dinner table, he was the only non-family member in attendance. He tried not to think about the fact that he had not packed any suitable attire for such an event, had not traveled with his valet, never presuming that he would be invited to stay for more than one night.

And he most definitely tried not to think about the woman seated next to him.

His future wife.

"—heard she and Richard are doing very well," came a voice from down the table. "Evelyn says in her letter that she is painting a great deal…"

"—truly, you are also an archer?" said a voice on the other side of him, chattering happily to Lord Leopold Chance. "What are the chances of that?"

Muffled, refined laughter followed.

Everything these people did was refined. Hell, Reginald had been raised in a baron's household—he was hardly a plebian unsure how to hold a knife and fork…but there was something intensely *polished* about these people.

Something about the way they walked. The way they held themselves. A confidence—no, it was not a confidence, but a certainty.

The Chances were absolutely certain of anything and everything they did. It was intoxicating.

All of them, that was, except his bride-to-be.

Reginald glanced at the woman next to him. She was eating silently, her gaze mostly fixed on her plate of roasted trout and lemon. Every now and again, she would look up—either to listen to something someone said, or to pick up her glass of wine and take a sip, then her eyes would return to her plate.

His eyes had barely looked at her plate. He was more interested in looking at her.

Dark hair. When he had first encountered her, Reginald had thought her hair merely brown, but he was wrong; there was a richness within it, almost a sheen of red. The curls appeared natural, flying away around her face out of control.

And her nose. Slight, and delicate, drawing the eye to her lips…

"I said, I hope your stay at Stanphrey Lacey has been comfortable so far?"

Reginald jolted. There was a man talking to him—who was talking to him?

Looking up, he saw that it was Viscount Pernrith. Miss Chance's father.

Right.

"Yes, yes, more than comfortable," Reginald said with a wide smile, hoping to goodness they asked him no further questions than that. Not when his mind had been so pleasingly occupied.

How had he never noticed the luscious shape of Miss Chance's lips before?

"I notice you do not have appropriate dinner attire," continued the viscount blithely. "Happens when one travels without one's valet, I suppose."

The man's wife, seated next to him, nudged him heartily in the ribs. "*Frederick!*"

"What I mean to say is that we are more than happy to lend you any additional clothes, should you need them," added the viscount with a wry grin. "As I was about to say."

Reginald drew himself up. Well, hang on now. He couldn't have the Chance family laboring under that misapprehension. Did they think him so poor that he could not afford clothes or a valet? Hang it all, that had not been the impression he had wished to create.

Beyond the fact that it was wrong, it was… Well. Not remarkable. And he'd wanted to impress this family. He just hadn't the patience, once he'd fixed his mind on his brilliant idea, to wait for his valet to pack and to sit in an accursedly slow carriage all the way here.

"I have sent a note to my valet in London, and he should be arriving tomorrow on the mail coach with a trunk of my clothes," he said brightly. "I had no wish to presume, and I doubt my horse would have permitted a large trunk."

There was some genteel laughter at this and a flicker of pride soared through him.

Yes, I could belong here. He could make this work. He had chosen well; the Chance family was accustomed to things being a little…irregular. But he could be happy here. He could restore his family's honor here.

All he needed was the hand of Miss Chance.

Reginald glanced at her again. She had not looked up as he'd conversed with her father, but by the tilt of her head, he wondered whether she had listened.

He wasn't sure if he wanted her to have paid attention or not.

Farther up the table was some… Well, he would not call it whispering. Murmuring, perhaps. Glances were cast his way, and one of the Chance cousins perhaps a few years younger than himself pointed uncouthly with a fork.

Pointed at him.

Trying to keep his expression steady, Reginald reminded himself that he was the imposition here. He was the outsider. Hell's bells, he had marched right up to this house and demanded—well, not quite demanded—the hand of one of their number. He could hardly expect the warmest of welcomes.

After all, the only reason they had invited him was because, once Miss Chance had given her consent, they'd had to.

Reginald drew himself up and smiled as he took another bite of his trout. He would become a part of this family; at the next year's summer house party, he was going to be right at the center of this brood.

And that had to start with the woman sat beside him.

He took a deep breath. This was going to be awkward, he knew, but it would only be as awkward as she allowed it to be.

Which, perhaps, would be a great deal. *Ah, well. The only way to tell was to try.*

"You look very well this evening, Miss Chance," Reginald began.

It was a safe bet. No woman he had ever met had disliked being noticed, and a gentle compliment he felt was better than an all-out charm attack.

That could come later.

But the conversation did not play out as he had expected. For a start, one needed at least two people opening their mouths for it to even be called a conversation. And Miss Chance remained mute, merely flinching ever so slightly as she continued to eat.

Fine, the compliment had been too vague. *Perhaps her silent condemnation is right*, Reginald thought darkly. After all, that could have been said about anyone.

"I like your…your collar," he said with a wry laugh.

Well, he was hardly a sartorial expert. Most ladies' gowns looked the same to him.

But now he came to look at her…

Miss Chance was dressed in a green gown, a light greenish blue that reminded him of a murky sea. There were ruffles in the sleeves, yes, but they were elegantly darted and there was lace trimmed down the front of her gown. The front of her gown that drew his eye to her—

Reginald snapped his attention upward and most unfortunately met the eye of Miss Chance's father. The viscount considered him a mite coldly, despite the subsequent nudge from his wife.

Despite his efforts of trying to smile, Reginald did not receive a smile in return.

"You like my collar," Miss Chance repeated quietly.

Perhaps it had not been the best choice of subject. Reginald tried to think desperately about his sister. What did she like to be complimented on?

"And your earbobs," he added. "Gold. Very pretty."

That gained a response. Miss Chance looked up and met his eyes, and a strange sort of twisting in his stomach made Reginald's jaw tighten.

She looked away and the twisting ended.

What the hell had that been about?

"Tell me about them," Reginald said desperately. Goodness gracious, he could not remember the last time it had been this difficult to converse with a woman. Why did she have to make it so…so difficult?

Was it possible that he had chosen the wrong Chance?

"Tell you about my earbobs?" Miss Chance repeated, as though ascertaining whether or not he wished to stick to his nonsense.

"—why would he choose her?" came a whisper that floated down the table.

"But did they know each other?"

"Irene told me they had never met before!"

Reginald could not precisely tell which Chances cousins were speaking, but their murmurs traveled farther than clearly they had expected—right to the ears of Miss Jessica Chance.

He could see her listening, see the flush of pink that tinged her cheeks, the pain flickering in her eyes, the downcast look. He watched how her fingers tightened on her fork, how she placed her knife down and ceased eating.

It was a strange sort of prickling discomfort that roared through his own body, but Reginald could hardly march up the table and demand that Miss Chance's own family apologize to her.

Not when he was the cause of such gossip.

"Earbobs," he said firmly.

The decidedness of his statement appeared to catch Miss Chance's attention. She looked up and smiled weakly. "You cannot truly wish to know about my earbobs."

"I find that learning about a woman's jewelry tells me a great deal about them," Reginald countered, delighted that he had managed to elicit a statement of more than five words from her lips. It should not really have been a victory, but it was.

Miss Chance raised an eyebrow. "Really?"

Ah. Here we are, back to single-word responses. Is this what our marriage is going to be like?

It was a strange thought. Reginald had taken a great deal of time selecting Miss Jessica Chance from the plethora of eligible Chance ladies but had spent almost no time at all considering what married life with her would be like.

Up to a point, it did not matter; it was marrying into the Chance family that mattered. Any Chance would do. Any Chance he could take.

Only now that he sat beside her and started to taste not the Chance food, but his personal Chance future did Reginald start to wonder whether he should have chosen another woman.

He took a deep breath. Well, there was no going back. He had made his bed, and before the month was out, he was going to lie in it. With Miss Jessica Chance.

The thought flared unexpected heat through his loins, but the sensation passed, and instead, he found himself looking into the waiting gaze of his future bride.

Reginald cleared his throat. "Well, take your mother, for example."

He did not bother to lower his voice; it was time that he started to impress the entire Chance clan, and he saw no reason why this could not be the moment. Out of the corner of his eye, he saw the viscountess lower her wineglass, her expression unreadable.

"My mother?" Miss Chance repeated, her own focus drifting over to the viscountess on the other side of the table.

Reginald inclined his head politely to the woman who would soon be his mother-in-law. "Her earbobs are clearly diamonds, and beautifully set. They match her necklace and the elegant string of diamonds within her hair. Yet they have been mended. Very well, yes, but you can tell that one of the diamonds in the necklace have been replaced. This is a sign of long ownership, and it is important to your mother. Why else restore them?"

Miss Chance said not a word, and neither did her mother. Perhaps that was where his future wife had inherited her reticence from. *Ah, inherited...*

"It was a gift—a parure, perhaps given by...by her father," Reginald hazarded, hoping to goodness he did not offend anyone through this ridiculous enterprise. "They suggest to me the sort of jewels one wears when one comes out into Society."

The viscountess inclined her head with a smile. "From my mother, in fact, but you are not wrong."

"Your bracelet, however, is quite different," Reginald continued, warming to his theme and wondering to goodness why no one was stopping him speaking such nonsense. "The coral is not diamonds—it's hardly worth one of the earbobs—but it is unique, special, unusual in its design. I would suppose it was given by a loved one without the funds for diamonds, but someone who knew you well, my lady. Someone who knew your tastes and wanted to gift you something that no one else in Society had. Someone... Someone precious to you."

For a moment, he thought he had gone too far. It was all very well, playing this parlor trick with friends who could guffaw when he was wrong and mock-applaud him when he was right.

It was the sort of thing that had kept them entertained on long nights. When he'd had friends.

But doing it here, at the Chances'? What if he was wrong—

what if he had offended?

Reginald saw to his horror that the viscount had reached out to hold his wife's hand with a yearning look in his eyes, and he was murmuring low.

Oh, no.

"—and not nearly as expensive as your diamond earbobs, I'm afraid," Miss Chance's father was saying in a low voice. "But I hope you never took that as a sign of my lowered love for you."

"Never," the viscountess murmured, lifting his hand and pressing a devoted kiss onto his palm.

Reginald was forced to look away from the blatant display of affection, heat searing his cheeks. *Dear God, that was a close one.*

His choice of direction to look away was at his future bride, and to his great surprise, she was looking right at him.

"Impressive," she said quietly.

"Goodness, I hope not," he said, unexpectedly delighted at her praise. "It's all just nonsense, really."

"Is that what you speak?" Miss Chance asked, her voice still soft. "Just nonsense?"

Reginald hesitated. This felt like a trick question. If he were in Town and a young debutante had said such a thing—not that a young debutante would be permitted to speak with him when the news got out—then he would consider it a gentle flirtation, and he would lower his voice and say that he spoke nonsense to everyone…except her.

But somehow, that did not feel right here.

Reginald swallowed and tried not to notice how Miss Chance's eyes flickered to his Adam's apple. "Mostly nonsense, but there is some truth in it. There are things jewels can tell us."

"And what do my earbobs tell you?" Miss Chance asked, a slight lift of her left eyebrow accompanying her question.

This could go one of two ways, Reginald knew. Either he would get this right and he would endear himself to his future bride…or he would get it wrong, and she would think less of him.

Not that it particularly mattered, of course. As long as she married him.

"Your earbobs," Reginald started slowly. "Your...your ear-bobs..."

They were beautiful, especially now that he was looking at them more closely, but there did not seem to be much detail. They were circular, golden earbobs—or dropped pendants, he supposed that was the correct term.

They were engraved but without much of a distinct pattern. No jewels had been embedded within them. They were simple. Elegant. Uncomplicated.

When Reginald shifted his attention to Miss Chance's eyes, it was to notice her blazing cheeks. Evidently, this woman did not get looked at much.

"Your earbobs are elegant and uncomplicated. Much like their owner," Reginald said in a low tone, trying his best to ensure that only Miss Chance could hear him. "I would hazard a guess that you selected them. They are the sort of adornment that will happily accompany any attire. Almost any color. You wear them often, almost all the time, in fact. You do not have to think about what you wear when you wear them be-cause...because you have something far more important to think about. You have a brilliant mind."

With a thrill of joy, he saw that Miss Chance's lips had parted in astonishment—something of a habit around him, he had to note.

"How could you know all of that?" was her question.

Reginald knew preening was an unattractive trait in a young man, which was why he was attempting not to do it. It was difficult, though. "Ah, to the well-practiced eye, much can be revealed."

There was a look of—well, not quite incredulity, but not far off. "I admit myself impressed."

"It's a game I used to play with my friends," Reginald found himself saying, the words somehow falling from his mouth before he could stop them.

"'Used to'?"

There it was—the spark of intelligence and insightfulness that he had hoped his future wife would not have. Miss Chance was looking at him curiously, her ability to pick up on the two words he had rather hoped she would not notice absolutely uncanny.

Reginald looked down at his now-empty plate. About now would be a good time for the Chance footmen to enter the room and clear the plates, providing a useful distraction.

But the wine was flowing and the laughter was raucous at one end of the table especially, and the footmen remained at their stations around the walls.

So Reginald smiled and delicately turned the conversation back to Miss Chance's earrings. "Was I right? Did you choose the earbobs yourself?"

"You… You can tell all that from my earrings?"

"I did warn you that it was mostly nonsense," Reginald chided with a wink.

The wink was too much. He realized it the moment he had done so, the light leaving Miss Chance's eyes immediately, replaced with a distant coldness, which was how he had started off the dinner.

Blast it to hell.

"Yes, you did," Miss Chance said quietly. "But you were wrong. The earbobs are my mother's. I borrowed them for the first time this evening."

Ah. Reginald could not help it; he glanced over to the viscountess, who was grinning. She raised her wineglass in a silent toast to him and her smile widened.

Brilliant. That was precisely what he needed.

Turning back to Miss Chance, he saw that she was picking at the remainder of her trout, turned from him now, as though wishing to make it absolutely clear that their conversation was at an end.

Which was not ideal when he would be marrying the woman in a few weeks. Though he wondered if he'd first need to get her father's explicit blessing.

"You must think me a fool," he said quietly.

For some reason, that statement gained Miss Chance's attention. Tilting her head toward him, she shrugged. "I... I do not know what to think."

That sounded slightly more positive. "Well, I hope that the next few weeks—"

"It is a strange man who would turn up here and request *me* for his bride," Miss Chance continued, as though she had finally been given permission to speak.

Her eyes fixed on his.

Reginald swallowed. Plain though she undoubtedly was, he was finding it difficult to remember that as he looked into her pupils. They were a shade of green he had never seen before. Not mossy, not emerald, but with a patina within them of gold and shimmering light.

They were... They were beautiful.

"I'm doing this all wrong," muttered Miss Chance, dropping her gaze.

Doing it all—doing what *all wrong?*

Reginald shook his head as though drunk. His head felt a little stuffed full of cotton wool, as though he'd dunked it underwater and was now having trouble ridding it from his ears.

What had just happened there? For a moment, he had thought—it had felt like—what had she said?

"Doing what wrong?" he murmured before he could stop himself.

Miss Chance's cheeks darkened to such a deep red, Reginald was almost certain he could feel the heat pouring off them. She said nothing, mutely shaking her head as she picked up her fork then put it down again.

Precisely what had happened to make her so self-conscious, he could not tell. Something had occurred and yet nothing had occurred.

What was going on?

Well, there was nothing for it. He was hardly a brute—he could not let the poor woman twist herself in knots if she had changed her mind.

Flickers of panic arched through his mind, but Reginald pushed them aside. His own family troubles notwithstanding, he would not permit a woman to marry him merely because he had asked and she had felt obliged.

Even though it would end all hopes of restoring his family's reputation if she broke off their strange engagement.

"Miss Chance," Reginald said quietly.

She did not look up. Perhaps that was all to the good. There was something most powerful in her eyes, something he did not understand.

"Miss Chance, why did you say *yes* to my proposal if you do not wish to be married?"

Reginald did not ask *"If you do not wish to marry* me" because he wasn't quite sure his ego could take the answer—but to his great surprise, Miss Chance looked up, her eyelids fluttering rapidly, and shook her head.

"I *do* want to be married. I will marry you."

"Yes, but—"

"Do you wish to rescind your proposal?"

Reginald stared, open mouthed. "No, but—"

"So there we are, then," Miss Chance said firmly, as though she were signing her own death warrant. "You wish to be married, I wish to be married, you asked me, and I said *yes*. That is all there is to it. That is all we need to know."

Reginald blinked. In his general experience, ladies were not so forthright, so business-like in their matches. But then, she was a Chance. Perhaps he should not have underestimated her.

"Right," he said aloud—uncertainly.

"Right," Miss Chance said, her cheeks still flushing. "Mama, it's time the ladies left."

It was a most outrageous breach of etiquette, with the Duchess of Cothrom right there, but it appeared that his future bride did not care. Not waiting for their hostess, nor her mother, Miss Chance rose from her seat and marched out of the dining room to muffled murmurs.

Reginald attempted to smile. "Gone to...to powder her nose."

Her father, the Viscount Pernrith, grinned from the other side of the table. "Ah, to be young and enjoy the first flush of romance."

Reginald's grin wavered, but only a touch. "Indeed."

Indeed. What had he gotten himself into?

Chapter Five

September 4, 1840

S ADLY, THERE IS only so long that a lady can pretend to have a megrim before her sister will march into her bedchamber and force her into a gown.

"Ouch!"

"My apologies, but if you keep wriggling like that, I am going to jab you in the head with a pin," Irene said smoothly.

Jessica glared at her sister in the looking glass. "By accident, I presume?"

"Perhaps?" said Irene with a laugh. "I bet you wish we all had our own lady's maids, but Wharton can only be spread so thin, I suppose. Come on, you're all ready. I don't suppose you are going to tell me why you were hiding up here all of yesterday?"

"And you would suppose right," said Jessica with a sigh, picking up her gloves and glancing about her toilette table in case she had forgotten anything.

She did not miss the eye roll that her sister gave her silently but decided not to pursue it. After all, it was not as though she could provide much of an explanation. Not one that she was willing to give.

"You wish to be married, I wish to be married, you asked me, and I said yes. That is all there is to it. That is all we need to know."

Those had been the last words that she had spoken to Lord Llyne, and they had been mortifying in the extreme. As though it were not bad enough that the man had decided to stay for the entire house party! As though it were not difficult enough to look into the eyes of a man who had decided, for goodness knew what reason, to marry her.

No, it had all been too much. His attempts to flirt with her, the looks he had exchanged with her parents…

No, Jessica had decided yesterday that it was much easier to plead a headache, and then a megrim, and merely remain in her bedchamber the entire day.

Her family had been concerned, in the main. Her parents had popped their heads in, Irene had banged on her door until Jessica had shouted at her to go away, and there had even been a note from Lord Llyne.

Devastated to hear that you are indisposed. I hope our conversation had nothing to do with it? Llyne.

Jessica had not replied to the note.

What could she say? *Yes, your mere presence is overwhelming me. You are so damned attractive, so damned self-assured, and I do not know whether or not to believe a single word you say?*

It was not exactly the picture of calm elegance she wished to portray.

But she could not stay up here forever, and the fresh autumn breeze that had blown in overnight was calling to her. Autumn was Jessica's favorite time of year: the chill in the air brought a renewal after the heavy heat of summer—a sense of relief she just adored.

Besides, Irene had yelled through her door yesterday that a gaggle of Chance cousins would be going hunting today, and she felt in need of a good ride.

"And you are certain you are up to this?" Irene asked, her voice full of concern as Jessica rose from her toilette table and pulled on her riding boots.

"I am sure," Jessica said shortly.

"It's just, whenever I have a megrim, the next day I'm—"

"I'm quite well."

"—absolutely useless. The megrim entirely exhausts me."

"Irene," said Jessica with a wry smile, wishing to goodness

that her sister was better at taking a hint. "I did not have a megrim."

Her sister's mouth dropped open as Jessica picked up her riding crop, swished it through the air with a satisfying *whoosh*, and started for the door.

It was as she'd stepped through it that her sister's voice called after her. "Did not have a megrim?"

Jessica sighed as she strolled down the corridor. She should never have told her, but she had been fussing so. "I just needed a day alone."

"'Alone'? At a house party?" Irene's voice was incredulous as she caught up with her sister. "I know you always need time alone, but here, I thought—"

"You thought wrong," Jessica said shortly as they reached the top of the stairs.

It was maddening. All her life, Jessica had needed time away from people—away from everyone. Friends, family—it did not matter. The world became overwhelming and she could no longer do anything or think anything because the noise in her head was just too much.

That was when she crept away, usually to her bedchamber, and spent a day…doing nothing. It was heaven.

Most of her family had grown accustomed to it now, although Irene of all her siblings found it the oddest. Jessica could understand why. She and Irene could not have been more different. Why, if there was a single moment that Irene was not with her best friend, the Duke of Aynor, it was a rare one. She didn't know how her sister put up with the lack of solitude.

"Well, I suppose a ride would do you some good," said Irene with a sigh beside her. "I'm going to wake up Teddy."

"I don't think she will want you to."

"Too bad," called her sister over her shoulder as she trotted along the corridor. "If you're not going to stay at the house and talk to me, *someone* has to."

Jessica smiled to herself as she watched the retreating back of her sister. They were so different.

"Miss Chance?"

She turned, glancing over the banisters at the person who had called her name—and was relieved that she had the banisters to cling on to.

It was Lord Llyne.

And not the Lord Llyne whom she had previously encountered. No, when the gentleman had first arrived at Stanphrey Lacey, covered in dust from the road and looking world-weary, he had not looked like that. When he had dined with the family, he had been wearing the same clothes, though a little cleaner. He had looked handsome, but not…

Not like that.

Jessica stared down with open mouth at the Lord Llyne who was standing nonchalantly in the great hall. He was attired in the smartest riding clothes she had ever seen. Clear and striking lines, elegant tailoring, boots that elegantly revealed his strong legs and a coat that was perhaps too tight across the chest. The muscular, broad chest.

His hair was better attired too. The dark curls were casually arranged around his face now, one lilting over his eye, and when Lord Llyne gently shook it away, his entire face looked wry.

Dear Lord.

The man was an Adonis. Surely, he knew it. Surely, he had dressed in such a way merely to point it out.

Jessica's fingers were trembling on the banister. And what was a gentleman who looked like that doing with a lady who looked… Well, like her?

All thoughts of how the shooting party would assist her in clearing her head were forgotten. No, she could not go—she could not ride alongside *that*!

"Miss Chance, I am so glad you are joining our party," said Lord Llyne pleasantly, his eyes raking over her in a similar manner to her own. "I trust you are recovered?"

Oh, she was never going to recover from this.

"'R-Recovered'?" Jessica croaked.

"Yes," he said politely. "From your megrim."

Oh, of course. The megrim she had told everyone she'd had. "Oh. Oh, yes. Much better. Thank you."

All she had to do was retreat back down the corridor to her bedchamber, and she could hide there. It was hardly the done thing for a daughter of a viscount to hide from her betrothed, but honestly she saw no other choice.

"I am glad to see you dressed for shooting," said Lord Llyne, his smile friendly. "I had hoped to enjoy the pleasure of your company."

Oh, blast. Jessica glanced down at her riding habit, the forest green a perfect choice until now. "I... I rather thought I wouldn't—"

"Right, then. Come on!" Her cousin Samuel, a man so good-looking that it was still a surprise to her that he never seemed to notice, grinned as he strode down the corridor toward her and the head of the stairs. "If we don't get out there soon, the beaters will have gotten bored and gone home. Ah, Llyne, you're joining us?"

"If you'll have me," said Lord Llyne with a laugh, inclining his head. "I'll have to borrow a gun, though."

"Not a problem, the gun room is this way," said Samuel as he started down the stairs. "Coming, Jessica?"

Jessica hesitated.

This was a mistake. She was attracted to Lord Llyne, more attracted than she had expected—and she was supposed to be making him attracted to *her*!

Not that her performance at dinner two nights ago had been that impressive.

Oh, she still cringed painfully every time she thought of the way she had attempted to be coquettish and had only succeeded in confusing the man.

"It is a strange man who would turn up here and request me *for his bride."*

She was making a fool of herself, that was all she was doing, and going shooting with Lord Llyne would only increase her chances of being an absolute idiot. No, she should stay. She should remain here, where it was safe.

"Miss Chance?"

Jessica blinked. Lord Llyne had stepped to the bottom of the staircase and was holding out his hand.

Swallowing hard and wishing to goodness the man weren't so charming, she descended the staircase, hoping with every step that she did not trip. Though if she did, maybe she could fall into Lord Llyne's arms. His strong, powerful—

"I need you," Lord Llyne said quietly as he tucked her hand in his arm.

Jessica cleared her throat, but her voice was still hoarse when she spoke. "You... You need me?"

He caught her eye and smiled, and she wanted to melt. "Yes. To show me the way. To the gun room."

Her shoulders drooped. *Do I have to embarrass myself at every possible opportunity?* "Of course."

It took about twenty minutes to get the family shooting party together. Uncle John and Uncle William were determined to attend, but the latter became distracted when the news that Cousin Thomas's bride had gone into labor on a sedate country walk—thankfully right beside the Dower House, where she was apparently now preparing for the arrival of her child.

"I'll just see that they have everything they need!" he called out.

Lilianna and Samuel bickered a good deal over a saddle, which Jessica tried not to smile at, and Thomas went racing past them on a steed a little while later, which made Frank and Gwen wonder just what name they would give the child when it was here.

All in all, there was enough noise and chaos to give Jessica a momentary reprieve from the intensity of Lord Llyne's looks— that was, until Uncle John called the gaggle to order.

"Come on, then!" he called out with a wink from his steed. "Those birds won't put themselves in the kitchen!"

General laughter mingled with the sound of horses' hooves as the seven of them trotted out of the stable yard and toward Stanphrey Lacey Forest, where the pheasants for today's shooting would be.

Jessica filled her lungs with fresh September air and started to immediately feel better. This was more like it. The skies open above her and the forest drawing her in, the movement of her mare, the renewed air, the freedom—

"I hope we can shoot together," came a low, honeyed voice.

Jessica almost dropped her gun.

She had not noticed how close Lord Llyne had moved toward her, and neither had she noticed just how quickly her family had disappeared into different directions. Samuel and Frank had gone to the left with Uncle William, and Lilianna and Gwen had disappeared to their right.

That left herself and Lord Llyne…ostensibly alone.

Oh, bother.

"Of course we can shoot together," said Jessica brusquely.

Lord Llyne smiled.

"In silence," she added.

His smile disappeared.

Well, what did he expect? This was a…a marriage of convenience, she supposed, though she was not sure why it was convenient, or whose convenience it was for. Who was doing whom the favor? She was a Chance, but he had a title. She was a wallflower, but he wished to—how had he put it? Make an excellent match?

"I don't want to waste time with a matchmaker and I… I thought you would accept my offer."

What precisely had he meant by that, anyway?

And despite Jessica's certainty that every time she attempted to warm this man up, she would only be cooling him down, she made a decision that the wallflower within her did not like.

She was going to talk to her betrothed.

"Lord Llyne," she said quietly as they rode along the path.

"Miss Chance," he returned with a winning grin.

Damn him, why did he have to be so good at this? "Lord Llyne, why did you propose to me?"

Jessica would have missed it if she had not been paying close attention. She would not have noticed the flicker of his pulse, the tension tightening then loosening in his jaw.

Small signs, perhaps, but signs of something. Signs that the man did not want to tell her the truth.

So when Lord Llyne said, "Why, I have already told you," Jessica was ready for her retort.

"You said you did not wish to waste money on a matchmaker," she replied, reminding the man of his own words. "But this— this marriage of convenience—"

"Is that what you wish to call it?" Lord Llyne returned softly.

Jessica swallowed. What she wanted to call it was *a marriage of devotion and desire*. She wanted the man to look at her and see her, truly her, not just a wallflower who was so desperate to be wed that she would accept just about anyone who asked.

Even if technically, that was true.

The cool air of the forest thankfully prevented her from reddening too much as she said, "I do not think it is a difficult question."

"I do not think my answer is insufficient," came the swift yet calm quip from Lord Llyne. "Do you and your family gain much excellent hunting in these woods?"

"Yes, we—" Jessica caught herself just in time. As she glanced over to Lord Llyne, it was to see him clamping down on his lips.

Oh, he thought he was so clever, didn't he?

"Well, I almost had you distracted." The man who would be her husband in less than a month grinned.

"Well, you do not have me yet," Jessica replied before she could think.

His lopsided grin was all too knowing, and it was a good

thing that her riding habit hid her décolletage because it would undoubtedly be burning red if anyone could see it. No one could, obviously, but Jessica could feel it, and it was most uncomfortable.

"I do not know why you are avoiding this question," she said quietly as they rode along.

"And I do not know why it matters so much to you," he returned jovially.

"Because—" Jessica bit back her words.

Because, she wanted to say, *this marriage of convenience… It's not how my family does it. We are Chances, and everyone who weds in this family has done so for love. Thomas, Lilianna, Evelyn, Leopold— even my parents! Eventually.*

Everyone married for love.

And here I am, unable to convince a single man to even dance with me, let alone fall in love with me, and I've…

Well, Jessica wasn't going to say it aloud, but she could say it in the privacy of her own mind.

She was so unlovable that she would have to accept a marriage of convenience or not marry at all.

"I chose you, and we will be married within a month," Lord Llyne said shortly—not unkindly, but without any sort of warmth. "I spoke to your parents when you were resting yesterday, explained I was a baron—it is true I was not forthcoming with that at first, to my regret—and they seem to have given their blessing. I thought you would be pleased."

Jessica almost snorted. Oh, yes, she was certain that her parents were delighted at the thought that they would be able to marry her off, and to a title, too. It would allow Irene to be more in Society, perhaps even Teddy to come out into Society fully.

Yes, this marriage was an excellent idea for the Chance family.

But what was it going to be like for her? Secrets? Lies? Her husband deciding that the truth was too much trouble to share with her?

Well, she'd had enough.

Slowly, Jessica slipped from her mare's back and stepped onto the leaf-strewn path.

"Miss Chance?"

"I am going to walk back to the house," she said quietly.

"You are?"

If she were not being so delusional today, Jessica would almost have said that Lord Llyne sounded disappointed. But that was surely because she was hopeful. Foolishly hopeful.

Heavy thumps—Lord Llyne had dismounted too. "Miss Chance?"

"If you don't want to speak to me, I have no wish to press my conversation upon an unwilling participant," Jessica said, hating that she had to explain herself. Wallflowers didn't have to explain themselves. They rarely had anyone to speak to. "So I will see you at luncheon."

"Wait."

It was not his word that stilled her, though that could almost have been enough. No, it was the hand on her shoulder.

Jessica stared at it, then the man to whom it belonged.

Lord Llyne was staring with an expression of...hope? Concern? Interest?

It was so difficult to tell. She had never been that good at understanding the expressions of others. Oh, feelings, feelings she endured deeply and could well comprehend the overpowering need to feel that others surely also experienced.

But telling what that emotion was, on the outside of another person's face? How was she supposed to do that?

Lord Llyne removed his hand, but only momentarily. Instead of grabbing her shoulder, he had now taken her hand in his and was pulling her off the path, away from the horses—*oh, Lord.*

Jessica gasped as the man who had proposed marriage to her just days before pushed her up against a tree. *This cannot be happening. Is this happening?*

"Miss Chance, you ask fair questions," Lord Llyne said in a

low murmur that thrummed through Jessica's whole body. "And I wish to give you fair answers, but...but I cannot."

"You cannot?" she breathed.

His gaze locked on to hers and a heat she had never known burned through her. There was such an intensity within that look, such a desperate wish to be open—or was she wrong? It disappeared before she could truly examine it.

"I have told you the truth, and only the truth, and I will always do that throughout our lives," Lord Llyne said quietly, making Jessica's knees quiver. "I want respectability, I want—I *need* respectability for my estate. There is no family so respectable as the Chances."

Jessica had to laugh at that. "You do know that my father is an illegitimate Chance, don't you?"

His eyes bore into her. "You think that matters?"

Her gasp caught in her throat. "No."

This was madness—they couldn't stand here like this, her back against a tree trunk and Lord Llyne standing there so...so delicious!

"And you are beautiful," Lord Llyne whispered.

"No," Jessica repeated in a whisper before she could stop herself.

His chuckle seemed to reach down into a deep part of her and pull desire from her, uncontrolled, unfathomable. "You are, if I say you are."

And before she could reply, before she could stop him, before she knew what he was doing or she was doing or whether any member of her family could walk over to them at any moment—

Baron Llyne was kissing her.

And not the gentle and genteel kiss on the back of the hand that Jessica had seen her parents share, oh, no. This was far more—more than anything.

His mouth crushed on hers and she gasped, parting her lips and letting him in as though he had been invited. Lord Llyne did not wait for a better invitation; his questioning tongue was delving into the warmth of her mouth and sizzling heat and pleasure in equal measure down her spine.

Oh, this was… This was…

Jessica grasped the lapels of his riding jacket, but though she had done so to push him away, to her great surprise, she found herself clinging to him all the more. She was moaning, whimpering as the sweet decadence of his kisses stirred her, and somehow, his hands were around her waist and his mouth was—

A cracked twig. A footstep. "Jessica?"

As though it had never happened, as though they had never touched each other in their lives, Lord Llyne was somehow five feet from her and waving. "We're over here!"

Jessica hastily brought a hand to her mouth as though she would need to cover the evidence. Would anyone know—could anyone tell what they had been, what *he* had been…

What they had shared?

"I said you are beautiful, and I meant it." For some reason, Lord Llyne's voice was cracked, his breathing irregular. "Now, shall we join your family?"

Jessica nodded, words impossible as her head span. Join her family? How could she possibly face anyone after…after what she and Lord Llyne had shared?

Chapter Six

September 5, 1840

THERE WAS SOMETHING so incredibly satisfying about seeing the ball *thunk* into the pocket. It was just a shame that it hadn't been the ball Reginald had been aiming for.

"Bother," he said aloud to himself.

Well. It might have been a bother. It might have been another word a little less suitable for the ears of ladies.

Not that it mattered—he was alone in the capacious billiards room in Stanphrey Lacey and had been for almost an hour. The days had slipped by and he'd found almost no opportunities to speak to Miss Chance—not that he particularly needed to.

Needed to, no. Wanted to… Well.

Heat flickered up Reginald's spine as he strode around the table, billiard cue in hand, attempting not to think about how he had pressed Miss Jessica Chance up against a tree and kissed her senseless.

Or she had kissed him senseless. He wasn't quite sure, even now, who had lost their senses the most.

Forgetting the kiss was impossible. Reginald had been interrupted by thoughts of it all day, hour by hour, finding it difficult to hold a conversation longer than ten minutes. He had been tormented by it at night, his mind replaying the moment as his fingers itched to feel the same heat.

It was a miracle he hadn't marched over to Miss Chance today at luncheon, pulled her from her seat, and kissed her again.

Reginald's jaw tightened. He lowered himself over the table, angled his cue, and took his shot.

"Bravo," said an unfamiliar voice.

He hadn't noticed the door open, but then, he had been focused on not thinking about Miss Chance's lips. So that was undoubtedly why he had not noticed two gentlemen enter the room.

Reginald straightened up and inclined his head in a polite bow before really taking in who they were. When his gaze settled on them, his chest tightened.

Ah. Miss Chance's father, the Viscount Pernrith, and her brother, Mr. Michael Chance.

He had been expecting this. In truth, he was rather surprised it had taken them a week to do it. Yes, he had explained he was a baron, but that had been in a rather public setting, and Miss Chance's parents had seemed glad to learn that news. No one had pressed him further at the time. Now, cornering him and investigating precisely why he had turned up at a private residence such as Stanphrey Lacey and proposed to one of their number? That would have been his first port of call, if some man had turned up and requested his sister's hand.

Though of course, the Blakley family had sufficient problems without worrying about being fastidious when it came to marrying off his sister…

"Gentlemen," Reginald said aloud, as pleasantly as he could muster. "Care to join me in a game?"

"You appear to be in the middle of one," Michael Chance said with a wry smile.

"Oh, I am merely practicing," Reginald said in return, matching the expression. Was it possible this was not as dramatic as he expected? Could it be mere coincidence that both Miss Chance's father and brother had shown up here?

"You two boys can play a game later if you would like," the Viscount Pernrith said quietly, moving to the other side of the room. "I want to talk about Jessica."

'Two boys.'

Well, Reginald should have expected it. Few fathers would permit their daughters to go about marrying men they did not know, and he had made a rumpus, turning up like this and requesting the hand of a lady he had never met before.

So, how would the man approach it? Remove his permission? Attempt to interrogate him about his past, about the reason for this swift marriage?

Reginald braced himself, his shoulders tightening and his fingers constricting around his billiard cue. Whatever approach the man took, he would be ready.

"I just want my girl to be happy," said the viscount quietly, his expression lost.

Reginald almost dropped his cue. He had not been ready.

"And I say again, you're taking this too much to heart, Father," Chance said with a sigh as he picked up a billiard cue of his own and approached the table. "Jessica knows what she is doing."

"Jessica is barely a woman."

"She is four and twenty, Father," countered her brother as he rolled his eyes at Reginald, who stifled a weak smile. "If she wants to go about marrying a man she barely knows, so be it. Perhaps she simply doesn't want to be a spinster."

"I would not care if she was. If she were happy at home, she would not see the need to leave me," said the viscount helplessly, dropping into a chair. "Do you not think so, Lord Llyne?"

Reginald opened his mouth, considered anything he could say to reassure this man, this father, then closed it again.

Poor fellow. Perhaps he should have predicted this; eldest daughter, first child to be married, it was no wonder the old boy was feeling a little out of his depth. He clearly didn't have any real questions for himself. The viscount was just worried about his daughter.

"And you, Lord Llyne," Miss Chance's father said with sudden sharpness that threw Reginald immediately off-balance. "I have to admit I had not heard of you, but I did my due diligence and checked *Debrett's,* and wrote to a friend who recognized you by description—you are the Baron Llyne. So, why do you wish to marry so swiftly? Why now? Why her?"

The movement of Michael Chance to Reginald's left suddenly halted. The room was stilled, the air thick, and he knew that his next words would have to be very considered.

He could tell the whole truth. He could tell some of the truth. He could lie. Apparently, this friend of the viscount's had not cautioned him against Reginald—so there was hope the news had not spread yet.

Reginald took in a long, slow inhale. He had known, hadn't he, that some of the truth would have to come out before the Chances would permit him to marry one of them? Oh, this family. He had longed to be a part of it for years, and his brother's shame had given him the perfect excuse—and now he was so close. So very close.

Looking up, he met the eyes of the Viscount Pernrith and knew precisely what to tell him. Even better, it would not be a lie.

It was not the whole truth…but it was the truth Reginald knew he would accept.

"I was not born the heir to the baron," Reginald said quietly. It was strange, saying it out loud. He usually spent so much of his time hiding this fact about himself. "I… My parents were not married when I was born. Not to each other, at any rate."

He had not released his gaze from the viscount's, whose steely focus somehow flickered with something. Something Reginald recognized.

After all, had he not seen it in his own expression year after year, in the looking glass?

"You are illegitimate," the viscount said slowly. That meant his friend had not written to tell him as much. He supposed such disreputable details were not made clear in a guide such as *Debrett's*.

Reginald inclined his head. Breaking the connection, he stepped around the billiards table and spoke in a light tone, as though he frequently discussed his parentage with relative strangers. "Yes, my father took a mistress, my mother. She was soon after widowed, but my father had married another woman and after five years and no children, decided to own me, legitimize me, make me his heir."

Strange, how the words could flow from him with seeming carelessness, as though the knowledge had not burdened him his whole life.

Chance stepped around the table in turn, taking his shot. "But I thought you mentioned—last night, at dinner, do you not have a sister?"

Reginald took a deep breath. "About a year after I was legitimized, my stepmother fell with child. Twins, a boy and girl. It made things…uncomfortable, shall we say."

Despite his better judgment, knowing it was a topic most delicate, he looked up.

The viscount's expression had softened. "A most uncomfortable situation for all involved, and I say that from experience."

The tension in Reginald's shoulder blades started to melt away. What was it that Miss Chance had said?

"You do know that my father is an illegitimate Chance, don't you?"

Perhaps, if he was going to find acceptance without explanation…it was here.

"Perhaps this will explain in part my need to act, I admit, a bit drastic when attempting to secure a good match. Being the illegitimate brother in a family is no easy task," Reginald said, his stomach swooping as he made the decision to say something perhaps too bold. "As I think you understand, my lord."

Chance missed. He missed his billiard's shot so hard that he almost ripped the baize.

Straightening up, cheeks pink, he stared at Reginald and raised a finger. "Don't you talk to my father like that!"

"Peace, Michael." The viscount had not moved from his chair. He had not lifted a finger. He merely looked at Reginald closely, his eyes slightly narrowed.

Reginald attempted to look a little cowed, which was not a particularly difficult thing because he felt it. This man...he understood, he knew what it was to be given a name later in life. He knew the distinct differences that were made, however subtly, between the son who was deemed rightfully there, and a son who was an interloper, even if no one said it.

The viscount grinned. "You know, I am impressed."

It was not what Reginald had been expecting. "You are?"

"You are?" repeated Chance incredulously.

Viscount Pernrith shrugged as he stood up. "The man could have said anything, mumbled on about seeing Jessica from a distance, falling in love immediately, all that nonsense—"

"Like you and Mama," interrupted his son with a grin.

Despite the son's height and maturity, he was cuffed around the head by his father. "The point is, he told the truth. And a man who does that has my confidence."

The viscount offered out his hand. "I suppose we ought to speak to the vicar here and write to ours back in London and get the banns started, then. Then you can wed as soon as three weeks, in either locale."

Reginald hesitated, but only for a moment. He took it, shaking the man's hand across the billiards table. "Thank you. I'd appreciate that."

"And the license?"

"I—I shall take care of that."

Reginald did not need to feel guilty—not really. It was not as though he had lied. The story was true.

It was just not, perhaps, the whole truth. The actual reason he wished to marry Jessica Chance, marry any woman. But apparently, the viscount had forgotten to press for the reasons why he had chosen his daughter specifically, for he seemed satisfied. He thought he had worked Baron Llyne out.

But he hadn't.

"Ah, who won?" came a sweet voice from the door.

They must keep the hinges in this place well-oiled, Reginald thought as he released his hand and turned to smile at—

Miss Chance. Miss Jessica Chance.

She was leaning against the doorway with a nervous smile. Her brother muttered something and received a thump in the arm from his father, so perhaps it was a good thing that Reginald had not caught it.

How could he, when he was too busy being transfixed by Miss Chance?

She looked… She looked lovely. How had he never noticed the way her smile brought a brilliance to her eyes?

"Come on. Let us leave the lovebirds alone," muttered the viscount, his face all delight as he pulled his son forward.

"Oh no, we're not—" Reginald caught himself just in time. Or perhaps not quite soon enough. Miss Chance had a raised eyebrow as she closed the door behind her father and brother. Apparently, the viscount's consent was enough for him to approve of his daughter being alone with her intended without a chaperone's presence.

There were many advantages, it seemed, to jumping straight to the proposal.

"We're not what?" Miss Chance said quietly, stepping into the cavernous room.

Reginald swallowed. Damnit all, but he was not supposed to feel this…this unbalanced when he was alone with Miss Chance. This was supposed to be a marriage of—of convenience, as she'd called it.

He wanted to be a part of the Chance family, and she was willing to have him. That was all there was to it.

So why did his knees feel mighty strange?

"Who beat whom?" Miss Chance asked quietly, picking up the billiards cue that her brother had deposited on a sofa.

"I'm sorry?"

"I presume you were playing with my father. He's a terrific shot," she said with an expression that was perhaps brittle. "But I have not seen you play. You might be even better."

Reginald tried to grin. "I'm not bad."

She laughed. "Confident, then? Have you been betting against my family?"

"I wouldn't be tempted by a bet when focused on trying to impress my future family," he answered, watching her quietly nodding.

What was she doing here?

Well, not here in Stanphrey Lacey, obviously, but the billiards room. She had been avoiding him the last few days, Reginald could tell. The number of times he had entered a room and she had scurried out of it, cheeks aflame—it was difficult to miss.

He had not understood it. After that kiss, that sultry, inflammatory kiss, there had been nothing more important to him than being close to her.

Reginald may not have liked to admit it to himself, but there it was. There was something about her that…that drew him to her.

It appeared the feeling had not been reciprocated.

And now she was here. What was going on with this complicated Chance woman? Did she like him or not? Did she regret accepting his proposal? Or was she excited about it?

The easiest way to find out would be to ask.

Reginald almost laughed aloud. *Ask? A woman? A direct question?*

That would be the last thing he would try. He was rather afraid of the answer.

"Have… Have you ever played billiards, Miss Chance?" he said aloud. Yes, it was his turn in the conversation, wasn't it?

A slight pink tinged Miss Chance's cheeks. "After… After what we shared in the forest, do you not think that you should call me 'Jessica' now?"

Jessica.

It was an intimacy Reginald had not expected. Oh, they were engaged, to be sure, but they did not actually know each other. He had presumed that he would be permitted to call her by her first name when they were married.

Perhaps not even then.

And there she was, standing on the other side of the billiards table, tantalizingly close, and yet somehow so distant, Reginald was surprised that he could even see her.

He swallowed, his throat dry. "Jessica."

Oh, that had been a mistake. Something had fizzled in the air as he had said that, his fingers itching around his cue stick to be holding on to, not unrelenting wood, but the soft and supple form of the woman before him.

Reginald swallowed again and almost coughed, his mouth was so dry. "I… I suppose you should call me 'Reginald,' then. If I am to call you by such an…an intimate name."

Miss Chance—or rather, Jessica's—cheeks were a brilliant red now, but she did not look away as she said, "I suppose I should…Reginald."

How was such an innocent sentence so—so erotic?

Reginald turned around with the pretense of chalking his billiards cue as he tried to tell his body to calm down.

She was going to be his bride, his wife. He could explore that side of things later. Much later.

When he was not in a house full of the woman's family, for a start.

When Reginald turned back around, he was master of himself and had a plan. He would speak of dull subjects. Nice dull, safe subjects, and nothing else. Cold, dry, boring—

"Do you wish me to teach you billiards?" he found himself saying instead.

Jessica's eyes sparkled. "You think you can teach me?"

No, Reginald wanted to say, his mind swirling into a blind panic. What on earth had he been thinking suggesting such a thing?

The trouble was, the late afternoon sun was pouring into the room and her flyaway hairs were shimmering like a crown and the way she put her hand to her curls, tucking one of them behind her ear…

Reginald swallowed hard and gripped his billiard cue as though it were the only thing holding him on the planet. "Of… Of course."

Well, what harm would it do? They were going to be married, after all. It would probably be a good thing if they had at least one topic they could speak on.

"This is a cue," he said, holding out his own.

Jessica smiled faintly as she stepped over to the rack, picking one out with inexpert fingers. "And that's what I hit the balls with?"

"Yes," Reginald said weakly.

This was ridiculous. When he had ridden up to Stanphrey Lacey and around the side of the house, he had been astonished at just how plain Miss Jessica Chance had been. After all, compared to some of her cousins—compared to her sisters—there was absolutely no contest.

He still believed that now, but in the opposite direction. She was clearly the most enthralling and enticing one of them all. The lilt of a smile in the corner of her mouth, the way her neck curved—

"And I want to tap all the balls into the holes?" she asked lightly.

Reginald was gripping his cue so hard, he was astonished that he had not broken it in half. "Before we start leaning over and caressing the long, hard—I mean, before we start playing billiards," he amended hastily, wishing he had a handkerchief with which to wipe his brow, "it's important that you learn the rules."

"The rules," repeated Jessica quietly, running her hands up and down the cue as she examined him.

Reginald coughed.

Dear God, did she have any idea what she was doing?

Surely not. Surely, it was only his filthy mind, he tried to tell himself, that was making him think of her hands on his—on his—

"I suppose it's all about scoring points," came her light voice.

Reginald whirled around. "What did you say?"

"Billiards," Jessica said innocently, pointing toward the cue rack where the points-counting board could be seen. "Is... Is that not so?"

She was a conundrum, Reginald realized. Here they were, in the billiards room with green leather sofas and armchairs, decades of cigar smoke embedded in the walls. The place was as masculine as it was possible to be.

And here she was, smiling nervously and talking about billiards as though that were the most important thing they had to talk about.

Not marriage. Not the rest of their lives. Not the kiss that had burned into him a need that he had not realized he would be possessed by.

Who *was* Miss Jessica Chance?

It was only now that Reginald was starting to understand how little he understood her. He'd had her down as a wallflower, and indeed, there were moments when her shyness overcame all ability to speak and she slipped out of the room, cheeks blazing.

None of her family seemed to notice. None of her family seemed to care.

But there were moments, moments like this, when Reginald could see something else. Something...not different, but additional.

And he was intoxicated with the challenge of discovering which was the true Jessica Chance.

"So," he said brusquely, attempting to distract himself from the woman who was becoming startlingly distracting. "Billiards. Points. Yes, right. So there, are two players—"

"You and me."

Dear Lord, did she have to be so distracting? "Yes," Reginald managed to say in what he considered to be a very calm voice, not at all preoccupied by her subtle movement as she stepped around the table. Her movement certainly had nothing to do with the reason why he stepped around but in the opposite direction, maintaining the same distance between them. "You use the cue—"

"This thing here?" Jessica asked innocently, lifting up her cue.

Reginald tried not to look at the way her fingers curled around the wood. "Y-Yes. You use the cue to hit the cue ball."

Jessica looked over the table. "So many balls."

Stay calm, man, stay calm—

"And which is the cue ball?"

"We have one each," said Reginald, grasping at the opportunity to keep the conversation light, and most importantly, not erotic in any way.

Jessica blinked up at him, all innocence. "So there is a pair of balls that we play with?"

Just about managing to transform his groan into a cough, Reginald looked up with as much nonchalance as he could manage. "Y-Yes. Yes. Every other ball is worth a number of points if you pot them, and there are cannons—"

"'Cannons'?" The elegant woman looked around the room as though seeking these particular weapons.

"It's complicated." It wasn't, but Reginald's brain wasn't entirely working right now, and he desperately struck out for shore. "Over the game, you rack up points, over there, by the rack, and when the table is cleared, the person with the greatest number of points wins."

"And that's it?"

"The rules of the game are always easier than playing the game itself," Reginald said with a wink.

Yes, that was it. *Flirt. Flirt! Woo the woman!*

Wait. Wasn't the whole point that I did not have to?

"And do you find playing the game enjoyable?" asked Jessica, stepping around the table and stopping just before him.

Reginald carefully placed the cue down on the table before he snapped it in half. "I suppose it's more fun when everyone knows what they're playing. When everyone knows the rules."

His breath was coming up short, which was ridiculous, but she was so close and the memory of that kiss was clouding his judgment. That kiss… That wonderful kiss…

"And do you treat life like a game?" came Jessica's quiet question.

Her eyes darted to his mouth as she spoke, and Reginald could have crowed to the rooftops. Was she thinking about that kiss too? Did she wonder, as he did, just what had possessed them to do it? Did she long to repeat the experience?

"I…" Reginald swallowed.

Did he treat life like a game?

His mind moved upward, despite himself, to the list he had written before arriving here. It was not something he would ever want read, not in this house, though there was no shame in it.

If Jessica Chance found it, his life would be forfeit. He certainly wouldn't be able to take both her father and brother. And maybe several uncles and cousins besides.

"You… You're not treating this as a game, are you?"

Jessica's voice was low, troubled, even, and it shot a bolt of discomfort through Reginald.

Not as a game, he could say. *But it is something I need to win. There's so much at stake—more than you could ever know.*

Perhaps he should tell her. But he couldn't. She, her parents, the whole Chance family—they would flee his company if they knew. His opportunity to become part of the Chance family would be over.

Reginald tried to smile as jovially as he could as he lied, "No, definitely not."

Chapter Seven

September 7, 1840

T HOUGH THE TEMPTATION was to run away and never look back, skirts flying, Jessica inhaled slowly and instead did something that any other day would be as easy as breathing.

She entered the library.

The thought flashed through her mind that she was being ridiculous as she crept rather than walked around an armchair and caught a glimpse of the man who, in a few weeks, would be her husband. Yesterday, her father had spoken to the vicar at Stanphrey Lacey and written to their vicar in London, where the first of the banns had been read. Her head had almost retreated into her shoulders as the whole of the congregation had turned to look her way. Reginald had smiled and nodded, seeming to enjoy the attention at her side.

Her future husband was seated in an armchair, one foot resting on his knee to better allow the newspaper to spread out, Lord Llyne's face furrowed in concentration. A line merely added to the attractiveness of his brow and his lips were pursed as his gaze flickered along the columns of the print.

Jessica swallowed. It really was most unfair that a man could look like that, so…so attractive, so intriguing, so elegant. The man had clearly had never made a mistake in his whole life. Only a man born to nobility, born to prestige, could lounge like that in someone else's library.

And it wouldn't have been such a problem if she hadn't found the man so enticing.

A flicker in her stomach, a tingling tension across her collar-bones that circled around her shoulder blades—Jessica knew it was wrong to feel such things for a man she hardly knew but… Well. He was to be her husband.

Which was precisely why she had braved the library, braved Lord Llyne alone.

Not Lord Llyne. *Reginald.*

Heat blossomed across Jessica's cheeks merely at the thought of his first name. The intimacy—it was something she had never shared with any man who was not a relation.

Reginald. Reginald. Reg—

"Reginald," Jessica blurted out.

It was a foolish thing to do, a foolish way to introduce her presence into the room, but his name had been so heavily echoing in her mind that it appeared her tongue had no ability to do anything else.

Lord Llyne—Reginald—turned around and his grin was broad. "Miss Chance. Jessica."

It should be illegal, Jessica thought darkly as her cheeks burned, *to feel this way hearing one's name spoken.* It was just a name.

Just a part of her. Just his lips curling around those three syllables, caressing them—

"G-Good hello," she said blankly, coming to a stop in the middle of the room and waving a hand vaguely.

"Good hello"?

If the library floor had not been so expertly carpeted with an Aubusson rug of the finest quality—only the best for Stanphrey Lacey—Jessica would have ripped it up and hoped to hide in the depths of the earth.

Good hello? What on earth was my mouth thinking?

"Erm…yes. Good hello," Reginald said with an expression that was either wry or cutting, Jessica couldn't tell. "You came here looking for something?"

For you, she wanted to say as she stood there like a lemon, stranded in the middle of the library with nothing in her hands.

What on earth did one do with hands, anyway? They couldn't just rest at her sides, that was ridiculous, she must have looked ridiculous—

"Jessica?"

"Book," she said aloud, regretting the decision to come in here and knowing she would never live it down.

This was ridiculous. In the billiards room, she had felt…different. The room had felt sensual, her bravery had suddenly come to the fore and she had spoken from the heart…

And then she had returned to her bedchamber. Played over in her mind the very scandalous way she had spoken to the man.

"So many balls."

Now all her shyness, all her wallflower tendencies, had re-turned and in full force. Now the very idea of being alone here in the library with a man to whom she was not related seemed disgraceful. Even if it was clear her father had given his consent for her to see Reginald without a chaperone present, she still imagined someone else appearing without notice, the scandal of being caught alone with a man who was not her husband.

And yet here she was.

She supposed she would just have to marry him.

"Jessica?"

"I… I tried to say *good morning* and *hello*," she said, her voice more breathy than she would have wanted it, but at least she was able to speak again. "And so I got muddled."

Muddled? Yes, that was the right word for how she was feel-ing right now. As though her mind were in quicksand, being pulled down and down until it would be impossible to think or say anything ever again.

And Reginald—

He was smiling. *Smiling?*

"Muddled is allowed," he said quietly. "I have been known to become a little muddled, in my time."

It was the kindness he showed, the very understanding and gentleness that made Jessica's shoulder blades finally relax.

Perhaps that was why the thought that had suddenly struck her managed to escape her tongue without any time for her to consider whether it was a good idea or not.

"Do you wish to accompany me on a walk in the grounds?" she asked suddenly.

Precisely why her mind had ventured in that direction, she had no idea. The library was surely the better place to attempt to get to know her betrothed: it was quiet, unlikely to be disturbed by her many cousins, and she could sit opposite him in a chair and examine his face as he gave answers to her many questions.

And that was perhaps why she had changed her mind. The thought of sitting opposite Reginald Blakley, Baron Llyne, as she... Well, *interviewed* was a soft word. *Interrogated* was perhaps more accurate to her plans.

Sitting across from him and demanding that he answer *all* her questions...

No, Jessica was certain she would not be able to face him. Perhaps walking side by side, it would be easier to speak her mind. Get her answers.

Get to know the man who had apparently decided she was his best matrimonial prospect.

"A walk? With you?" Reginald blinked.

And shame, blinding, scalding shame rushed through her. For a moment, Jessica couldn't even see the gentleman seated before her, she was so self-conscious.

He did not even wish to walk with her. Had she made such a fool of herself that—

"I would like that very much," said Reginald quietly, rising to his feet and reminding her once again—*how could I have forgotten?*—just how tall and imposing the man was. "Shall we?"

Jessica swallowed, her hesitation momentary, but the moment seeming to elongate out for miles.

He was offering his arm.

His arm. Before she'd met Reginald, the only gentlemen's arms she had ever taken had been her father's and her brother's.

She had never touched another gentleman.

And here Reginald was, expecting her to just…just take…

The wave of panic was anticipated, but no less overwhelming. *This is why you're a wallflower*, Jessica told herself sternly. *This was why you hadn't found a husband in all those years of being out.*

This is why it does not make sense that this man wishes to marry you.

Taking slow, deep inhales, Jessica forced the ground to stop spinning and her eyes to focus more on the man who sighed slightly now, bending his neck forward.

Was it possible…

Was Reginald disappointed that she had not eagerly grasped his arm?

"Thank you," Jessica said softly as she half-stepped, half-tripped toward him.

It was a good thing that the man's arm had already been extended, for if she had not been able to grab it, she may indeed have fallen. As it was, Jessica's hands grasped a strong, unyielding arm that immediately bore her weight, steadying her and preventing her from spilling to the carpet.

There was something intensely secure about the man. The heat was to be expected—Jessica had known that she would flush the moment she was in any sort of contact with the man. Thoughts of that kiss, a kiss that would surely not be repeated until they were wed, flashed through her mind.

But it wasn't just her own body that was warm. Reginald's too seemed to be fiery, heat pouring through his sleeve into her arm.

Jessica lifted her head and her lips parted as she caught Reginald's. There…there was something there, something he wished to say.

"Jessica," he said quietly.

All her life, she had wanted romance. All her life, she had dreamed of moments like this—but now she was in them, Jessica found the heat prickling, the intensity of his gaze too much.

She pulled her hand away and exhaled into a brief smile. "Shall we?"

Not waiting for her betrothed to reply, Jessica marched out of the library as quickly as possible while still, just about, being polite.

It was a close-run thing, though.

Drawing deep lungfuls of air, she waited for Reginald to join her on the patio outside the salon. When he did, Reginald looked… Well, not *saddened* by their physical separation. There was even a twinkle in his eye, though Jessica decided that she was not going to notice it.

No, all she had to do was walk and talk, and learn more about the man who would be the father of her—

Jessica almost tripped over her long skirts as she violently pushed the thought away. *No. One thing at a time.*

"The grounds here are quite spectacular," Reginald said, clasping his hands behind his back as he started to meander down a path. "I suppose you have seen them change over time."

Yes, perfect, Jessica thought, eagerly moving onto the neutral topic. "I-I have, indeed. The poplars along there have grown a great deal the last ten years."

"How wonderful for you and your family, to grow up in a place like this," said Reginald with a grin. "Stanphrey Lacey, it is a wonderful place to call home."

Jessica attempted to smile. "Yes."

There was a great deal more she could say. She could point out that she had only come here for the first time when she'd been nine years old. She could share that her father had never quite been treated the same, not until she'd been about fifteen. She could reveal that her father's birth had stained the relationships with the broader family, that her and her siblings' lack of titles made them instantly different from the others.

But she didn't. After all, this walk was intended to aid her in a greater understanding of her betrothed. Not to rake up family dissent.

"Did you grow up in a place like this?" Jessica asked instead, allowing her fingertips to trail through the wide, herbaceous border, petals of different shapes and textures tickling at the whorls of her fingerprints.

"Like Stanphrey Lacey? Oh, no, I cannot imagine there are many places like Stanphrey Lacey in the whole of England," Reginald said with a brightness that was perhaps too false.

It was flattery, she was sure…and yet there was something more. A greater depth to his words that she could not quite untangle as their path swept to the left, losing the house behind a tall beech hedge.

"Tell me about your home," Jessica said, a little startled at just how bold she was being.

It was not a question she had ever asked anyone else. She had never spoken for long enough to someone outside the family to even consider asking it.

"My home?" Reginald spoke lightly, as though he were asked this question every day of the week. "Well, I have taken lodgings in London just off—"

"No, I meant—well, where did you grow up?"

Jessica had not thought it a particularly personal question. After all, she would happily relate the fact that she had been raised in Pernrith House, London, and had spent a great deal of time there attempting to grow chrysanthemums to not much success.

For some reason, Reginald would not quite meet her eyes as they followed the gravel path into the Winter Garden, now mostly sparse in the heat of the summer. "Oh, not in London."

Jessica waited what she considered was a polite stretch of time, then cleared her throat. "And… And your family. Do you have brothers, sisters?"

"Yes." Reginald's voice was not exactly curt, but it did not invite further conversation.

Which was precisely the point of this walk, Jessica could not help but think ruefully as their steps continued, crunching on the gravel as the only audible accompaniment to the burgeoning sounds of nature. A blackbird sang, heralding the growing heat, and the slightly nectar-drunk hum of a cascade of bumblebees filled the silence.

It wasn't what she'd wanted to fill the silence, but all attempts to encourage Reginald to speak had ended poorly.

Jessica bit her lip, trying not to allow the feelings of worthlessness overtake her. She was a wallflower, yes, but it was not entirely down to her alone to maintain a conversation. The least he could do was ask questions if he would not answer them.

"I apologize." Now his voice was stiff, awkward, uncomfortable. "I do not find speaking of my family that easy."

She glanced at him and saw, as though in a looking glass, the tension around the mouth, the fear and discomfort in the eyes. It was startling, seeing her own awkwardness painted on the face of another.

"I have no wish to pry. I just—"

"It is a reasonable question and I have no reasonable answers," exhaled Reginald with a wry tenderness that disappeared as soon as it had come. "It is just... I did not grow up in a place like this. For my early childhood, I lived in... Well, I would not call it *poverty*, but only because my mother had too great a respect for herself to speak of her situation in such a manner."

Jessica's eyes widened. "I... I see."

She absolutely did not see. How could a baroness be living in such difficult circumstances?

Perhaps... Perhaps Reginald's father had lost his fortune. Yes, that would explain it: the hesitancy to speak of his family home, the poverty or not quite that he spoke of. Maybe the Llyne estate homes had been sold?

Which raised another, far more pressing question—and not one that Jessica could quite work out how to ask.

Where on earth where they going to live, then? Did Reginald have an income, since inheriting the barony?

It was not exactly acceptable to pry into another person's

finances—Jessica had been raised to know that. Yet at the same time, she *was* to wed the man. Surely, her father had ascertained the facts of the matter and had been satisfied. After all, he would not let her marry a pauper.

"Things are different now," Reginald said in a voice that was far too bright and cheerful to be *actually* bright and cheerful. "The barony is in good shape, and my sister, I am sure, will be delighted to meet you."

Ah. Another sister.

Not that Jessica had anything against a sister-in-law, she reminded herself hastily. It was more… Well. She already had three sisters. An extra brother, now, that would be—

"I am afraid my brother will be unable to attend our wedding."

The sentence was spoken so rapidly as the pair of them encircled the Winter Garden and moved to another sweeping lawn, that Jessica barely caught it. It was only as her mind slowly caught up that she understood the sense of it.

"Oh," she said blankly, unsure exactly whether she would gain any answers to her questions if she made them. "He… He is on the Continent, then? A Grand Tour, something like that?"

If she had not been looking for it, Jessica would not have spotted the hitched breath, the flash of pain that cast a momentary shadow across Reginald's handsome features.

When he spoke, it was vague, with sorrow in the corners of his tone. "Something like that."

Do not ask again about his brother, Jessica made a mental note. Clearly, something had occurred between them, something painful—something he was unwilling to speak of.

And though she had absolutely no right to pry, though it was hardly her own business, Jessica could not help but think that in a way it *was* her business. He was to be her brother-in-law, after all. He was a part of the Blakley family. She would need to know, would she not?

But perhaps…

Perhaps, and the thought was an unpleasant one, perhaps most marriages in good Society were not like the ones her family enjoyed. Openness, honesty, deep, romantic love… Jessica knew how rare these things were in a match, and yet she was surrounded by parents, aunts, uncles, and cousins who had all found these characteristics in their own partnerships.

Perhaps she was not to be so fortunate. Perhaps she and Reginald would be pleasant to each other, cordial, even…but there would always be a gap between them. Perhaps she would never truly know him. Perhaps Reginald did not want a wife who knew everything about him.

Perhaps he would not want to know everything about her.

And a wash of loneliness, of deep disconnection, of knowing that she was truly alone and no one in the world would wish to know her fully, careered over Jessica.

The sensation was so unpleasant, so jarring, that she halted in her tracks.

"Jessica?"

Reginald had halted in turn, his brow crinkled with concern.

But not true concern, Jessica tried not to think. How could he truly worry about her if he did not truly know her? If he did not allow her in?

"Are you quite well?" Reginald asked softly.

No, she wanted to say. *No, I'm a wallflower and I'm getting married to a man I don't know—who won't* let *me know him.*

The words would have done her no good, even if she'd had the bravery to speak them.

Somehow, the ambiance of her unspoken thoughts appeared to have been communicated through her expression, for Reginald sighed and dropped his gaze for a moment before returning it, bashful, to her face.

"You expect better of me, I know," he said quietly. "But you will have to trust me, Jessica. There are secrets in every family, and some…some are not for me to tell. You would not wish to embarrass my brother by forcing me to speak of his shame, would you?"

Cheeks burning, Jessica shook her head. To think, she had almost asked him again.

"Thank you." Reginald's smile was eager now, natural, and the crinkles in his brow had smoothed. "You are fortunate. There is not a single scandal in your family. You do not have to fear the truth."

It was true; it was difficult to imagine the idea of keeping secrets in a family. Jessica had never known such a thing; her family had always been kindhearted, respectable, and absolutely aboveboard.

True, some of the whispers she had overheard about her cousins' courtships were that they had been a little sudden, but…none had been as fast as hers.

"I want you to trust me," Jessica whispered, hating that she couldn't put any additional strength into her voice but knowing she had to speak to ignore the rushing thoughts in her mind. "But that doesn't mean you have to tell me everything. Secrets are…are allowed between a husband and wife, after all."

"Not mine," Reginald said with a ferocity she had not expected. "My secrets, scant as they are, will never be held back from you, Jessica. I—"

"Jessica—Jessica Chance, where are you?"

Jessica's heart skipped a beat. There was a tension in her mother's voice, a tension she had not heard in years. Why, it sounded just like when Michael had almost threatened to leave home—to emigrate, Lord knew why.

"Mama?" She did not know when she began running, but she did know that Reginald had grabbed her hand and started to run with her, almost pulling her along as his longer strides took him ahead of her. "Mama, what is it?"

"Jessica—there you are, I've been looking all over," said her mother as she paced up and down the terrace, wisps of hair flying around her face. "He's here!"

If only her lungs were not crying out in agony, if only her legs were not pained at the sudden exertion, Jessica was almost certain that she would be able to concentrate. Here? Who was here?

"Your cousin Thomas, his baby is here!" cried the Viscountess Pernrith, clasping her hands together as she beamed. "It was a difficult birth and he was not expected for a good few weeks, but—"

"Mother and baby well?" asked Reginald swiftly.

Jessica barely had time to glance at him curiously—that a man should ask that—before her mother had thrown herself into the startled man's arms.

"Mama!"

"Oh, isn't it wonderful? A new baby in the family, a late summer child," cried Jessica's mother, pushing herself back from Reginald's shoulders and grinning. Reginald's jaw was slack. "They're in the Lodge. Darling Victoria wanted some privacy and hardly wished to be moved after such an effort, but we can all go tomorrow and visit them."

The only topic of conversation around the dinner table that evening was the arrival of little baby Thomas. Uncle William gave a speech that had Uncle George weeping. There was much hilarity over attempting to select middle names for the new-born—every cousin wished for their own name, naturally—and Jessica sat amongst it all in silence, smiling wanly at those around her, trying to absorb not only the arrival of a new Chance, but the conversation she and Reginald had shared that afternoon.

And when the Pernrith branch of the family was permitted a visit the following day—after the Cothrom and the Aylesbury and the Lindow branches, naturally—and Reginald peered into the basket that held the squirming new life, Jessica's stomach jolted.

There was an expression of delight in Reginald's eyes, pure and unseen before, and that was when she could no longer hide the truth from herself.

If this marriage went as planned—if, in short, she married him and became Baroness Llyne—then he would be the father of her children. When she brought a child into the world, if God was that good to her, then it would be Reginald standing by her shoulder, proudly welcoming in her family to meet the babe.

It was a thought which would require much consideration and—

Reginald looked up and caught her expression, his cheeks pinking as he murmured, "Every child is such a gift."

Jessica's stomach dropped out of her body. *This can't be real. It can't be!*

Wallflowers like her did not find future husbands like him. So what was the secret? What terrible disadvantage to Reginald was there…and when would she discover it?

Chapter Eight

September 8, 1840

IT WAS ALL going incredibly well, and that could only mean one thing.

Well, not the letter burning a hole in his pocket. The letter from his brother—well, more of a note—was short, perfunctory, and galling.

Reginald—awfully sorry to be delayed in returning home. Do not worry, nothing to concern yourself with. I'll explain all when I'm home. Peter

Explain it all when he got home—the cheek! As though he could explain away treachery…

But if one ignored the letter entirely and focused instead on the game before him… everything was going incredibly well.

Reginald grinned as he leaned back after hitting a particularly impressive shot on the billiards table. It was fast becoming his favorite room here at Stanphrey Lacey, a place that was calm, cool, and without—

"Reginald Blakley, how dare you lie to me!"

It was perfectly natural to flinch. Reginald did so instinctively, ducking down and holding up the billiards cue as a defense against the marauding—

Jessica?

"Jessica?" he said, unable to hide the surprise in his tone. "What's wrong?"

"Don't you dare talk to me! Is it true?" Jessica snapped, her eyes narrowed and her fists clenched at her sides.

Reginald opened his mouth…then closed it again. *"Don't you dare talk."*

Well, how on earth was he supposed to explain anything, then?

There was a snort of laughter from the other side of the billiards table. "Someone's in trouble," said Jessica's brother in a singsong voice. "Someone's in—"

"Say another word, Michael, and I will stick that billiards cue right up your—"

"Steady on, sis!" said the young man as his jaw dropped and he reflexively took a step back. "What has gotten into you?"

It was a fair question, though Reginald was glad he had not been the one to ask it. Jessica looked…strange. Her cheeks flushed, yes, but not in the same way they normally were. They were often tinged with the delicate blush of embarrassment, but this was different. Bolder, a darker red—and there was no hint of shyness in her eyes, as there usually was.

She stood there, grasping the billiards table with her hands, looking like an avenging angel who had just been informed of all his sins.

Reginald swallowed. *Surely, not all of them. Where had she found the time?*

"You," Jessica said, and it was a malediction that made Reginald take another step back. "You lied to me!"

"Ah," he said weakly. "Well."

What was a gentleman supposed to say about that?

Yes, yes, of course I lied to you!

And a great number of lies had been told, now he came to think. Oh, Reginald did not typically like to catalogue these things, but as Miss Jessica Chance looked as though she could quite readily tear the billiards table apart with her bare fists, perhaps it was time to take stock.

So: he had lied to her about precisely why he had wanted to marry her.

He had not told her how he had come to choose her, out of all her cousins.

He had lied about his parentage—that was, he had told others in the family about it, but not her. Surely, she considered that an omission?

He had certainly omitted the exact nature of his brother's absence from the country.

Reginald tried, desperately, not to clench his own fists. That brother of his was the root problem of all this. It had been *his* foolish treachery that had meant he, Reginald, had had to take this outrageous step to secure the family's name.

Which…he had also not told Jessica about.

So, he wondered as he looked up into his intended's irate face, which of these lies, or lies by omission, had she discovered?

"You," Jessica said, raising a hand to point at him—Reginald took another hasty step back. "You have been lying about the gambling debts you've been racking up with my family!"

"Ah," said Reginald in a sweep of relief.

"Ah," said Jessica's brother, his utterance sounding a tad less relieved. "You know, I think I'll just go and—"

"You can stay right there, Michael Chance," Jessica said darkly, and Reginald was not surprised that the young man remained rooted to the spot. "Gambling! What would Mama say?"

"Mama never has to know."

"Oh, so you would once again like me to keep a secret for you?"

Reginald's head darted back and forth between the arguing siblings and tried not to smile.

Well, considering what it could have been, it was not much of a secret, was it? A few pounds here and there, and between family too—or at least, men who would soon be his family. What did it matter?

No, considering the little lies he had already told, along with the gaping lies of omission, he was fortunate indeed that Jessica had not uncovered any of them. If that occurred, he rather thought it would be his own billiards cue which would disappear up his—

"—greatly disappointed in you," Jessica finished.

Much to Reginald's surprise, as he did not consider a sister's disappointment to be that great a threat, Michael hung his head.

"I am sorry, Jessica," he said humbly.

The statement appeared to rid the young woman of all her ire. She deflated, took a deep breath, and said, "Right. Well. Good. Now go away."

Reginald stiffened. "No. What about our game?"

"Got to go. Sorry, old man," said Michael hastily, clapping Reginald on the arm and giving him a brief grin before adding in a whisper, "Just apologize as soon as you can get a word in edgeways. Works every time with my sisters."

The rogue winked and then stepped out of the billiards room.

Ah. So perhaps the humble apology from the young man was not precisely what it appeared.

Clearly, Jessica was well aware of this, however, for she sighed heavily and before Reginald could protest, picked up one of the billiards balls and moved it from hand to hand. "He always apologizes, even when he doesn't mean it. *Especially* when he doesn't mean it."

Reginald cleared his throat. "Ah, well, you know. Brothers."

There was still a tension in the room somehow, but he could not quite put his finger on why. The afternoon sun was starting its journey back down toward the horizon, though it would be hours before it dipped out of sight. The warmth was pleasant this side of the house, and until a few minutes ago, the room had been full of his and Michael's laughter as they'd played for another shilling. A shilling he had been about to win.

And now...

Now it was different. Oh, Jessica brought a sort of uncomfortable heat in his loins whenever she walked into a room, but this was different even to that.

There was a sharpness to her eyes, her expression one Reginald had not seen before. Almost as though she were preparing to say something. Something she did not wish to express.

Perhaps Michael was right. An apology, that would fix it. Whatever this was.

"I am sorry," Reginald said, finding that he was, much to his own surprise. "I should not have told you I wouldn't be tempted by a bet."

"I don't care about the gambling," Jessica muttered, still moving the billiards ball from one hand to the other.

"You... You don't?"

It was not often that Reginald was bewildered, but the word was particularly apt in this moment. She did not care about the gambling, and yet she had marched into the room like a Valkyrie.

So what was the problem? Why was she now examining him as though attempting to look through his skull into his very thoughts? And why was there a prickle of anticipation in his body that made him sense an incoming storm?

Jessica sighed and placed the billiard ball back down on the table—at least three inches, from Reginald's judgment, from where it had been. "It's not the gambling. It's the not knowing."

The not knowing.

His mind was working swiftly, but clearly not swiftly enough, and Reginald found to his great distaste that he was being left behind in the conversation.

"'The not knowing,'" he repeated, hoping that by saying the phrase aloud, it would unlock its secrets for him.

No, he still did not understand. Was he supposed to have told her about the three pounds her brother owed him, and the half a crown he owed her father? The sums were so small, he had honestly forgot them entirely until she had marched into the room.

Surely, that could not be it...

Jessica swallowed, her throat bobbing in a way that distracted Reginald to no end. He wasn't supposed to be looking at the curve of her neck, not thinking what it would be like to press kisses there, to taste her pulse—

"I wasn't going to ask this, but I can't help myself," she said in a rush, drawing Reginald's attention unexpectedly back to her face. "But finding out from my father that you've been gambling with him—"

"It was just for a few coins—"

"I know." She was smiling now, and Reginald could hardly tell whether he should have been concerned or delighted. "I know, but it…it made me realize how much I don't know you. Not in the way I want to. Not in the way I would want to know my husband."

"My husband."

Something strange happened to Reginald's spine when she'd said those words. Small, perhaps generally innocuous, and yet they made his spine tingle and his shoulders crack.

He was to be her husband—and she was right, she did not know him. That had all been on purpose, but…

"Why me?"

Reginald's whole body tensed. He could not have heard that correctly, could he?

Jessica was leaning her palms elegantly on the billiards table now, her head tilting to one side as she examined him, watched him, as she waited for the answer to her question.

He swallowed. "I beg your pardon?"

"I told myself I would not ask. I told myself it did not matter," Jessica said, and there was a lightness to her voice that spoke not of nonchalance, but of great and delicate care. "But finding out from my father—I know 'tis only for a few shillings, but it made me realize just how little I know. And so I wanted to start at the beginning. Why you chose me. Why… Why did you choose me, Reginald?"

Oh, hell.

It was the question he had hoped she would never ask.

Foolishness, Reginald knew. It was only natural that she would seek the answer to that question eventually. He had hoped—idiot that he was—that Jessica would only brave the question once they were married.

And now here he stood, forced to either lie or confront her with a truth that she would not like.

"Well?" Jessica said quietly. "You didn't draw me out of a hat, did you?"

Reginald forced a laugh, more to break the tension in his own chest than anything else. "Oh, no, most definitely not."

"So there was some reasoning behind me as a choice?" she persisted.

Damn her intellect, and damn her inquisitiveness.

Not that Reginald could put much heart into the thought. It was natural for her to wonder, was it not? And now here he was, standing in the billiards room and hoping desperately that someone would interrupt them.

"Was that your mother calling you just now?" he tried hopefully.

Jessica did not even turn around, her gaze never leaving his face. "No, it was not. Why don't you want to tell me? Is... Is it bad?"

Bad? "No," Reginald said, mostly truthfully.

That was it—*mostly* truthful. As long as he could stay on the side of mostly truthful, he would probably be fine.

Probably.

"Look, I could have picked anyone," began Reginald, sweeping his arms into an expansive arc as though to demonstrate that in many ways, there was no story here whatsoever.

It did not work. A flicker of pain, a shadow, and then a frown all hovered over Jessica's face in quick succession. "Am I supposed to feel flattered? Grateful, that of my more beautiful cousins and sisters, you chose me?"

"No! No, that's—that's not what I meant!"

Reginald tried to grin. He had little experience in flattery; that was, he had a great deal of experience in flattery, but not of this kind.

No, the flattery he had utilized in the past had meant nothing. A smile in the street, a laugh during a dance, a whist player who enjoyed their time at the card table or a dinner partner who was not bored by him…

That was the flattery he had typically used.

This was different. He was, Reginald was starting to realize, actually interested in Jessica's good opinion of him. Not merely because they were to wed, though that was helpful. But because… Well. Because it was Jessica.

So. He would need to flatter, and he could not lie. Had any gentleman ever been in such a pickle?

"I had heard of your reputation," Reginald said slowly, carefully selecting every word and examining it in the privacy of his own mind before speaking it to ensure that it was both mostly true—and unlikely to offend. "Your reputation in Society, I mean. Everyone has heard of Miss Jessica Chance."

She frowned. "They may have heard of me, but I doubt they spoke of me often. They frequently forget to invite me events to which they welcome my entire family, despite bearing no ill will toward me."

He still couldn't believe the cheek of anyone so thoughtless. "That is awful, truly. But I heard of you regardless. It was a name that sung melodiously in my mind. A name that stuck with me."

And there it was—the smile. He was always able to create a smile.

"Oh," said Jessica, her smile paired with a delicate flush in her cheeks. "I see."

No, she did not, Reginald thought heavily, but perhaps that was the best way. Yes, it had been her reputation that had first made him think of her, out of all the Chance cousins who were currently available for matrimony.

Her reputation as a wallflower.

Miss Jessica Chance was a wallflower. And that meant, Reginald knew, that she would not have received much attention in the past from interested gentlemen. Why, she may not have received much attention at all. She would crave it, be willing to welcome it from a quarter she did not know at all because she had received so little.

She would, in short, be grateful for it. For him.

It had all seemed so simple at the time. Reginald had thought himself clever, in fact, to have found a way to calmly and dispassionately choose the woman who would restore his family's fortunes and perhaps even become a companionable person with whom to live.

And now…

"That was before I met you," he said unguardedly.

Jessica stiffened, her whole body expressing the sentiment that her mouth soon did. "You have altered your opinion of me?"

"I have, indeed," Reginald said, and he stepped forward as the truth was more easily tasted on his lips. "For since I have been at Stanphrey Lacey, I have been captivated by your…your beauty."

He had not expected that particular word. He had intended to say 'geniality.' She was, after all, a pleasant person to be around. Very pleasant, in fact. Far more pleasant than he would have expected.

But he had not lied—Jessica's beauty had captivated him in that moment and he had spoken from the heart. As Reginald had stepped forward, the sunlight streaming through the windows had shifted and Jessica had been lit up and—

She was beautiful. It was a beauty only discovered through knowing her, Reginald realized. Knowing her and looking at her, truly looking at her.

Oh, it was easy enough to look over her. Wallflowers were accustomed to being overlooked, and he rather thought Jessica had slipped into the habit of becoming part of the background. There were so many of her sisters, after all, who took center stage, with their fashionable lips and their loud, pleasing chatter. And that was before the cousins entered the fray.

But Jessica… Jessica was different. She had an elegance around the mouth, but one had to spend a great deal of time looking at it before one realized just how perfectly balanced it was with her chin. Her jaw was soft, and together with her high brow, it rendered a face that was so perfectly proportioned, it almost felt impossible.

And those eyes—those eyes sparkled with intelligence, a trait Reginald could not help but find painfully attractive. She had wit, did Jessica, and it was only in moments like this when she was open to him that he could see it.

Reginald swallowed. And then there was her…her form. The curves that swept past people so often that they probably did not account for them.

He was accounting for them now. Remembering, in fact, when his hands had been clasped on her—

"My beauty?"

Reginald blinked. Jessica was staring with an expression that was not so much incredulous as disbelieving.

"You tease me," she said quietly, and there was a discomfort in her voice that was the audible accompaniment to the way she crept into herself. "I do not want to be chosen from pity, my lord. Not that. Never that."

It was astonishing—moments ago, she had been glowing, both thanks to the sunlight and the confidence he had wrought in her.

Now the wallflower Miss Jessica Chance was smaller, quieter, less vibrant, as though desperately hoping not to be noticed. As though she were becoming part of the background again.

Reginald stepped forward once more, closing the gap between them that was now but a few feet. "Beauty, yes. Have you never examined yourself in a looking glass, Jessica? Surely, you must see what I do."

"It is Irene who is beautiful, not I," she said dismissively, so swiftly that Reginald wondered whether this was a sentence she had trotted out before.

"She has her advantages, yes. But you are more," Reginald found himself saying, utterly truthfully. "Your beauty lies not only in your curves, but in your character."

Perhaps saying 'curves' had been going too far. Jessica's lips parted—those painfully kissable lips. Why hadn't he kissed her again since the ride in the forest?

"You cannot mean that," she whispered.

Reginald grinned, trying to keep the rogue out of his expression. "And why not? You are to be my wife. It is only right for me to enjoy the fact that my wife-to-be comes alive when she is truly herself. Your beauty, Jessica, it is incomparable to others'. It's... It's you. It's who you are, and it makes me want..."

"Want what?" she asked after a beat.

She seemed mollified by his words, but her cheeks were flushed.

And his words had been true. Reginald knew that for a certainty. The fact that he had never said such things to any woman before was most startling, but then, he had never felt this way before.

Hang on...

"You mean a great deal to me, and I know you will mean just as much to my family," Reginald said in what he hoped was a slightly more appropriate tone. Well, they were not married yet, after all.

"To your family?"

Her tone was inquisitive and Reginald knew, at some point, he would have to tell her about his father, his parentage, how the whole thing had come to be.

But not now. Not today. And certainly nothing about his brother.

And so he spoke quietly, imbuing his voice with an intimacy that did not feel anywhere near so forced as he had expected, and spoke truths.

Truths, yes. Not complete truths. But what wife wished to hear the complete truth from her husband?

"Our marriage will make a great difference to my family," Reginald said honestly, holding her gaze.

Because she would save it. Her connection, her Chance name, that would reduce the gossip, the speculation about his brother's loyalty.

She did not have to know that, of course.

Jessica frowned as she looked deep into his eyes, the moment elongating into silence that was not uncomfortable.

Reginald looked steadily back. He would have to hope she could see the sparse truth he had spoken in his eyes, for if not…

"I am honored," she said softly, her attention dropping to her hands. "I-I hope you are not offended by me asking about this."

"No. No, it is only natural," Reginald said with a deep sigh of relief.

She had bought it, then. She had believed him.

One more day down. One day closer to the day that he would make Miss Jessica Chance his bride.

One more day that he had avoided spilling the truth.

Chapter Nine

September 10, 1840

SO MANY THOUGHTS had whirled around in Jessica's head the last few days that she finally capitulated and went to bed early. When she awoke, therefore, head heavy and temples throbbing, it was with a great relief that after dressing she sent a note downstairs in the hands of Wharton, her and her sisters' lady's maid, to say that she would not be descending for breakfast.

Lord Llyne. Reginald. The man was an enigma. An enigma wrapped in a puzzle. An enigma wrapped in a puzzle behind a locked door, and he was inside, holding the key.

What did he truly want with her? Why her, of all women in the Chance family—of all women in Society?

It was confusing to the extreme, and the worst of it was that Jessica knew she was attracted to him. There was a…a way about him that made one want to sit at his feet and smile as he spoke, and that, she thought firmly, was pathetic.

She may have been a wallflower, but that did not mean she was willing to lavish her attentions onto anyone who walked by.

It was all greatly confusing. The marriage was agreed, but she could break it, if she wished. But should she? Was suspicion of a man she hardly knew sufficient cause to break such a thing?

Jessica could not help but grin as the gentle knock on the door ten minutes later revealed Wharton had returned with a breakfast tray.

"Almost as though I'm a married lady," she said with a weak

grin as she propped herself up against two pillows, fully dressed, and welcomed the tray of hot buttered toast, a pot of jam, a pot of marmalade, and a pot of tea. "That's what my cousin Liliana does now she's married, all the wives. They have breakfast in bed."

"Well, you'll be joining them soon, won't you, miss?" opined the narrow-faced maid with a beaming look before heading to the door. "I'll be back shortly to help you dress, after I help your sisters."

Jessica did not turn around to watch her go, staying perfectly still in horrified shock.

Because her maid was right. In a few weeks, she would be married, and she would also be having breakfast in bed, like all married ladies did.

Oh, goodness.

The thought did nothing to improve her headache, and so when Irene bounded up into her bedchamber calling out that she needed to borrow a pair of gloves, Jessica raised a hand to her throbbing head and winced.

"Do you not have your own gloves, Reeny?" she asked her sister peevishly, as her sister rummaged through the chest of drawers on the other side of the room.

"Oh, yes, but we're going into Stanhampton today, all of us, and I have lost both the lefts of my pairs—ah, there they are, can I borrow these?"

Jessica would have offered Irene her own head if it meant she would go away. "Of course. What do you mean, everyone is going?"

"Well, most of us. Not Thomas or Victoria, of course, with the new baby at the Lodge, and maybe one or two others have their own plans once we get into town. But the rest of us came up with the plan last night, after you retired early. You're welcome, too, of course." Irene looked her over. "If Wharton can help you get ready in time."

"No, that's quite all right. I...I'll stay. I don't feel up for a drive today, I don't think. It's my head again."

"You won't mind being left alone?" It appeared that it was only now that her sister had considered the implication. "I mean, should I stay with you, keep you company, that sort of thing? I could read to you, I could tell you what I can see through the window, I could sing—"

"No," Jessica said, perhaps a little too hastily. It was an open secret in the family that Irene's musical appreciation was second to none, but so was her musical ability. In the opposite direction. "No, I thank you, but I believe I shall doze most of the morning. Are you all going to Stanhampton for the morning?"

"For the whole day, Uncle William says. Something about spreading about the family money in the place," Irene said breezily, pulling on her sister's gloves. "Goodness, these are lovely. We might be back for afternoon tea, definitely for dinner. You don't mind being alone with the family gone?"

She would welcome it, though it was hardly the sort of thing Jessica could say. "I do not mind," she said, completely truthfully. "I hope you have a wonderful time. And come back with both gloves."

Irene pulled a face. "Not likely, given my current run with gloves, is it? Feel better soon, Jess."

And that was that. The whirlstorm that was her sister and her incredible glove-losing skills rushed out of her bedchamber, and silence reigned once more.

For a while, it was precisely what Jessica needed. She closed her eyes and allowed her mind to drift away, trying to ignore the throb of her temples. A bird sang gloriously outside. The room lightened, warmed up as the day continued fine.

But after what felt like an age Jessica opened her eyes again, she saw it had only been an hour—Wharton had no doubt peeked in on her and left her alone, as her clothes were laid out for her on the chair in front of the dressing table.

Quite unaccountably, Jessica was bored.

Bored.

Her temples no longer throbbed and she was to be alone all day, the family gone to town. There was no reason why she would have to stay up here, was there?

She quickly dressed, perhaps not quite reaching all the buttons on her back that Wharton would have reached for her. But she had no desire to ring for the maid, even if it meant her hair was a bit messy as she attempted to pin it up without assistance.

An empty house. It was something Jessica had craved, though she had been unable to put words to it, from the moment her branch of the Chance family had arrived at Stanphrey Lacey. Oh, her family was all very well—in truth, she rather suspected that she had a very pleasant family, all things considered.

But there were so many of them. On and on, every room one entered, there was bound to be someone in it. Privacy and silence were in short supply.

Until today.

Jessica smiled to herself as she stepped down the sweeping staircase and walked along the corridor toward one of her favorite places in the manor. Her footsteps echoed into the still silence, the heat somehow keeping the air stilted. Other than the servants, who seemed to manage to keep themselves out of sight most of the time, she was all alone here. All alone, not to be interrupted, able to do whatever she wanted.

Her fingers reached out for the door of the place she had longed to come since arrival, but it had always been so busy, so frantic. And now—

"Ah, Jessica," said Reginald with a smile as he turned to see who had entered the portrait gallery. "Your sister informed me you were unwell before they left. I trust you are feeling better?"

It was all Jessica could do not to faint away, which would not have spoken well of her health, and almost certainly led to some dramatics, including Reginald picking her up and carrying her upstairs to—and she had to swallow at the mere thought of this— her bedchamber.

The image flashed in her mind. Her cheeks pale, her loose

hair tumbling down her shoulders as she wilted against Reginald's broad chest, her whole body in his arms as he gently lowered her onto her bed and leaned forward to brush away—

Jessica shook her head momentarily, as though attempting to rid her ears of water.

She did not understand. They were all meant to be—the house was supposed to be empty—had not Irene said that they had all planned on leaving?

"Is everything quite well?" Reginald asked, peering at her with furrowed brows indicating what appeared to be genuine concern.

All the *family* had gone to town. Why had she not noticed the flaw in her sister's statement?

Reginald was not family, and so Irene had not thought to include him in her mental list of those taking the carriages to Stanhampton. And that meant he was here.

That meant the two of them were alone.

It was most remiss of her mother, to be sure—of all the aunts, too. To be left alone in the house, without a chaperone! Well, there was Wharton, but she was no doubt busy mending several of her sisters' clothes.

Perhaps her mother approved of Jessica spending time alone with her betrothed, as her father did. The banns had started to be read, after all. This marriage was going to take place.

Or perhaps everyone had made the same mistake Irene had. Perhaps they had all forgotten Reginald.

Jessica swallowed, the sound seeming to echo in the impossibly long portrait gallery. Forget Reginald? Forget a man that tall? That broad? With that twinkle in his eye, that searing magnetism that surely drew every woman under the age of five and forty toward him?

Heavens.

"I... I thought you had gone with my family to Stanhampton," Jessica managed to say, navigating speaking and walking two paces forward with great difficulty.

How did he manage to do this to her?

"Oh, I was worried about you. I did not wish to leave you here alone," came the quiet reply.

That made her smile, at least. "Alone, other than the butler, the housekeeper, footmen, underfootmen, maids, lady's maids, valets, the cook, kitchen maids, a scullery maid or two, I would suppose, laundry maids, gardeners, stablehands, groundsmen, and our steward?" Jessica asked lightly.

She had not intended to injure, and yet that appeared to be the effect of her quip. Reginald's cheeks flushed with color and he looked away for a moment before turning his blazing gaze back at her.

"Yes," he said simply.

Well, what on earth was a lady supposed to reply to that? Goodness, the man was impossible—and even more confusingly, he was standing right before one of her favorite paintings, the one she had come to stand before.

Maybe something of her thoughts showed in her face, for Reginald turned back to the frame and said quietly, "Magnificent, isn't it?"

Jessica half-sighed as she stepped forward to join him beside the painting. It was large, at least ten feet high, and perhaps six feet wide. The frame was a masterpiece, all gilt gold and furls and twists, but it was the painting itself that always drew her whenever she visited Stanphrey Lacey.

Four boys—well, two young men and two boys, really. The older two had to be nearing the time when they would go off to university, and the younger two appeared to be squabbling, each attempting to get closer to the middle. They were standing in a garden—a garden not too unlike the one currently flourishing in the grounds.

"Your father and his three brothers, I suppose," Reginald said quietly. "I can see the resemblance."

It was not so impressive a statement. A small plaque had been attached to the bottom of the painting years ago, before Jessica could remember, with the inscription: *The sons of the Duke of Cothrom: William, John, and George.* She could remember the additional plaque that had been attached beside it, remember her father's face when he had first seen it, when her Uncle William had proudly taken the Pernrith family to the portrait on their second visit.

And Frederick.

Jessica had not understood the significance of it then. She understood now.

"Strange, that the names of the four brothers were made over two plaques," mused Reginald, clearly utterly blasé about the whole thing. "Especially when your father and your Uncle George, they look around about the same age."

"Yes," Jessica said quietly. "Well, there's a story there. I am surprised you do not know it."

Perhaps she should not have been. Oh, her mother had always said that there had been a great to-do about her father's legitimization when it had happened, but that had been so long ago. There were plenty of people who had surely forgotten.

Not her father, of course.

"'Know it'?" repeated Reginald, his brow furrowing as his hand glanced across hers.

Jessica gasped.

She should have been wearing her gloves—the gloves she had thoughtlessly loaned to her sister, now miles away.

She might have not needed to wear gloves indoors, at home, particularly when she had thought herself the only one in the building, but it would have prevented the searing heat that flashed across her knuckles as Reginald brushed past them.

Did he feel it too? Was that why his eyes had glittered, just for a moment?

"The painting, the two plaques," prompted the man she was to marry in a few short weeks. "Will you tell me the story?"

Jessica hesitated, but only for a moment.

"Never be ashamed." That was what her father had always said.

"If you're ashamed of where you've come from, you'll learn to become ashamed of where you're going."

"There is only a month's difference between my Uncle George, and my father," Jessica said aloud, looking up at the two young boys. Her father's eyes were sad, even in the painting, even as a small boy.

For some reason, Reginald did not appear to need any further explanation. "Ah. You are happy to speak of your father's initial illegitimacy, then."

She could not help but stare in surprise. "How—How did you…?"

"Your father is not the only man born without a name but given one as he grew older," Reginald said, his smile not quite faltering.

And that was what Jessica noticed. Precisely how his smile did not falter—as though he were well-practiced, in fact, in ensuring that his smile in that moment did not falter.

Quite why she did it, she did not know. Jessica slipped her hand into his and squeezed his fingers.

There was an answering squeeze—and though she had intended merely to squeeze his hand then release it, to show comfort and retain propriety, somehow, Jessica did not wish to. She stood there, staring into Reginald's eyes, his warm hand encircling hers, and did not pull away.

Reginald was the first to break the moment, and he did so by looking back at the painting. "Your father was illegitimate. A half-brother."

"Y-Yes." Jessica inhaled deeply and mirrored him. Her father as a child looked out at the painting with joy at being included, yes, but also confusion as to why. It broke her heart. "He always knew he was, and his brothers…they grew to accept it. Uncle William first, many years ago. It was he who, upon inheriting the duchy gave the estate of Pernrith to my father. He decided to give all his brothers titles, give them permanently for their own heirs."

"I did wonder," said Reginald with a wry look. "It is unusual.

But people say the Chances are unusual—not in a bad way, of course."

"My uncle thought it was fairer." It was all Jessica could think to say, when her mind was still reeling from what he had said mere minutes ago.

"Your father is not the only man born without a name but given one as he grew older."

So did that…did that mean—

"Yes," said Reginald quietly, once again demonstrating that peculiar habit he had of being able to read her mind. "Yes, my parents were not married to each other. I was legitimized as a young boy when my father's wife could not have children."

Jessica swallowed, but there was no bitterness in the man's tone. If anything, he sounded…calm. At peace. "But you said— you had a sister."

His laugh was bright, too. "Yes, about a year after I was formally legitimized and brought into the family, my stepmother started having children. Three in all—one died very young, but my father was delighted at the other two. I was still his heir, and now he had a larger family. It was all he ever wanted, I think. You do not remark on my parentage."

The last sentence was hardly accusatory, but it was curious. Jessica was all of a sudden very conscious of the fact that she was still holding hands with the man.

Aside from that kiss, that heady kiss, it was perhaps the most intimate she had ever been with a gentleman.

"I see no reason to remark on it," she said aloud. "Judging a man on his birth is hardly fair, and it's rarely correct. Some of the most dissolute gentlemen in Society are, from what I read in the newspapers, from the best families without a stain on their bloodline. My father is one of the best men I have ever known. I suppose you might fall into the latter category."

She risked a glance and saw to her relief that Reginald was smiling.

She had made him smile. Why did that light a blaze in her

belly and make her fingers tingle?

"You flatter me with the comparison," he said lightly.

"You have earned it." And exactly why she was telling him this, Jessica did not know. She flushed as she continued. "I mean, you have been nothing but honest and honorable. You have asked for my hand and I…I am grateful."

"I do not merely want your gratitude."

And what on earth was she supposed to say to that?

Before Jessica could manage a flustered reply, Reginald continued. "I admit myself impressed by the Chance family. Oh, I knew you were respected and esteemed, I knew that you had one of the most elegant family trees, an ancestry that went all the way back to the Conqueror…but I admire more than that. Your family's acceptance of your father, the way you could not tell to look at you all now, the sincerity between you—the way you were raised, it is quite wonderful."

Quite wonderful.

Jessica was not sure why she did it. There she was, standing before a painting of her father and uncles, the picture of almost happiness, hand in hand with a man who was willing to marry her—quite unlike any other man she had ever encountered—and she was about to do something reckless.

She was going to be honest.

"I would not call it all 'wonderful.'"

The words had been quiet, but they had echoed around the large portrait gallery as if she had shouted them.

Reginald let go of her hand. "Why would you say that?"

He was meandering now, away from her, just as she had expected. Why, oh, why had she let her guard down—why had she allowed herself to be so truthful?

He had stopped now before a painting that Jessica knew almost as well as the first. "You and your sisters?"

Jessica moved to stand beside him, stomach twisting as she wondered if she could avoid any more truth-telling. Well, other than this. "Yes."

They had been young when this had been painted—Jessica could remember it clearly, but Gwen couldn't recall it at all.

"You all look so happy," Reginald said quietly, and there was no malice in his words, no accusation, just interest. "You all look happy now. Was it not so?"

"It… It's not that I am not happy…" *Oh, blast, where is one supposed to find the words?* "It's more that—well, one can feel lonely in a crowd. When one is around so many people, so many vibrant, handsome, charming people…it is a challenge to be noticed. You can feel ignored, not because people are purposefully ignoring you, but because…" She should never have attempted this. "Because there is always someone more interesting. More charming. More adventurous. More intellectual. A painter, or an archer, or a Society beauty. There's always—"

"Always a distraction," Reginald said, and his smile was genial, and comforting, and somehow spiced. "You've been lonely, then."

I'm lonely now. That was what Jessica wanted to say, but it felt like a disservice, a betrayal of her family to speak so.

It was not their fault she was a wallflower. It was not their fault she struggled to maintain a conversation with someone for three minutes together.

"I was lonely," she said aloud, tamping down the thoughts as best she could. "But it is not the worst thing in the world. I am accustomed to being ignored."

For some reason, Reginald's brow had furrowed. "But, Jessica—I mean, no one who sees you, truly sees you, could ever ignore you."

One way or another, her breath was catching in her lungs, every movement of her ribs painful as Jessica stared up into his dark eyes. "I-I beg your pardon?"

"Anyone who sees you as I do," he repeated quietly, and he had taken a step toward her, and Jessica had retreated but her back had hit the gallery wall right beside the frame, and she could not retreat farther, "anyone who truly sees you, Miss Jessica

Chance, would never wish to ignore you. God, it's all I can do to stay away from you."

Jessica gasped, unable to help herself, and the sudden movement of her breasts grabbed Reginald's gaze and she burned, burned to be looked at by him.

Truly looked at. Truly seen.

"Then… Then don't."

He did not appear to understand her. "Don't what?"

His voice was a growl and hers was only a whisper when Jessica managed, "Don't stay away."

It was a miracle that she was able to get all three words out, for Reginald moved, pressing her against the wall and capturing her mouth with his own.

And oh, it was heaven—it was heaven to be so desired, to find herself devoured, to feel his hands on her waist pulling her into him as his chest pressed against her breasts, pinning her against the wall as his lips teased pleasure out of her in roaring waves.

Jessica whimpered, splaying her palms against him then curling her fingers around his lapels to bring him closer. Oh, he could never be close enough. His kisses were fiery and his left hand was gently sliding down her gown to cup her buttocks and all she could think was *more, more, more—*

"Jessica," Reginald groaned into her mouth, as though he were entirely at her mercy. "Jessica…"

"Reginald," she moaned in turn, her whole body sparking with sensual bliss, his mouth moving now to trail kisses down her neck.

Oh, God, how had no one told her that it could be like this? Her body was alive, alive in a way it never had been before, and though his left hand remained cupping her buttocks, his right hand was moving up, slowly caressing her breast as his mouth nuzzled her décolletage, and a servant could walk in on them at any moment and yet she did not care, and if not for the wall, Jessica would surely be falling, falling—

A crash—a roaring, echoing noise that near deafened her.

Jessica started as Reginald pulled away, staring with dazed eyes at the large painting that had slipped to the floor.

"Oh… Oh, dear," Jessica said weakly.

The painting was not damaged—it had only been knocked off its hook—but it had been their passionate kissing, Reginald's ardent caresses that had done it.

When she looked up with nervous eyes, it was to see her future husband grinning.

"Well, now that we've done all the damage we can," he said blithely, moving to press her back against the wall and grinning as Jessica gasped, "I'd like to keep kissing…"

Chapter Ten

September 11, 1840

"MY GOODNESS," GROANED Reginald, placing his hands on his stomach theatrically. "I do believe I shall have to send a note to your cook, Your Graces, and request that they cease their impressive concoctions immediately. My poor valet will have to adjust all my waistcoats!"

There was good-natured laughter around the large dining table as all the plethora of Chances chuckled at his pronouncement.

"Nonsense, you need feeding up," said the Dowager Duchess of Cothrom gracefully. "I always say—"

"Mama," interrupted her eldest son with more than a little of an eye roll. "You do not need to worry about feeding up men marrying into the family! You have a grandson now. You can worry about feeding him."

"Oh, I think it quite important that I feed up everyone who comes into this family—after all, am I not still, in a sense, the matriarch, even if I've stepped aside for my dear daughter-in-law?" His mother grinned. "Besides, I will happily accept any compliment that comes my way, even if it is technically for our cook. Lord Llyne, another ice?"

"Your Grace, I am utterly undone, as are my waistcoat buttons," said Reginald with a grin as a few of the younger Chances snorted. "I am considering skipping the port and cigars and having a footman roll me up to my bed forthwith."

More laughter, though there was none emanating from the

beautiful woman seated to his left.

Against his better judgment, Reginald glanced at Miss Jessica Chance. She was smiling. She was also flushing.

"Absolute nonsense," she murmured under the raucous chatter that had erupted down one end of the table—a debate about the cheese course, it appeared. "You have never looked so...so trim."

The flush of pink on her cheeks told Reginald that it had taken Jessica a great deal to compliment him in that way, and he rather enjoyed it.

He rather enjoyed her. Dear God, but he had not expected this. Go to the Chance family manor, easy, select his bride, fine. But actually start to...to care for her? To admire her, to see her wit and respect it, to see her loneliness and wish to change it? To see her beauty, to see it unfurl before him and then taste those lips and know that no cuisine, not even from the Stanphrey Lacey Cook, would ever compare?

Reginald swallowed and shifted in his seat. "I thank you."

Jessica inclined her head and yet said nothing. Her hand slipped to her side and almost without thinking, he mirrored her and took her hand, squeezing it.

Squeezing it as she had done in the portrait gallery before they had...

Well. It had been fortunate, indeed—or *unfortunate*, a matter of opinion—that they had been interrupted by a well-meaning footman, investigating the source of the clatter, before he had managed to get his hand up Jessica's skirts.

So close. His whole body had throbbed with unrequited need the rest of the day.

And now here he was, seated beside her at dinner, remembering that moment, how his body had thrummed, how his manhood had twitched, how her breasts had felt under his eager palm—

"You look a tad warm, Lord Llyne," said Jessica's brother from the other side of the table. There was a mischievous twinkle to his eye. "Something heating you up?"

Jessica immediately dropped Reginald's hand as he said, "In fact there is, Mr. Chance. Guilt."

"'Guilt'?" Chance spoke so loudly that the rest of the table—and there was a great deal of them—quietened to hear them. "Goodness, you astonish me. What, precisely, are you guilty of?"

Reginald was very careful not to even glance at the beautiful woman beside him, but even in his peripheral vision, he could see that she was flushing most deeply.

Did she believe that he was about to announce to her entire family, at dinner, precisely what they had been getting up to in the portrait gallery?

Never fear...

"I am guilty of overstaying my welcome, I regret to say," Reginald said quietly, hating that he had to say it, but knowing that the feeling had been overcoming him for some time. "I have imposed. I arrived here with no invitation, merely the hope of gaining the hand of your fairest flower, and now I have done that, I suppose, even though the reading of the banns have only just begun, I should be returning to—"

He was not permitted to finish his sentence.

"Absolutely not," said the dowager duchess firmly.

"Not an imposition at all—tell him, Frederick," said Jessica's mother just as firmly.

"If anything, *we*'re the imposition, making you part of our entertainment!" That was Jessica's brother, and he looked genuinely aggrieved at the idea that Reginald might depart.

"We still haven't gotten to know you—those Pernrith Chances have kept you all to themselves," protested a cousin whose name Reginald could not quite recall in this moment. "I mean, fair's fair."

"What Frank is trying to say," said Lady Liliana with a wry smile, "is that you are very welcome to stay and you must not dream of leaving merely due to propriety."

"Yes," said Frank, yes, that was her name, with a snort. "Most of us don't follow propriety any—Sammy, that hurt!"

"And what my nieces are attempting to say," said a genteel woman whom Reginald knew was Aunt Dodo, "is that you are no imposition, and you are very welcome to stay for the rest of our time here. Is that not right, Cothrom?"

All eyes turned to the patriarch of the family. Or he would rightfully have been, if he had not prematurely passed his title on to his son. The family still seemed to think of him in that way, though, a mark of respect for a man so long the head of such a brood.

His temples were gray and his eyes were sharp, and Reginald swallowed to see himself inspected so closely by a man who demanded and received such respect.

Uncle William—or the Dowager Duke of Cothrom, as Reginald rather thought he should consider him—inclined his head. "You do us great honor by your presence, Lord Llyne. Do not deprive us of it now."

There was applause, and cheers, and laughter, but none of it mattered nearly so much as the hand on his knee.

On his knee?

When Reginald turned to Jessica, she was flushing, but she was also smiling.

"Stay," she said softly.

His pulse skipped a beat.

And that was the trouble, wasn't it? If this was still all a marriage of convenience, a plot, a clever plan to secure and guarantee his family's place in Society, then perhaps he could stay. If it was all merely a laugh, a charade, then Reginald could stay at Stanphrey Lacey for weeks on end, awaiting the three Sundays for the banns to be read, entertaining himself, and ensuring that he convinced Miss Jessica Chance that he cared for her and would marry her.

That had been the plan.

The plan had been upended. As Reginald stared into Jessica's brilliant eyes, his gaze darting to her luscious mouth, he knew that this had ceased to be a marriage of convenience. When that had occurred, he did not know.

He did know that he cared for this woman. That the plan had been to use her, and now he wanted her for herself.

Love…that was perhaps too strong a word. Certainly desire, certainly admiration. A need to be with her, a strange urge to protect her, to try to convince Jessica that she was worthy of his desire and admiration.

"Stay," Jessica repeated under the noise of her family. "I… I would like you to stay."

And that was when Reginald knew that he would. How could he say *no* to her? How could he leave this woman who was starting to mean more and more to him?

Besides, it all worked, didn't it? He needed her; his family needed her. His brother's disgrace would soon be out into the world, and if his sister were ever to hold her head up high as she stepped into Almack's, she needed a sister-in-law who could present her. Who would always be accepted by Society. A Chance.

Surely, he could not be guilty of using Jessica, of needing her for his plan, if he was starting to care?

"Besides, we need you," came a voice that cut across his thoughts.

Reginald's head jerked round. "I beg your pardon?"

"We're going to skip port and cigars," said Michael Chance cheerfully, pushing back his chair, "and go straight to the dancing. Jessica, you'll lead us out, won't you?"

"L-Lead you all out?"

Reginald did not need to look around to see the fear in his betrothed's eyes; he could hear it in her voice, sense it in the shifting air. He knew her all too well.

Her hand had gone from his knee now, *more's the pity*, and she was holding her hands together before her as though they could shield her from an incoming storm.

His eyes raked over her face. Jessica was nervous, uncertain—

she had clearly never been asked to lead a dancing set in her family before.

And that fact alone was enough to make him do what he did. How was it possible, after years and years, that his Jessica—that Jessica Chance, eldest daughter, had never led a set at a family dance? Surely, they had danced together countless times, but in all those dances she had never been asked to lead?

It was ridiculous. It was almost insulting. And it was what propelled him to rise from his chair, hold out his hand, and say, "Will you give me the honor, Miss Chance?"

Perhaps it was a mite formal. There was a titter from someone at the other end of the table, then an "Ouch!" when the Chance in question was presumably elbowed by a neighbor.

Reginald did not look away from Jessica, his hand outstretched. She was staring at it, as though the rest of the table did not exist.

For a heart-stopping moment, he thought she was going to refuse him.

And then she rose, skirts sweeping and lips breaking out into a shy smile as she said, "Y-Yes."

There were cheers and arguments between two sisters about which of them would have to dance with their eldest cousin, and calls from one of the aunts that no ankles were to be broken this time—which didn't bode well—and Reginald and Jessica, hand in hand, were swept away on the tide of Chance cousins as they poured out of the dining room and down a corridor.

Reginald could not help but laugh, the exuberance and the joy of the family overtaking him, and Jessica laughed with him and dear God, he could do this forever.

I could do this for the rest of my life.

It was a passing thought and not one that he decided to pay much heed to—not as they all burst into a room Reginald had never entered and which turned out to be a rather cavernous ballroom.

"How large is this place?" he muttered to Jessica as Lady

Liliana was beseeched by a great number of cousins to play the pianoforte for them, a request she was vehemently rejecting.

"Larger than you would expect," Jessica rejoined with a wry look. "Look, if you don't want to—"

"I want to."

He spoke with passion modulated by her clear discomfort. There were shouts and laughter echoing around the ballroom now as cousins divided into pairs, those who had married into the family being squabbled over as no one really wished to dance with a sibling, and he could see the noise crowding Jessica's thoughts.

Reginald stepped closer, wishing to pull her into his embrace and shield her from the cacophony.

But she smiled. There was a clarity in her expression, a fierce determination, that he had never seen before.

"No one has ever asked me to dance before," she murmured as Lady Liliana started playing an old-fashioned country dance on the pianoforte in the corner.

Reginald almost staggered as she pulled him over to the top of the set that had formed. Never—never been asked bef—*never?*

But there was no time for that. The music had reached the point where he would have to dance, actually remember what to do with his hands and feet, and Jessica had left his mind very little room for those actual thoughts.

He was not usually one to fear a dance. Not that this was fear—and yet it tasted like fear. The frantic beating of his heart, the tension in his shoulder blades, the shiver of panic that was roaring through him…

And it all faded away as Jessica stepped forward, nerves in her eyes yet boldness accompanying it, and took his hand.

The music slowed, their movements reduced, and Reginald grinned as he felt the clasp of Jessica's fingers around his own.

This was… This was everything. This was a moment of perfect clarity, as though time had decided to stay still so that he could relish every single second. She was smiling, her expression full of trust and contentment.

And then she was stepping back.

The pain of their separation was visceral and it was only when Reginald realized that it was the movement that the dance required, and not a statement of her desire to be close to him, that he managed to calm.

Dear God, if this is what a few seconds in a dance can do to me...

"You look...strange," Jessica murmured as they stepped together again, arms encircling each other for a brief moment before they were all too soon divided by the progress of the dance.

Reginald tried to speak, but his mouth was dry, his throat naught but sandpaper. "Argh... I... Erm..."

Christ alive, he had to better than that!

She was looking up at him now with a quizzical brow. "I beg your pardon?"

What on earth was wrong with him? "I... I feel strange," Reginald said honestly, unable to tie up his words into something more delicate or impressive.

Her delight was unadorned. "Good. I would feel lonely, feeling strange all by myself."

What was it she had said? Reginald tried to think as they stepped through the motions of the dance, his fingertips fizzing every time they came into contact with any part of his partner.

"No one has ever asked me to dance before."

He had not believed it then and he could hardly believe it now. The idea that no man had ever seen the beauty of this woman, the elegance, the entrancing nature of her smile, the way she listened so carefully to anything you said, really listened...

There was something almost erotic about the way Jessica Chance paid attention to a man when he was speaking.

And it wasn't just that. It wasn't the mere sense of being attended to that made Jessica all the more alluring. It was how she responded, her brilliant mind, the wit she somehow kept hidden until it was right there in front of you, dazzling you, so bright, it was almost difficult to see her.

Perhaps that was how she had managed to go through so much of life without being noticed.

One could not stare straight at the sun.

"You are very quiet," said Jessica as they promenaded down the set, the cousins laughing or chattering away without much heed to the music. "I am usually the quiet one."

And I am usually the one with too much to say, Reginald could not help but think. *But you've staggered me, Jessica. I can hardly breathe when I am with you, and that is…*

Well. Most confusing.

"I don't know what to say," he managed to voice aloud.

Jessica's face did not fall, not exactly, but she did not look so content. "And yet I am usually the one with nothing to say."

"Oh, I have a great deal that I could say," Reginald said before he could stop himself. "I could say that you are beautiful, and a wonderful dancer, and I'm—I'm intoxicated by you, Jessica."

It was the wrong thing to say. At least, it appeared to be the wrong thing. Jessica looked down at her feet, no longer willing or able, it seemed, to hold his gaze. When she stepped forward and raised a hand to meet his own as the dance required, she did so without looking at him. Without looking at him at all.

Pain twisted within Reginald. He had spoken the truth—it had poured from him without much control—and yet it had somehow displeased her.

"I—I am sorry," he said, hardly knowing how to fix this. How could he fix this when he did not know precisely how he had managed to break it?

"Why?" She had whispered the word and was now, much to his relief, looking at him.

The trouble was, the way she was examining him made Reginald feel as though he couldn't feel his feet. It was all he could do not to trip over.

Never fear: if she kept looking at him like that, he was going to have a third leg…

"Because I… I thought I had offended you," Reginald said a little lamely.

And she smiled and all was forgiven and he could have flown to the moon on the joy that filled him when Jessica said, "I'm intoxicated by you, Reginald. It's just… I thought I was alone in that."

"You are not alone," he breathed as they stepped together, his hand on her waist.

The dance required them to separate after a beat and Jessica attempted to do so, her natural instincts following the rhythm of the music—but Reginald kept such a hold on her waist that she was unable to do so.

Reginald stood there, his Jessica in his arms, and wondered precisely when this woman had become his. When this marriage of convenience had ceased to be convenient, and the emotions flowing through him had started to be most inconvenient.

A snort—a laugh, a stifled sentence.

"What are they doing?"

Reginald blinked. Then he suddenly realized what he was doing and hastily released the furiously flushing woman.

"My apologies," he said gruffly, trying not to catch the eye of any of the cousins—most definitely not her siblings Miss Irene or Mr. Chance, one of whom was grinning, and one of whom was glaring. "I didn't mean to—I didn't think—"

"I know," Jessica said softly, and though the dance did not require it, she placed a hand on his arm. "I know."

And she did know. *And that is the damned trouble*, Reginald could not help but think as the dance came to an end and the ballroom erupted into delighted applause.

"Truly excellent, no one stepped on my foot this time—"

"—much better this time, Samuel. You almost managed to—"

"Frank, no, you cannot dance in trousers next—"

And amongst it all, as Lady Liliana demanded that someone else take over at the pianoforte for the next dance so that she could waltz with her husband, and footmen poured in with little glasses of sherry on trays, and one of the aunts popped her head in and ordered them to have as much fun as possible but to keep the noise down after midnight, Reginald stood there with Jessica's arm slipped through his and realized…

Realized it had all gone wrong.

He couldn't do it. At least, he could do it, but it would be for completely different reasons now.

He had selected Jessica to be his bride to be useful. To use her name to protect his. To ensure his sister could find a husband. To prevent their brother from entirely destroying everything that they were.

And now…

Now he cared about her. Jessica Chance was a very special woman, and it simply wasn't right to treat her in such a way anymore.

No, marrying her would be wrong.

And yet, not marrying her would be wrong. Reginald did not quite understand the flurry of feelings jostling for notice within him, but a great deal of them were demanding that he marry Jessica on the morrow and make sure she could never discover the worst of him and leave him. The very thought, the very idea of her not being by his side…

Reginald looked down at the beautiful woman beside him, and a smile crept over his lips, unbidden. He had to find the words, even if he could not articulate them well. He had to try to explain just what she was starting to mean to him. That she was beyond compare. That he had never felt so…so himself, so comfortable in her presence.

That he wanted to take her to his bedchamber here and throw her on the bed and strip her of all her clothes and kiss every—

"Reginald?"

He jolted, almost dropping Jessica's arm at the surprise at her murmur of his name. "Jessica."

It was an instinctive response, another one that surprised him.

Since when had his instinctive response to someone saying his name become to say her name?

"Reginald, what…what are you thinking?" Jessica's clear eyes were bright, and curious, and there was no archness in her brow, just honesty. "Right then, you were thinking something…something important. I could see it in your expression. What are you thinking?"

For a moment, just a moment, Reginald hesitated.

What was he thinking? What was he thinking, pulling a woman like Jessica into a plan like this, tying her forever to a family that was traitorous to the Crown?

"Nothing," he croaked, hating himself. "Nothing. Shall we have another dance?"

Chapter Eleven

September 12, 1840

J ESSICA GAVE OUT a long, languid sigh as she watched the autumnal breeze rustle the top leaves of the oaks down the avenue.

And it *was* an autumnal breeze. For the last few days, she and her sisters had attempted to persuade their father that the summer had lingered, that the growing evening chill should be ignored, that the final harvest of apples was not to be considered.

But the signs that summer was over and autumn was finally here could no longer been ignored. The cooler temperatures were allowing for more of the hunting the family was enjoying, and the mantelpiece was groaning with the growing number of invitations being sent on with requests for the presence of a Chance, any Chance, at every event for the rest of the year.

Any Chance they could take.

Jessica smiled as the bustle of several footmen and maids behind her in the great hall filled the place.

"—two more trunks for Miss Irene—"

"Did anyone clean the guns for Mr. Chance?"

"—haven't seen it for a while. Is it possible his lordship left it in the library?"

There was always such a to-do whenever the Pernrith branch of the family decided to return home. It was no surprise, in a way. They were the most numerous of the four branches.

Still, that did not explain why they were quite so disorganized.

"I swear, there is not a single left glove in this place." Irene sighed as she approached Jessica by the large windows. "I don't know where they are running off to."

"You keep losing them," Jessica reminded her sister with a wry expression. "What I don't understand is how Gwen, who keeps losing her right gloves, isn't finding yours. Surely, between you two, you could make a few whole pairs."

"Careful now, that's got the dragon in it!" Irene rushed off in a flurry of skirts and Jessica chuckled as Reginald joined her by the window, his eyebrows raised.

"How is it possible," he asked genially, "that I have been here for weeks and have not realized that this family keeps dragons?"

"It's just Gwen's dog, Petal," Jessica explained with a laugh. Well, she had never had to explain this to an outsider before, had she? She had never been intimate enough with anyone for them to need an explanation. "Do not raise your eyebrows, we all call dogs dragons. I blame Maude."

"Maude—your oldest cousin, I believe?"

Jessica considered pointing out that technically Maude was her aunt Alice's daughter from her first marriage, adopted by her Uncle William so long ago that whole years could go by without her remembering that fact.

She did not bother. Maudy was family. Where a person came from did not matter. What mattered was that she was one of them. *One of us.*

"Yes, Maude," Jessica said aloud as a pair of maids bickered behind them about how exactly to carry a trunk out to the waiting carriages. "I think she wished for a dragon as a pet, not a dog, and so decided to call her dog 'Dragon.' When her brothers were born and they were learning their animals—"

"I can quite see how the situation occurred." Reginald laughed, glancing over his shoulder at the yelping box that was carefully carried by a somber-looking footman out through the main door onto the drive. "Such a great deal of luggage for your family. I thought—I had hoped you would be staying with the rest of the family. The banns have been read at the local church, so I assumed that was the plan. Then again, your father said he wrote to your London parish to begin the readings as well."

A tug at her stomach made it impossible, immediately, for Jessica to reply.

It was always this way. She would not say it, for fear that her father may overhear. She had no wish to upset him, after all.

But it was like this every year. Every year, the Pernrith branch of the family was invited to the summer house party of the Chances just like all of them. Every year, they would come, and it would be wonderful, and they would have such a marvelous time that she and her siblings had no wish to go home.

And every year, about a fortnight before the house party was officially over, her father would decide to leave.

She had never asked him about it, and Jessica never would.

She thought perhaps, with him initiating that the banns read locally as well as in London, this year might be different, that she and Reginald might hold their wedding here at the end of the family gathering. But it appeared not.

"No, we are leaving this very afternoon," she said aloud. "We shall have to make arrangements for the wedding, but the banns can continue without our presence and we can return here, perhaps. Or the London location will work just as well. I suppose your sister will be glad to see you?"

It should not really have been a question, not really. Jessica could not imagine any sister not looking forward to Reginald returning home. He was such… He was so…

Every moment with him was more entertaining than the last. Just when she had thought she had understood him, all of him, there was something new. Something fresh. Something more to discover.

"I suppose she will, when I return," Reginald said quietly. "But not today."

There was something strange in what he said, and it caused Jessica to glance over her shoulder and take in the plethora of luggage, trunks, carpet bags, and boxes that were slowly disappearing into the two baggage carriages that the Pernrith Chances had brought with them.

There was her brother's gun set and Gwen's and Irene's trunks, and her own things, of course, and her mother's lady's maid had already taken Teddy and her own belongings out…

But there was nothing in the grand hallway that did not belong to them. In short, Reginald's belongings were nowhere to be seen.

"But…you are not leaving?"

"I was going to," Reginald said quietly, stepping closer to her to lower his voice.

Jessica's breath hitched at the nearness.

"You were going to?" Jessica could not understand it. It was most strange for the man to turn up at Stanphrey Lacey without an invitation in the first place, but to linger without her…

"I was hoping," he continued, his voice now a delicious murmur, "that I might persuade you to stay."

Stay.

"Stay?"

Reginald's expression was one of longing, just for a flash of a moment. She was certain she could not have misunderstood, but it was gone before she could truly interrogate it.

She was, after all, supposed to be making the man fall in love with her. That was going to be rather difficult, from London.

"Yes, stay," Reginald said quietly. "I thought—well, if you and I decided to stay, not only would we be able to continue the banns at Stanphrey Lacey's church, you would still be under the protection and guidance of your extended family, and it would afford us more time to…to be together. To get to know each other better, before the wedding. To be…alone."

Alone.

Jessica's sharp inhale was lost in the noise of the room, but she was certain that the gentleman staring at her mouth had noticed it.

Alone.

"I don't think that's such a good idea," was what she really should have said.

After all, the one day they had been left alone at Stanphrey Lacey, they had revealed family truths, held hands, and kissed so furiously against a wall that they had dislodged a painting.

It was hardly auspicious.

"You can decline, obviously," Reginald said as he took a half-step back, his attention now directed to the window. "It was just a thought. I have no wish to impose."

"I would like that." Jessica had not meant to speak hastily, but she did, before the man could get quite the wrong idea about her hesitation. "I took the time to consider not because I do not wish to spend more time with you, but because…because I think I may wish to spend time with you a mite too much."

It cost her greatly to be so bold, and yet the reward was instantaneous.

Reginald's smile could have burnt down a building. "Thank you."

He'd thanked her and yet he could not know, could he, just how much his words meant to her? How everything he did was starting to mean so much to her.

It was cruel, in a way, that she would start to fall in love with a man to whom she was already engaged.

She could not dream of catching his eye when she'd done nothing to catch it in the first place.

"Jessica Chance, if you have any knowledge of your sisters' gloves, I beg you to give us peace and let us know."

"Mama," said Jessica swiftly, turning while placing a hand on Reginald's chest and then removing it as though scalded. "Mama, I have decided to stay."

"Stay?" Her mother blinked as though she had started speaking gibberish. "Stay what?"

"Stay here. At Stanphrey Lacey," Jessica added in way of further explanation.

Her mother did not look as though she fully understood. "But you can't. I know the banns have been read, but your father decided we are leaving. They've been read back in London without us present as well. We can discuss the details of the plan going forward at home."

"I am sure Victoria would appreciate some assistance with the baby, and I can walk over to the Lodge every day, and—"

"You wish to *stay?*"

Jessica swallowed. It was most unfair of her mother to sound so incredulous—but then, she supposed it was an odd request. She had never asked for such a thing before. The noise of a Chance house party was usually more than enough to drive a wallflower back home at the soonest convenience.

"As you said, Father already had the banns begun here. It makes sense for me to stay for the rest of the readings, even if we wind up marrying in London. And... And I can continue to plan the wedding. With Reginald. Lord Llyne," Jessica amended hastily, determinedly not looking at the man standing beside her.

It did not matter. Even without turning her attention to him, she could feel the weight, the heat of his focus upon her neck. That was surely the explanation as to why her cheeks were flushing and heat was cascading down her neck.

"With...Reginald?"

My mother has absolutely no right to speak like that, Jessica thought furiously. No right at all to give her a sidelong look, to glance at her betrothed and to wink—wink!—at her daughter.

"Well, I quite understand," the Viscountess Pernrith said blithely. "You know, your father and I—"

"Yes, I know the story, Mama," Jessica said with a wry smile.

"My darling, the carriages are packed and the dragon isn't going to wait patiently much longer," her father called out from the front door. "Come along now."

Jessica looked hurriedly at her mother. "Please, Mama."

For a moment, she thought her mother might ignore her plea and request her immediate presence inside one of their carriages.

But the Viscountess Pernrith beamed. "Of course, my child. Ask one of your uncles to bring you back with them when they return to London, won't you?"

"Darling!"

"Yes, Fred, I'm coming," called her mother, and Jessica glowed, hardly able to believe it. "See you in a few weeks, Jessica—yes, yes, I'm coming!"

Jessica accepted her mother's embrace and her two kisses on the cheeks, then watched through the window as she ordered a footman to remove her eldest daughter's possessions from the carriage.

She spoke with the viscount, who frowned but nodded, looking up to catch Jessica's eye in the window.

"Why hasn't Jessica come out yet?"

"What is Jess doing there?"

"She's not, is she?"

The cries and confusion of her siblings barely carried on the breeze, but Jessica was able to catch most of it, and she smiled with a twist in her stomach as the carriages pulled away and started their journey back to London.

It was the first time she had ever been without her family.

The thought jolted her painfully. Well, she was still with family, really—but there was something different about parents and siblings to cousins and aunts and uncles.

Something separate. She was the only Pernrith Chance here. The safety net of her sister, Reeny, who so frequently rescued her from the unpleasantness of awkwardness, was gone.

And Reginald was here.

"You know," Jessica said quietly, her voice barely making it over a whisper, "this...this marriage of convenience is starting to become more and more...convenient."

It took a great deal of effort to bring herself to look up as she spoke. Precisely what Jessica wanted to see in Reginald's face, she did not know.

Delight? Joy? Reserve?

She certainly knew what she did *not* want to see.

Distaste. Awkwardness. Embarrassment.

All she saw was an open expression and slightly lopsided smile, which was completely impossible to decipher.

And then Reginald took her hand.

"Good," he said gently.

Jessica's heart fluttered and she knew she had never felt this way for any gentleman before—more than that, she never would. What she was sharing with Reginald, what she knew they would share, was so precious that she did not wish to sully it by even considering that another man would make her feel this way.

But did he feel what she felt? Did his pulse skip a beat whenever she walked into a room? Did his soul sing whenever they were together?

"You know, now that you have decided to stay with me—at Stanphrey Lacey, I mean—we probably should put a little more thought into the wedding beyond the banns," Reginald said, taking Jessica's hand and slipping it into the crook of his arm as he led her through the front door and out onto the drive.

Jessica glorified in the way that he kept her close so instinctively. No waiting for permission, no hesitation, just a silent declaration of intent.

"I suppose we should," she agreed as their steps meandered across the gravel onto the wide sweeping lawn. "Though I hate to tell you that my mother will have arranged the vast bulk of the decisions by the time we return to Town. I would not be surprised if she changes the venue to London, even if it means asking the vicar here to join us there. Not the normal way of things, perhaps, but the Chances do things differently."

"That they do." Reginald's chuckles hummed through her side, they were so close together. "Should I be worried? Your mother appears to me to have excellent taste."

"Oh, she does. But if you were hoping for a small, quiet wedding with only family," Jessica said, her lungs tightening, just for a moment, "prepare to be disappointed."

She was not going to think about it. She was not going to picture the hundreds of guests that her mother, a former flourishing rose of the Season, was going to invite. She was not going to imagine all those eyes staring, all those voices whispering, wondering how on earth the wallflower Chance had managed to snag a husband.

"I would have thought that a wedding with only your family would be, by definition, not a small or quiet wedding," Reginald pointed out wryly as they walked past a croquet match that undertaken by a number of cousins.

So far, a physical fight had not broken out, but Frank was playing, so it was only a matter of time.

"I suppose you are right." Jessica giggled, shaking her head ruefully at the thought. "Having four siblings and eleven cousins does make for a rather rowdy party. I always looked forward to a quiet home outside London—not too far from my family, but not too close that they could drop in unannounced."

"It sounds like Llyne Hall might be perfect for us, then."

"Perfect for us."

Tingles roared across Jessica's body, her whole skin overtaken by the smallest of phrases.

"Llyne Hall?"

"Yes, it's the barony's seat in Kent. About a day-and-half's carriage ride from London, so easy enough for a week's visit, but not sufficiently close for a surprise tea party," said Reginald with a grin. "It's nothing to this place, obviously. Only an eight-bedroomed manor on an estate of a hundred acres or so."

Only.

"It sounds...perfect," Jessica murmured, tightening her grip on his arm.

Was this truly happening? Every now and again she had to almost pinch herself to believe that this was happening, that this wonderful man had chosen her, out of all the women in the world, and was going to make her so happy.

She tried to surreptitiously pinch herself as they rounded the corner of the croquet match—in which Frank was shoving Samuel sharply and yelling about cheating—and started toward the parkland.

No, that pinch had definitely hurt. She was not dreaming.

"I don't know—I suppose I should, but there is no better time to ask—I don't know what it is you want from life."

Jessica looked up. She had been distracted by a herd of deer just visible through the trees, but now she was looking at him, it was to see nervousness on Reginald's brow.

"'Want from life'?" she repeated.

"Well, I am to be responsible for your happiness," Reginald said firmly, as though this were something he discussed every day. "Your father has made that very clear to me."

Jessica raised an eyebrow. "My father?"

"Your sister Irene has made that very clear to me," he amended, and their laughter rang out across the parkland, startling the deer and making them disappear into the more densely planted trees. "She instructed me, and I quote, 'to keep her happier each day than the last.' So I ask again, what do you want from life?"

What *did* she want from life?

What a question. It was not one she had ever seriously considered. She wanted a great deal, she supposed, but quite what, she did not know.

"I want… I want to be loved," Jessica said, cheeks burning. Before Reginald could say anything, she continued. "And I want to love in return. I want to…to have my own home. To invite family, friends when I want, but to have it to myself with…with the person I love. I want to read every book every written, and hear all the music, and…and build a home. A place I can feel myself, where I never have to worry about being a wallflower because that is precisely where I belong. That… That is what I want from life."

It was quite a speech, and already, Jessica was regretting a few of the phrases she had chosen. What gentleman wanted to marry such a bore as that?

"And, you know, throw parties," she added lamely.

His laughter filled her and reassured her in equal measure. "Jessica Chance, you can't lie to me. I know you."

And he did. He did know her.

"I agree with the building a home," Reginald said, wistfully now. "I want our children to grow up in a home where they are exuberantly loved. Wanted, adored, not just tolerated until they can be grown."

A twist, a shudder low in her gut. Jessica swallowed it down and did not quite understand it. *Our children*. It was a heady thought, so heady that it made her head swim.

"—other than that, a quiet life," Reginald was saying. "I am not much one for Society, though I suppose it has its uses. I like… Well. Country living. Riding, hunting, long walks. There are some very pretty cliffs near Llyne Hall, and some wildflowers there you just don't get anywhere else."

And Jessica's breath caught in her throat. "Country living."

It was all she had ever wanted. All three of her uncles had been wealthy enough for a townhouse and a country estate, and technically, her father had Wickacre—but that had been let now for over a decade to provide a steady income for her parents' growing brood. They had never been able to go to the country when London grew hot and unpleasant, except when they were invited to Stanphrey Lacey.

And soon… Soon she would have a home in the country. A place where she could walk uninterrupted on their hundred acres. A place where she could see the sea.

"I've never seen the sea," she said aloud.

"'Never seen the—'" Reginald halted, his astonishment evidently too great to consider the additional task of walking. "'Never seen the sea'?"

"When would I have seen the sea?" Jessica rejoined with an awkward laugh. "I've always wanted to, but Papa wouldn't take us to Brighton, and—"

"I want to give you the sea."

She stared—stared at the earnestness in his face and the depth of candor in his voice. "I beg your pardon?"

Reginald stepped closed, placing his arms around her so that he did not so much pull her into an embrace, but he placed one around her. One hand lifted, cupping her cheek. "Jessica Chance, I want to give you the sea. I want to give you rolling hills and wildflowers and space, space to be yourself and to know yourself and to know that you are worth the wildflowers and the rolling hills and the sea."

Jessica could do nothing but stare up at this man. He was... He was...

He was dipping his head to kiss her, but while there was passion in the kiss, there was something more. Reverence, and need, and desperate respect, and a holding back, but only because there was so much desire to dam.

When Reginald lifted his head, Jessica could not help the little whimper of disappointment that the kiss was over.

"We are going to have such a good life," he murmured.

Joy burst within her and Jessica hardly knew how she could stand there without shouting to the heavens. "We are?"

"We are," Reginald said with a low chuckle. "Full of—of laughter, and happiness, and seashells, and—"

"And respect, and honesty, and wildflowers," she added, swept away by the rush of words that he had said.

And he hesitated. Precisely why she did not know, but he hesitated. When he finally spoke, his voice was gravelly, his hand no longer cupping her cheek but brushing a curl out of her eyes.

"And respect, and wildflowers," Reginald said quietly, his expression a little pensive. "And honesty."

Chapter Twelve

September 14, 1840

REGINALD KNEW THAT it would injure him. Knew that reading the words again would be painful, that the moment could cloud the rest of his day.

Nevertheless, as he sat in the drawing room while a few Chance cousins played a quiet game of whist and Lady Francesca leaned over a large notebook, scribbling away furiously, Reginald pulled the letter out of his inner waistcoat pocket, slowly unfolded it, and allowed his eyes to fall on what appeared to be hastily scribbled words.

> *Reg,*
>
> *I can assure you that the plan is going exactly as I had expected, and I am hoping that you are continuing to trust me. Remember the time we played pirates? It all seems so long ago, doesn't it?*
>
> *I am safe here in Paris, for now, though I expect you are hoping to see me as soon as possible. I will return to England soon, I promise. London holds a great many delights for me, the foremost of which is your and our sister's company.*
>
> *You will have many questions—I know that, and I beg you to keep them to yourself. Believe no rumors. Ignore the gossip.*
>
> *Trust me.*
>
> *This letter will be taken to Calais by one of my connections, and I can only hope that it reaches you safely. Apologies, I cannot give you my exact whereabouts.*
>
> *I remain your loyal brother—*
>
> *Peter*

Reginald stared at the letter longer than he knew he should have. It had been disconcerting indeed for the missive to make its way not only through Paris, across France, but to him here, at Stanphrey Lacey. He supposed it was only right that his butler was forwarding things on to him, but to read his treacherous brother's words while here, in the sanctity of the Chance manor house…

He sighed, folding up the letter and dropping it into his lap.

How very like Peter. He should have known that his younger brother, younger half-brother, would wish to rebel one day. All the signs had been there—playing pirates, indeed. If that was what his brother called 'borrowing' their neighbor's rowboat and accidentally sinking it, then he supposed it had been piracy.

And now the man had gotten himself into far more trouble.

Reginald tightened his grip on the chair arm as he tried not to think about the punishment for traitors to the Crown.

It was hanging. And if his brother were ever found…

"There you are," came a gentle, cordial voice.

Reginald did not so much start as jolt, a movement that he hoped Jessica did not notice as she approached him across the drawing room. "Jessica."

"Reginald," she said with a smile, flushing as one of the cousins nudged the other and they giggled.

It was rather intimate, he supposed—they had fallen into it without much thought, and now the idea of calling the woman about whom he so cared 'Miss Chance' seemed ludicrous to the extreme.

"What is that?" she asked curiously.

Reginald shoved the letter from Peter into his pocket as swiftly and as nonchalantly as he could manage, which was not very. "Nothing."

She frowned. "It looked like—"

"Just a dull letter from my steward," lied Reginald brightly. "I would much rather look at you."

"I wondered whether you wanted a walk," Jessica said softly, dropping into the chair beside him with only the hint of a flush in her cheeks. "But only if you wish it."

Only if he wished it.

That was the trouble, wasn't it?

Oh, perhaps he should have expected it. Perhaps Reginald had been naïve to think that he would not start to truly care for Miss Jessica Chance once he met her. He ought to have *hoped* for this. He'd just been so distracted by the need to achieve his goal, he hadn't thought to consider his own happiness.

But of course that should have been his end goal… Focusing only on the goal of taking a Chance wife all seemed so ridiculous now.

Jessica beamed, her grin becoming uncertain as he did not reply.

She was so beautiful. So gentle. Reginald had never met a woman who was so…so good, without expectation of reward or recommendation.

And he was marrying her for all the wrong reasons.

Reginald swallowed. "A walk. Fine."

It appeared she did not need greater encouragement, which was all to the good because his throat appeared to be closing up and it was taking all of his concentration to put one foot before the other.

The corridors of Stanphrey Lacey were becoming as familiar to him now as those of Llyne Hall. The vase that stood on the pedestal on the corner; the impressive landscape painting of the grounds at the end of the corridor; the wide bay windows that allowed such light into the Long Gallery.

It would be a wrench to leave this place. The question was: would he be leaving with a betrothed, perhaps even a wife by then…or wouldn't he?

Reginald cleared his throat as they stepped out into the grounds, a chill in the air. He had not permitted himself to even consider that possibility until now, and it was his damned feelings for her that were prompting him to do so at all.

He cared about her. Truly cared about her. Reginald glanced to his left and saw the innocent smile, the refreshing joy of a woman who believed that all was right with the world.

And what he was doing was wrong. His affection was clouding his judgment, making him wish to scramble for a special license and marry the woman tomorrow...but that would be unfair on her, wouldn't it?

"You know," Reginald said, forcing himself to start voicing the concerns that were racking his mind, "I do worry about you, you know."

Jessica did not frown, exactly, but the way she chewed her inner cheek gave her a quizzical expression as she said, "Let us not walk. Let us sit."

Walk, sit—it made no difference to Reginald. This would be a conversation of discomfort, but the fact that he had not had it was weighing him like...like the letter in the inside pocket of his waistcoat.

Oh, damn.

Jessica led him, her fingers casually slipping to intertwine with his own, over to a part of the Stanphrey Lacey gardens that he had not entered before. It was, it seemed, a kitchen garden.

The place smelled wonderful. The heavy rains that morning had left the place dew-dripping, the scent of fresh nature hanging in the air like a mist. The herbs around the edges of the redbrick walls scented the breeze that drifted by them, and there were late apples and pears groaning from the branches of the fruit trees to their left. On their right, rows and rows of vegetables—potatoes, leeks, tomatoes, beans, and what appeared to be a strange sort of cabbage.

And right before them, over an arbor, was a bench.

"I come here sometimes to think," said Jessica softly as they gently sat side by side on the bench. "Or steal fruit, depending on the season."

Reginald could not help but smile at that. "I imagine that both are pleasant here."

"The strawberries are usually out of season by the time we have the summer house party, but there are usually a few to be found, if one really looks," she said, her gaze drifting out across the neat rows of plants. "Anything really precious can usually be found, if one looks hard enough. And in the right place."

Oh, hell.

He had found her. Quite unlikely though it was, and when he had not even been expecting it—but he had found her, this precious thing, and he was going to harm her if he were not careful.

Right. Focus. Say what needs to be said—without saying what mustn't be said.

How hard could it be?

"You said you worry about me." Jessica had turned slightly, her knees brushing his leg as she examined him closely. "Why?"

Reginald took a deep breath. Then another. Each one put off what he knew he had to say.

"It isn't something small, is it?" Her words were not a question, more a statement, and there was a serious look in her eyes now that Reginald remembered well from when they had first met.

This was Jessica at her gravest, her most careful. Her most vulnerable. This was what she had been when he had first met her, before he had been able to draw her out of her shell.

"My future wife," he said quietly, "will have a difficult time of it in Society. The…stain of illegitimacy—"

"We don't call it that," Jessica interrupted.

It was so unlike her that Reginald turned to her, his eyes wide and his lips parted. "We don't?"

"You forget, you are not the only one here who understands what it is to live after legitimization," she said calmly, as though she discussed such things all the time.

His memory flared. Her father. Perhaps she did discuss this sort of thing all the time.

"Being born on the wrong side of the blanket—it's not a

crime. It's a fact of life, and it happens to far more people than you may think," she continued quietly. "My father knows that. I know that. You should know that."

And he did. In a way.

Oh, no one had ever mentioned anything at Oxford when he had gone up. His friends there had never even obliquely referred to the fact that he had only gained the title of Lord Reginald around the age of ten.

But it was how they didn't mention it that had always rankled Reginald. The way they had never asked about his father, ignored all mentions of his mother. They had never invited him to house parties or shooting parties, presumably—he had always guessed—because they did not wish to be placed in the awkward situation of declining a reciprocal invitation.

"Your father is a good man," Reginald said quietly. "But he is unusual, you must know that."

Jessica's expression was wry. "I do indeed."

"So you must know that for most people, his background, his story—my story—is one to be ignored at best, commented on behind hands more often, and inspiring the cut direct at worst," Reginald continued, forcing himself onward even though the pain of his words was discomforting. "I would not wish to force that onto you. I—"

I care too much.

That was what he'd been about to say. That the pressures of his life were not ones to share, especially not with a woman who was so shy, she barely blossomed into herself surrounded by her family, miles from Town.

Reginald swallowed. And the other thing that he hadn't said, that he wouldn't say because it would put her in too hard a position, was this.

I love you too much to marry you.

It would be a scandal. He knew it would be: a gentleman breaking off an engagement to a lady—it was inconceivable by most. Oh, it happened, but only among those people who did not understand the importance of these things.

There was only one thing for it. Leave and hope that distance would loosen the bonds that had somehow crept between them.

"I feel…I feel…" Blast it all to hell, why couldn't he find the words?

Because you're a coward, a horrible, little voice from the back of his mind shot out. *Because you're just like your brother: when things get difficult, you turn tail.*

It was a terrible thought.

"You know," said Jessica quietly, "sometimes, when I need to get my thoughts in order and I can't help but feel itchy inside, I go for a ride."

Reginald blinked. "A ride?"

"It helps me get my thoughts in order, and I know you, Reginald. I can see into your mind."

Now there *was a terrible thought.* "You can?"

Jessica's laughter was precisely the tonic he needed as she rose to her feet and gestured to a door in the corner of the wall. "I can, indeed, and I know that you are worried about the upcoming wedding."

"I am?" he said weakly, following her and wishing to goodness he had more gumption.

This wasn't how it was supposed to go. He was supposed to tell Jessica that though he cared about her deeply, it was precisely because he cared about her that he had to leave. Had to break this connection they were building.

Instead, she was leading him happily to the stables, where they were going to go on a romantic ride, just the two of them.

Blast it all to hell.

"It is natural to be worried about such things. At least, that is what my cousin Lilianna says," Jessica said brightly as she mounted her mare from the steps provided by a silent stablehand. She was not in a riding habit and so was obliged to ride sidesaddle. "After all, it is a big change, for both of us."

"Yes," Reginald said wretchedly, hardly knowing how on

earth he had managed to get here.

He mounted the gelding he had brought with him, a bright little thing who clearly hadn't been exercised enough, for he jolted a little as they trotted out of the stable yard. It was easy enough to bring the beast under control and provided an excellent distraction.

The trouble was, when Reginald looked up in delight over the fact that he had not been bucked, it was to see the approving look of a woman who meant far more to him than any woman had any right to.

"What are you worried about, exactly?"

The question was spoken in softness, in curiosity—in precisely the sort of tone that Reginald would have expected from a woman of Jessica's sensibilities and gentleness.

And there was no good answer.

Dear God, what could he say? That he was worried he cared about her too much? That his affections, his desire was clouding his judgment so utterly that he was no longer able to make a good decision? That his sister was depending on him to keep the family, his family, respectable—and that keeping the secret of their brother's treachery was tearing him apart?

The weight of the letter in his waistcoat's inside pocket was growing, bearing him down so heavily that Reginald was surprised his horse was able to carry the pair of them.

What had he been thinking? That he could march up here, to Stanphrey Lacey, pick out a bride as though she were in a catalogue at a modiste's, and expect her to be delivered gift-wrapped with no other consequences?

No. No, this had gone on far enough.

"I leave for Town tomorrow," he said abruptly.

He had clearly spoken so abruptly that Jessica started, her horse jumping forward in disquiet. If it had been another woman, perhaps it would have been a terrible accident—what a fool he'd been—but as it was, the expert horsewoman calmed the mare with a gentle pull of the reins, a whisper in the ear, a gentle touch.

Reginald looked away. Honestly, it was ridiculous to be envious of a horse.

"I thought you wanted to stay here, with me," Jessica said quietly.

Hesitation only built the tension in the air between them, but Reginald could not bring himself to say what he had to. That he hoped whatever feelings she may have for him would fade, with distance, with time, with a lack of him in her life. That she would feel the need to break off the engagement, but if not, he would do it—and soon.

Before the news of his brother's treachery was splashed across the papers.

Reginald sighed, and his gelding echoed him. Whatever his brother's so-called assurances proved to be, this was going to be a scandal, one way or the other, and it was he who had damned Jessica into it.

If he broke off the engagement, she would be considered spoiled goods.

If the news came out about his brother, she would be tainted by association.

If they wed and the news about his brother came out after, she would be ruined along with the rest of the family.

He could not hope for the story to never come out. Even if it didn't, and he finally told her after it was too late for her to back out, she'd never forgive him.

Reginald's head hung low, the tension in him rippling out through his whole body. What had he done? This plan of his, he had thought it so clever, so positive; he had seen only beneficial outcomes for himself and his family.

He had given no thought to the faceless Jessica Chance at all.

He glanced over. The beautiful Jessica Chance looked back at him, concern in her eyes, concern for him, though he did not deserve it.

Well, it had to be done. Hopefully, if he left soon, he could break off the engagement quietly. Perhaps the news had never reached Society—maybe London was none the wiser. With a start, she remembered her father had written their vicar back home, and he'd begun the banns there, too. Well, she could always say it was she who had changed her mind, not he. After the news came out about his brother, she'd be well justified. As long as her family didn't talk, no one need ever know they'd spend time unchaperoned during their engagement, and perhaps she could be viewed as chaste still.

Then she would be free: free to marry someone else. Free to marry someone who deserved her.

"You look so serious, Reginald. I do not believe I have ever seen you so," Jessica said, her lips pursed. "I suppose if I ask you to stay, then…then you won't."

And it was her disbelief in him, in herself as a power to hold him here, that finally cracked Reginald's heart open and made him face the truth.

He loved her. He loved this woman, and he would do anything she asked—which was a danger, but a danger he could no longer deny.

"I will stay," he croaked, no strength in his voice.

They had circled around the main parkland now and were meandering back to the house, and the afternoon sun lit Jessica up with a glow as she smiled, her cheeks pink.

"You will?"

"I will do anything you ask," Reginald admitted, no longer able to hide the truth now.

Anything, anything she asked. He belonged to her now, even if he'd thought he'd been brave enough and good enough to give her up.

"You say that as though…as though I am important to you," Jessica said, her voice low.

"You are." And Reginald knew he was barreling toward something dangerous and yet he could not stop himself. "Jessica, I l—"

"There you are!"

Reginald almost fell from his horse.

"Sorry about that. Didn't mean to startle you," said Lord Samuel Chance, eldest son of the Marquess of Aylesbury, with a wide grin on a gelding himself, roaring up to them in a blaze of hooves and snorting horse. "We were going to have a game of charades. The rain's coming in and the rest of the afternoon will be a total washout. Will you join us?"

Charades? Pretending to feel things, do things, and then have other people guess what they were until you were found out?

Reginald cleared his throat. "I...I do not think so. I have a letter to write."

Which was true enough. He would have to instruct his servants back at Llyne Hall to halt the preparations for a mistress, at least for now. He had to decipher the nonsense within his heart before too long.

"What about you, Jessica?"

"No, I thank you," murmured Jessica, her gaze dropping to her hands, her shoulders slumping, all the spark in her diminished as though she were a candle blown out by an icy gust.

"Well, fair enough—we'll be in the ballroom. I think there'll just about be enough room in there," said Lord Samuel blithely. "Last time we played charades, Frank almost burnt down the morning room, do you remember?"

Reginald's attention flickered between the two cousins. "Burnt—burnt it down?"

"It could have happened to anyone, Frank says." Lord Samuel shrugged. "See you later, then!"

With a kick of the man's heels, the horse and rider galloped off in the direction of the stables.

Well, that had been close. *If I had not been interrupted,* Reginald thought with a wry smile, *I could have accidentally revealed a wonderful, frightening truth.*

"What were you going to say?" asked Jessica innocently, patting her mare gently on the neck as she looked curiously at him.

Reginald stiffened in his saddle. "Nothing."

"You were definitely going to say something."

"No, I don't think I was. And if I was, it doesn't matter. And if I had even thought about it, no, I didn't," blathered Reginald, utterly unable to stem the tide of nonsense that was pouring from his mouth. "But your cousin's right, you know. There is definitely rain in the air. Shall we head for the stables?"

There was a deep and entirely merited look of suspicion in Jessica's eyes as she beheld him for a moment without saying anything.

The moment lengthened. After a few more frantic inhales, Reginald wondered whether he should just come clean about the whole plan now.

Look, he could say, *I didn't want to mention this, but I chose you from a list of potential spouses merely to hide the fact that my brother has betrayed the British to the French...*

No. No, he could not see that going down well.

"Yes, let's head to the stables," came Jessica's voice, cutting through his thoughts. "And do not think that you have escaped me, Lord Llyne."

Reginald tried to laugh, but even to his ears, it sounded weak. "Escaped you? Why would I want to escape you?"

Jessica's gaze was steady. "I have no idea."

Chapter Thirteen

September 15, 1840

J ESSICA KNOTTED HER fingers together again and sighed heavily as she looked out of the window. Rain was pouring down the glass panes, the whole of Stanphrey Lacey covered by the torrential downpour all morning. It was so dark in the drawing room that Nicholls had been forced to send in footmen about an hour ago to light the lamps.

She sighed again.

"If you sigh for a third time," said her cousin Samuel's pleasant voice, "I shall set Frank on you."

"What did you say?"

"I'm just saying," Jessica's cousin said hastily under the irate look of his sister Frank, who had a pencil in her mouth and was staring into the distance again. "What on earth has gotten into you, Jessica?"

What, indeed.

It was not as though she could quite put her finger on it. Something was wrong, wrong with Reginald, and she could not understand what it was that she had done wrong.

The plan had seemed so simple. Make Lord Llyne fall in love with her.

How hard could it be? People fell in love with her cousin Lilianna all the time. A few gentlemen had even had the misfortune to fall in love with her sister Irene, which had only ever ended in tears. The gentlemen's tears, that was.

Jessica had been certain that it could not be that difficult to make a gentleman fall in love with her. He'd already asked her for marriage, which was more than any man had, so she thought she'd have an easier time of it than she otherwise would have. His attention had already been focused her way. She had been pleasant to Reginald, she had bared herself—that was, she amended hastily in the privacy of her own mind, she had been open and honest with him, which was more than she had ever done for anyone else, including some members of her own family.

She had even kissed him. Multiple times.

Her toes curled in her satin shoes. Several kisses, each of them fantastically wonderful and utterly unforgettable.

And then he went around saying things like he had on their ride.

"I leave for Town tomorrow."

Evidently, she had missed something.

Jessica cast a curious glance at her cousin Lilianna, who was focused on the book in her hands and seemed unaware that she was being observed.

Exactly how did ladies like Lilianna do it? How did they captivate the attentions of young men, often accidentally, it seemed?

Was it mere beauty? Or was it something more?

And the worst of it was—though now she'd thought that, there were several worse things—was that she felt an uncomfortable need to be close to Reginald at all times. Just sitting here in the drawing room and not knowing where he was... It was infuriating. It was like an itch she could not scratch, a deep-seated hunger that she could not sate.

Not without going to find him, at least. And what sort of reception would she gain?

"Jessica?"

Because it was she who was always drawn to him, wasn't it? Jessica was the one with this gnawing, aching feeling in her whenever she was apart from him. She was the one who had had a quiet word in her cousin Victoria's ear and ensured that she would always be seated beside Reginald at dinner. She was the one who watched him whenever he moved around a room, tracing his steps as though she were a prowling tiger. She was the one who—

"Jessica!"

Jessica started. Whether it was the shouted name or the click of the fingers just before her eyes, she was not sure.

Her cousin Samuel was glaring. "You've not been listening to a word I've been saying, have you?"

It would have been easy to lie. Lying was wrong, but it was extremely tempting in this moment.

"No," said Jessica awkwardly, her shoulders slumping. "No, I have not."

How could she, when her thoughts were trailing a man who seemed utterly confusing, a man who would be marrying her in a few weeks—just one more banns needed to be read before they could—and yet he did not seem to wish to discuss the wedding at all?

She swallowed hard. It was not a good sign.

He... He *was* going to follow through on this marriage, wasn't he? Surely, Reginald, Lord Llyne, would not do the unthinkable and actually decide to...break this engagement?

"You look a little tired," said Samuel quietly. "It's not like you to be so inattentive. Quiet, yes, but I thought those keen eyes silently took in everything."

Jessica pounced upon the excuse with relief. "Yes—yes, I do feel warm."

Well, it was not exactly a lie.

"Perhaps you should go and lie down," suggested her cousin. "And rest."

The thoughts that spun into Jessica's mind had a lot to do with lying down—and very little to do with resting.

Dear Lord, what had gotten into her! It could not simply be blamed on Reginald's intoxicating presence, could it? The poor man had no idea that she was so brazen in the privacy of her thoughts.

And it would have to stay that way. The very idea of him finding out… No.

"Jessica?"

"I beg your pardon?" Jessica said hastily, blinking twice in an attempt to focus her mind.

It focused on a very concerned Samuel. "Right, off to bed with you."

"I don't need—"

"Then go and find something to do. Sitting here, doing nothing while it rains outside, no wonder you cannot keep focused on one thing for a full minute together," said her cousin determinedly. "I don't know…just go somewhere and do something."

Jessica swallowed. "Yes. Right."

It was only when she had risen and stepped halfway to the door that she realized that her cousin's recommendation had not included doing anything outrageous with a certain young man, which was a pity. Still, it had not been forbidden.

So, where was Reginald?

It took her almost ten minutes to find him—which, given the large size of Stanphrey Lacey, was actually quite quick. He wasn't in the music room, the library was full of Frank and one of her inventions, and the gun room was of course empty. None of the Chances could go hunting in this weather.

And so it was a rather obvious conclusion when she opened the door to the billiards room that she would find him here. And she had. All she had to do was make some light conversation.

"There you are."

Jessica had not intended to speak in such a sultry voice. Had it sounded sultry? Really, she was hoarse, her breath completely taken away by the sight of Reginald in tight trousers leaning over a billiards table.

It would be too much to fan herself, wouldn't it?

Before she could decide what to do, he had turned around, a vague smile on his face. "Jessica."

"Don't tell me, you want to take him away for a romantic horse ride," quipped another one of her cousins, stepping around the table with a sardonic expression. "Samuel told me all about it."

"Be quiet, Zander," Jessica said hurriedly.

Her cousin smirked. There was a particular type of smirk, she decided, that was somehow only created by men, and created only to distract and irritate their relatives. How did the pest do it?

"Once the rain has let up, I would not be adverse to a ride. But only after I have finished trouncing your cousin," Reginald said conversationally, a wicked grin of his own spread across his face.

Jessica stifled a giggle as her cousin said hotly, "You are not *trouncing* me—don't tell her that! We're neck and neck, and at any moment—"

"Yes, yes, at any moment, you will suddenly find the form that you have never demonstrated," jested Reginald with a snort.

Stepping into the room, Jessica glanced at the score. "It doesn't look neck and neck to me."

"That is because I always bring my brilliance for the second half of the game," retorted Zander, his face flushed and his color high. "Besides, you're distracting me. If you've only come to distract me, please go."

"Believe it or not, I did not come here looking for you, Zander," Jessica said sweetly. "I came looking for Reginald."

She caught his gaze and wondered how it was legal for her to spend any time in his presence with other people. Surely, anyone could sense the heat in the air?

Perhaps that was what chaperones were for. To make sure the heat stayed in the air *between* a couple tempted to take the steam to new heights with physical contact.

Apparently, at least one person picked up on it. "And that is the unspoken request that I leave—just do not tell my mother," Zander said forebodingly. "The last thing I need is for her to know that I left the two of you unchaperoned."

"Oh," Jessica said disappointingly. "Perhaps, then, you best stay."

"It *would be* a problem if she found out, but as she's never going to find out, it's not a problem," said her cousin with a grin as he handed Jessica his billiard's cue. "To be continued, Llyne?"

"Yes, I'll be happy to trounce you later," said Reginald with a grin.

Something twisted, molten hot, in Jessica's stomach as the men exchanged polite nods. The door shut, which was the noise that informed her that her cousin had left the room.

All her attention was fixed on her betrothed.

It was all so...strange. Some days, Reginald looked at her with blazing heat, and it was all she could do not to launch herself into his arms and beg him to take her. Not that she would ever do that, of course. That would be ridiculous.

And some days he looked at her with... Well. Aloofness. As though they were mere acquaintances who had bumped into each other in a coffee house after both attending a house party of a mutual acquaintance five years ago.

It was most odd, and not something she had yet managed to untangle. Perhaps she could now.

"The wedding approaches," she said in a bright voice. "One more Sunday of the banns, and then we're free to set a date."

The response was more than a little underwhelming. "Yes, I suppose we are."

"And... And preparations will need to be made." Why couldn't she just ask him outright? What was holding her back?

"I suppose your mother is doing an excellent job of just that in London," Reginald said brightly. "If that is where we are to have the wedding instead of here. If there is anything in particular that you want, be sure to let her know."

The words had formed and slipped from her tongue before she could stop them. "I want you."

The words hung in the air, the atmosphere already warm and wet due to the late summer rain, but it was different now. Heady, and intoxicating, and strange—Jessica had never felt such a frisson before.

The way he looked at her...as though he had already removed the vast majority of her clothing with his eyes and would have no compunction in doing the same with his fingertips.

Jessica swallowed. *Do not look at his hands. Do not think about him slowly peeling off your clothes. Do not imagine—*

"Have you come here to be taught a lesson, Jessica?" Reginald asked in a low voice.

She had intended to walk forward and give him the billiards cue, but something in his tone made her feet stumble and her breath catch.

He hadn't said—surely, he could not have meant—

"A billiards lesson," Reginald added, as though it were perfectly obviously what he had been saying all along. "I seem to remember that you have not played."

Her mouth was dry when Jessica swallowed. *Yes, yes, obviously, that was what he meant. Of course he could not have meant anything else.*

"If you are willing to teach me," she said aloud, relieved that her voice betrayed none of the quaver of her desire.

Reginald nodded, removing his jacket calmly as though he frequently stripped off his clothes before women to whom he was engaged. Which was ridiculous. The man had never been engaged before.

At least, she did not think he had. *Was that the sort of question a lady could ask?*

"Right, you have a cue," he said, nodding at the large stick in her hand. "Time to work on your stance."

Jessica was utterly helpless as he strode confidently toward her, unsure precisely what he was going to do and utterly certain that she would allow him to do it. This man, he...he had a sort of power over her, a sway that she could not articulate, nor could it be defined. He was...attractive, and not just in his looks. In so much more.

"So you're going to want to lean over the table, like this," said Reginald quietly, demonstrating the move with his cue in his hands, the table end resting on his fingers. "Do you see?"

Jessica swallowed.

Yes, she did see, and far more than perhaps the gentleman had intended. It was truly impressive, the way his trousers tightened around the man's buttocks at this angle. Every inch, every sinew of his thighs appeared to bulge through the material, highlighting his strength, his—

"Jessica?"

"Trousers," she blurted out, cheeks burning the instant she realized her own indiscretion. "I mean…table. The table. It is acceptable to…to touch the table? To balance the cue," she added wretchedly.

Dear Lord, he will think me some sort of heathen!

That was, Reginald already knew her to be, did he not? Their frantic kissing in the portrait gallery was surely sufficient evidence of her wayward ways, was it not?

The grin on his face was all too knowing. "Yes, it is permitted. Come, stand beside me and copy me."

It is just a billiards table, Jessica attempted to convince herself as she stepped over to his left and leaned over the table as she aped it. It was not as though she were leaning over…a bed, say…

"Not—not quite. Lift your shoulder."

Jessica attempted to lift her shoulder. This angle was most disagreeable; it did not appear to be natural at all.

"Your other shoulder."

Her other—how on earth was she supposed to do that and not tip over? "Like… Like this?" she attempted.

When Jessica glanced up, it was to see Reginald's smile. "Almost, but not quite. Here."

Precisely what was going to be 'here,' he did not elucidate. Instead, he moved.

Jessica gasped. He had moved behind her, placing his back against hers, his bent knees against hers, his arms moving alongside her own, until—

Until he was flush against her.

It was all Jessica could do not to whimper with the intensity of his presence. Reginald's heat flowed through his clothes and hers as though they were wearing nothing. She was breathing him in, that mingled scent of cedarwood and something entirely Reginald utterly overwhelming her. Was that her pulse at her wrist, or Reginald's as he carefully, slowly, slid his fingers along hers?

Dear God. She could never have conceived of something so intimate while two people had their clothes on.

And if he didn't move soon…

"Feel the line of the cue," Reginald whispered, his breath blossoming over her ear and neck. "Feel the angle of it."

Jessica swallowed. There was only one angle she could feel, and it was where his hips were interlocked with his own. How could he possibly talk in this position?

"And now, movement," he murmured, pulling back her right hand on the cue in a slow, steady flow.

It was a very slight movement indeed and to an observer—not that Jessica wanted an observer right at this moment. It was probably a shift of only a few inches.

It was so much more to Jessica. Oh, to feel the friction of the two of them, to feel the power and command that Reginald had over the billiards cue in her own grip…it was too much, and yet she craved more.

Oh, she craved more.

"And then, when you are ready, when you are certain where you want the ball to go," Reginald continued, his voice low and seductive against her ear, "you…release."

Jessica gasped as with a sudden violent flick, both Reginald's right arm and her own rushed forward in a controlled jab.

"It is like…poetry in motion," she whispered, the words slipping out before she had the opportunity to check them for an iota of sense.

"It is?" Reginald had not moved from her, his body true against hers and still heating her from one moment to the other.

Jessica tried to nod, but that only seemed to make things worse. Her cheek brushed against his own, sparks tingling out across her skin, and it was heady stuff, her mind giddy, all rational thoughts about propriety disappearing under the buzz of desire.

Because it *was* desire. Try as she might, she could not pretend to herself that it was anything else.

"Do you understand?"

Jessica did; she was starting to understand herself better and better with every passing moment. The trouble was, she was not sure whether she was brave enough to do what she wanted. These desires, these needs, they were still so new to her.

So new, and yet so natural.

"Jessica?"

Perhaps it was her own imagination, but it sounded to Jessica's ear that Reginald's voice was a little…breathless.

Twisting slowly so that Jessica's buttocks rested against the billiards table, she found to her delight that Reginald had not moved—putting her right in his arms.

"Reginald," she said quietly, looking up into his brilliant eyes. "I think I do understand. Do you?"

She knew she had been far too forward—painfully forward. Wantonly so. Why, no Chance would surely ever be so brazen.

The billiards cue fell to the carpet, but she paid it no heed. Reginald lowered his lips to hers in a kiss so reverential, so worshipful, that Jessica could do nothing but throw her arms around his neck and pull him closer. She did not want his reverence—at least, she did, obviously, but she wanted so much more.

His heat. His need. His desire.

She wanted to feel as though she were the most important woman in the world.

Her wordless question appeared to have been answered as Reginald deepened the kiss, teasing his tongue along the slit of her mouth and welcoming himself in to delve deep in the soft center of her mouth. Jessica moaned with pleasure as his tongue sparked sensual bliss throughout her body, one of his hands on her waist and the other attempting to cup her buttocks, pressed hard against the edge of the billiards table.

Yes—this was what she wanted.

Jessica tilted her head, welcoming him in even further, and gasped in his mouth as Reginald suddenly lifted her buttocks and placed her actually *on* the billiards table.

Her eyes snapped open, though she had not noticed herself closing them. She saw his wicked smile and knew that she had succeeded.

This was what she had wanted: raw desire. And that was what she was getting.

"Oh, Jessica," Reginald said in a ragged voice before he pressed into her again.

Somehow—even amongst the many layers of her skirts— Jessica had encircled Reginald with her legs, her ankles crossed against his buttocks, and the hard press of him as she clung to him was intoxicating. There was a strength and a potency within him that she had never felt before, his hands pulling pins from her hair, his mouth trailing kisses down her neck, and all Jessica could do was attempt to breathe because her lungs were catching with every passing second as heat flowed to between her thighs and—

A thump.

Reginald froze, his face nuzzling into her décolletage, one hand almost at her breast and the other still entangled in her hair.

Her chest heaving with every inhale that she managed to pull into her lungs, Jessica stayed otherwise completely still as the sound of footsteps grew closer and closer.

"I don't suppose they're outside. It's still pouring with rain," came Maude's voice down the corridor. "Maybe they're in the billiards—"

"No! No, they're not." Zander's voice joined in, much to Jessica's relief as she sagged against the strong plane of Reginald's chest. "No, I think I saw them in the library. Shall we go and investigate?"

The library. On the other side of the house to the billiards room.

The footsteps passed by the door to the corridor but swiftly receded again. Another thump, the sound of a door closing. Then there was silence.

Jessica swallowed.

She was sitting on the edge of the billiards table with her hair half down, pins cascaded over the green baize, her ankles around Reginald's hips, and his lips on the tops of her breasts.

It was not a sight she wished for anyone to see, though she would very much like to stay here.

Reginald lifted his head, and there was a rueful smile playing on his lips. "That was close."

"Too close," Jessica said quietly. "I... I suppose we should stop."

"Yes," he said softly. "We should."

Neither of them moved an inch, then both exhaled and chuckled.

"I... I never thought it could be like this." Precisely why Jessica had thought it acceptable to speak out her very thoughts in that moment, she did not know.

She *did* know that Reginald's eyes widened, just for a moment.

"'Like this'?" he whispered.

"Like this," Jessica whispered. "This... This perfect."

Reginald lowered his head and she lifted up her lips, desperate for another taste of this man she still did not quite understand.

Chapter Fourteen

September 17, 1840

"BUT YOU HAVE to admit, travel around the world is becoming far easier and far more dependable," Jessica was saying, her eyes alight. "And—why are you looking at me like that?"

Oh, bother. Reginald had been attempting to keep his bald-faced admiration to himself, but apparently, he had not managed it. "Like what?"

"Like…" Evidently, she could not think of the words. That, or she did not wish to share it. Her cheeks flushed, that delicate pink that Reginald now knew so well, and her eyes dropped to her hands. "It does not matter."

Everything you think matters, Reginald wanted to say—but then, they were not alone.

Dinner had been delicious, as it always was. He had been forced to decline second helpings of everything and had then spent an enjoyable half an hour drinking port and exchanging stories with Jessica's uncles and male cousins. When the ladies had joined them in the drawing room an hour ago—

Reginald blinked. His focus had just caught sight of the long-case clock in the corner.

It had not been an hour ago. It had been three hours ago. Hell's bells, where had the time gone?

"Anyway," came Jessica's sweet voice, which immediately drew his attention, "I think it perfectly possible that in the future, travel across Europe will be so commonplace that it will not require nearly so much planning and will be available for almost all. Do you not think?"

I think, Reginald wanted to say, *that you are the most fascinating creature I have ever encountered.*

Every time that he believed he had plumbed the depths of Jessica Chance's character, she surprised him. It should not be possible to do so, and yet…here she was.

"Where is everyone?" Jessica asked, glancing around them.

The pair of them were seated on a sofa near the unlit grate, and until recently, they had been surrounded by a great deal of cousins. Lady Francesca and Lady Lilianna had been playing cards, both of them growing more and more irritated with each hand, a trio had been exchanging tales of the best—and worst—balls they had ever attended, and the dowager duke and the Earl of Lindow had been chattering away happily about a potential scandal that was about to erupt in Parliament.

But now…

Reginald blinked. "You know, I don't know."

Somehow, at some point, most of the family had disappeared. He had not noticed them go; he had been far too entranced by Jessica's conversation. But now the drawing room was almost empty. Just himself, Jessica, and her aunt Lady Lindow remained.

The Countess of Lindow was seated in an armchair, hunched over a notebook with a pencil rapidly scribbling. She looked up. "Frank, I've solved it! Frank, I've—Frank?"

"She's gone," Reginald said helpfully, as though the woman could not look around the room and discern that particular piece of information for herself.

The countess blinked. "She has?"

"She has, and so has almost everyone else," added Jessica helpfully.

Reginald tried not to notice just how close his knee was to hers.

It was foolish, in a way. After their entanglement in the billiards room—on the billiards table—it felt mindless to be so entranced by the closeness of her knee against his own.

And yet… And yet it was entrancing. *She* was, Jessica. She was intoxicating. Each and every moment that he spent with her was a moment he wanted to savor. Part of him seemed to know that he would not be able to keep this pretense up forever. At some point, Jessica would discover the truth about him, about his family, and this closeness, this intimacy that he was so relishing— it would all be over.

Then he would have naught but the memories.

"Well, I suppose my calculations will wait until tomorrow." The countess yawned, closing her notebook on her pencil. "Goodness, look at the time."

Reginald made a show of looking, though he had already realized just how late the hour was. "My word!"

"It's bed for me, and I'd advise the same to you two," said the older woman as she rose. Then her breath hitched. "That is— different beds. Obviously."

He did not need to look around at the woman seated on the sofa beside him to know that Jessica's cheeks were burning. He could almost feel the heat from here. "Obviously."

"Yes. Well. Good," said Jessica's aunt with an awkward grin. "Goodnight, then."

"Goodnight, my lady," Reginald said solemnly. Well, for all that the rest of the house party called her 'Aunt Dodo'—a familiarity he had not permitted himself—she was not his family, after all.

"Goodnight," came the breathless voice of Jessica beside him. Evidently, she had not managed to move past the embarrassment of the 'separate beds' recommendation from her aunt.

Reginald could not help but grin as the door shut behind the older woman and they were left alone. *Well, it wasn't the worst suggestion, was it?*

Silence settled onto the room like a warm blanket. It felt comfortable, staying here with Jessica as the clock ticked closer to midnight. Being with her anywhere felt remarkably comfortable.

Comfortable, that is, other than the fact that you are constantly fighting your instincts to bed her and pleasure her until she screams your name, Reginald reminded himself.

Other than that.

"I suppose we should take my aunt's advice," Jessica said quietly.

When Reginald turned to her with a raised eyebrow and a delighted expression, she burst into giggles and nudged him with her knee.

"Not like that! I just—"

"I know what you meant," Reginald said genially, heartened by her expression.

There was something so… No, the word was not *innocent*. He may have used that descriptor for her before, but he had seen too much of Jessica's raw desire to now use it.

There was something intensely *honest* about Jessica. What you saw was precisely what you got. There was no artifice in her, none at all. Not like himself.

The thought was painful and Reginald attempted to ignore it, but it was almost impossible to do so. How could he permit himself to continue on with this lie, this charade that his family was nothing but respectful?

Her father would surely have not permitted him to make his suit—well, his almost immediate proposal—if he'd known. Would not have let the banns be read without objection. The whole family would not have invited him to stay here, at Stanphrey Lacey, would not have welcomed him in with open arms, if they had known just how much he had kept the truth from them.

And here she was, Jessica Chance, seated beside him and looking up with such…such adoration. There was no other word for it.

Reginald swallowed. He knew that she deserved to know the truth.

The trouble was, there were two truths now. It was true that his brother's traitorous actions had betrayed the Crown and would ruin his family name.

It was also true that he was irrevocably in love with Jessica Chance.

So. What was it to be? Both truths? Or only one—and if so, which one?

Or would it be best to simply hold his tongue?

"You look awfully serious, Reginald," said Jessica quietly.

Reginald tried to smile naturally, but unfortunately, he had forgotten what that was supposed to look like. Did one's eyes have to be quite so wide? "I do not feel serious."

"And yet you look it, and you have never been able to hide what you are feeling in the time I have known you," she returned, only a very slight pink in her cheeks belying how bold she was being, going against her wallflower nature. "Would you like to tell me about it?"

Yes, he wanted to say. *Good God, I wish I had told you about it from the very beginning. I wish I could always be as open with you as you are with me.*

It was admirable, that quality, in here, but it also rubbed against the falsehoods in him, reminding him just how much a liar he was.

"No," Reginald said heavily, knowing the response he would receive. She would pout, she would argue, she would rail, she would state that as his betrothed, it was his duty to tell her everything—

"I understand," Jessica said softly.

If he had not been so securely seated on the sofa, he might have fallen off it. As it was, Reginald turned, shifting his whole body so he could face her. "You... You do?"

Her shrug was light, drawing his attention momentarily— fine, more than momentarily—to the thrust of her bosom as her chest moved. "You are not obliged to tell me every passing thought that strikes you. As I've told you before, even between a...a husband and wife, there must be some privacy." A delightful little line appeared in Jessica's brow as she considered this. "Would you want to tell me everything? Every thought that flashed by, every meander of your mind?"

It was startling and most disconcerting, this sensation. Reginald had never realized it before, but...yes. Yes, he wanted to unburden himself fully to this woman. To be seen, utterly seen. To know that there were no secrets between them, that she could ask anything and he would immediately tell her the secret.

If his damned brother had not existed, then he would have said...*yes*.

He did not want anything to be between them.

Jessica was smiling. "Besides, you will hardly want to know everything I think."

"Yes. Yes, I would," Reginald could not help but say, but the very thought that she would think so of him cut him to the quick. "Jessica, your mind is truly incredible. Your ideas about European, about international travel—you do realize that I have never heard anyone speak in such a way?"

Her flush was one of delight now—he was starting to be able to tell them apart. "You flatter me."

"Flattering it may be, but I promise you it is the truth," he said firmly. "You think I admire you for your looks, and I do—"

"*Reginald!*"

"—but it is your mind that makes you truly unique," Reginald continued, speaking over Jessica's mortified interjection. "You must know that is why I... why I..."

The words were so close on his tongue. So close, and yet he could not bring himself to say them.

I love you.

Where did that lead? Reginald had been in half a mind to break off the engagement a few days ago, and now he was teetering on the edge of revealing his heart for her.

This was madness. This was intoxication. This was—

"Ah, I do apologize, Miss Chance," said a voice from the door.

Reginald would have sprung back from Jessica if he had been as close as he wished to be. As it was, the sudden intrusion of the Chances' butler by the door, a pair of footmen behind him, was still quite the imposition.

"We came to close the drawing room for the night, Miss Chance, but I see that you are still up," the butler said with a bow in their direction. "We shall come back, then."

"We shall be going up directly," said Jessica. "Up to bed. I mean—"

"Separate beds," interjected Reginald hastily, heat burning across his torso.

"Yes, yes, separate beds."

"One bed would be ridiculous." He tried to laugh, hating the look of agonized discomfort on the servants' faces.

"Yes, yes, ridiculous, two beds—"

"Two beds in separate rooms!" *Dear God, why can't I stop talking?*

"Of course," the butler said, cutting across them both and causing Reginald's shoulders to droop in relief. "I shall return in an hour and close down the room. Good evening, Miss Chance, my lord."

The butler and the red-faced footmen disappeared, the last to exit closing the door behind the three of them, and Jessica fell against the back of the sofa.

"Oh, dear Lord."

"Yes, that did rather get away from us, didn't it?" mused Reginald, attempting to grin.

Yes, that's it, keep it light. Do not focus on the fact that you just tried desperately to convince a butler that you were not going to bed a woman of the family he serves…

The silence that fell about them now was at least less awkward than their ramblings at the servants, but that was not saying very much. Eventually, he would have to say something, obviously, just as soon as he worked out what the words should be. At that time, he would say something. Any moment now.

Any moment.

"You know, I was very suspicious of you. When you first arrived here at Stanphrey Lacey, I mean."

Reginald's focus snapped to the woman beside him. "You were?"

Jessica nodded, her smile lilting and her presence enthralling. "Oh, yes. What man decides to turn up, uninvited, to a family house party and request the hand of a woman he has never met before?"

It was difficult to nod, but he just about managed to. It had been rather a reckless idea, hadn't it? "I am that sort of man, I suppose."

"It was natural to feel suspicious, and I... I did not know whether you were the sort of man I could trust," Jessica continued, her wallflower tendencies overcome as she stared steadily at him. "I did not know whether you were the sort of man who could make me happy."

Reginald swallowed. Was... Was it possible that after all his agonizing, all his concerns that he should break off this engagement—as outrageous as that would be—that Jessica... that *she* was going to break it off?

The pain of the thought was like a dagger to the heart and just as unwelcome.

And just as unexpected. Why did it hurt so much, the thought of losing her?

"You have earned my trust," Jessica said simply.

He stared, expecting more. "I... I have?"

Her smile was a little too knowing. "You do not have to sound so surprised."

"No, no, not surprised," Reginald said hastily, the lie swift on his tongue.

"The way you have treated my family, your behavior while you have been staying here, every moment you have proven yourself to be an honorable young man," Jessica was saying, her eyes bright as she looked at him with... There was no other word for it: *adoration.* "My mother was a tad concerned at first—"

"I knew she didn't like me," Reginald said in an undertone.

Jessica laughed as she tapped him playfully on the arm. "She does like you! It's just—well, I am their eldest daughter, and none of us, not even my older brother, has married yet. It is her first time, letting a child go free. And you—you have earned her trust. She is happy now that you are going to marry me. That you are going to care for me, for the rest of my life."

Reginald tried to swallow again, but for some reason, his throat wasn't working. "Yes. Yes. Care for you."

And the damnedest thing was, he *did* want to care for her. Considering he'd almost hoped he wouldn't care much for his bride, due to the fact that he'd be dragging her into his family's scandal, it was frustrating in the extreme to fall in love with his future wife, but there did not appear to be any way to prevent it.

What man could help but fall in love with Miss Jessica Chance?

"And I realized I had never—you probably don't even care," she was saying, her throat noticeably bobbing as she swallowed. "But I thought you should know. I thought it might be important. You have earned my trust and my... my admiration. And I wanted you to know."

Jessica's gaze did not waver as she stared, and he could see the veracity of her words in every syllable.

She did trust him—and admire him, and what man did not enjoy being admired?

The trouble was, he was not worthy of her admiration. Damnit, Reginald had lied to her, her and her whole family, from the moment he had arrived here. He had been lying to Society for weeks, from the moment he had received the discreet notice from the law courts.

His brother was a traitor. He would be caught soon.

And here she was, the woman he cared about more than he dared to admit, telling him that he was admirable.

Damn.

"I know my regard means nothing to you," Jessica said suddenly, and she reached out and took his hand in hers.

Reginald looked down at the interlocking fingers, twisting with an emotion he was not going to allow himself to name.

"But I wanted to let you know," she continued softly. "You're important to me, Reginald, and I do not like keeping my esteem for you a secret. I feel like you are owed the truth in this matter. I... I care about you. Very much."

Well, there was no choice. He would have to say it.

"Jessica," Reginald said, his mouth dry.

She looked up at him with such trusting eyes that a fierce surge of protective instincts threatened to overwhelm him. She was so precious. He would do anything, anything to protect her.

Even if that meant protecting her from himself.

"Yes?" Jessica prompted, after he had fallen into silence.

Reginald swallowed. What he had been about to say was suddenly no longer appropriate, but he wished desperately to say something. Something had to be said.

He had to tell her how he felt. How conflicted he felt. How twisted he was inside, how desperate he was to please her and yet he worried that by attempting to do so, he would rain down disgrace onto her family.

"Just say it," she whispered, her wide eyes not leaving his. "Whatever it is you want to say."

Reginald opened his mouth, and the floodgates opened. "I love you."

Jessica's gasp caught, just for a moment. "I... I beg your pardon?"

She was really going to make him say it twice, wasn't she? Well, he could hardly blame her, and now the admission had been made, there was nothing more that he wanted to do than keep telling her. Keep telling her over and over again that he loved her.

"I love you," he said in a rush, his lips broadening into a grin. "God, I love you, Jessica. I love the way you look at the world, I love your gentleness, and your compassion—"

"Reginald," Jessica said quietly.

But it wasn't enough to stem the tide. "When I'm with you—dear God, when I'm with you, I am absolutely useless. I cannot think of anything else—"

"Reginald—"

"And it's even worse when I'm *not* with you," Reginald admitted, unable to stop himself from laughing. "Do you know what it is, to have your mind always drifting off to wonder where you are, and if you're well, and—"

"Reginald!"

He halted. "Yes?"

Only then did he notice just how her eyes were blazing—only then did he spot the signs. The dilated pupils. The way she was leaning into him.

"Kiss me," Jessica ordered with a whisper.

He did not need telling twice. Pulling the sumptuous woman into his arms and almost weeping with relief now that they were touching again, Reginald poured upon her lips a series of achingly sweet kisses—until she parted her lips and showed him that she wanted more.

Far more.

She was sweet, tasting of honey and need, and it was enough to stiffen all the sinews Reginald had been attempting desperately not to stiffen. Her touch, feathering down his neck to his shoulders, only stoked the fires that were swiftly burning to a white-hot flame.

"Jessica," he breathed, his voice jagged and his need aching.

"Reginald," she whispered, taking one of his hands and—

He could not help but groan. Dear God, she had placed it on her breast.

Jessica looked up, immediately worried. "I-I am sorry, I—"

"Never apologize for encouraging me to touch you," Reginald said darkly, capturing her lips before she could reply.

At least, before she could reply in words. Her response was

easy enough to understand as she pressed her breast into his hand and clung to him, her tongue teasing along his own as her kisses became bolder.

Dear God. He was inflamed, utterly unable to stop himself from kissing this woman.

Exactly how they had managed to become horizontal, Reginald did not know. Precisely when her gown had become unbuttoned at the front, the edges of her chemise showing, Reginald did not know. Why the floodgates had suddenly opened, Jessica giving herself and more to him in a new way, Reginald did not know.

But he did know one thing. He loved Jessica Chance. He loved her, and the best way to love her now was to let her go.

He couldn't do this to her—he cared too much. Marrying Jessica would be condemning her to a life of stares and scandal, of disdain and dishonor.

He would not do that to her. He had to break this off.

"Jessica," Reginald said, his heart breaking as he looked at the woman he would, never see again. "I—"

"I think," Jessica interrupted, her smile nervous yet remaining. "I think we should go upstairs."

He exhaled heavily. *Tomorrow, then.* Tomorrow, he would tell her precisely that he could not marry her, that she could not ask why, but she had to trust that he had her best interests at heart, that her family would surely keep quiet the fact that they had ever been alone together, and her reputation would remain intact—

"Upstairs to my bedchamber," Jessica continued, her eyes never leaving his own. "The two of us. I... I think it's time you took me to bed."

Chapter Fifteen

JESSICA HAD JUST done something utterly outrageous. She had propositioned a man!

A man she would soon marry, yes, but that did not decrease the level of scandal that she had stepped into. What sort of respectable woman went about suggesting that a man should take her to bed?

Jessica watched Reginald's motionless face and her spirits sank. Even worse, what woman suggested that a man should take her to bed…and then found herself rejected?

"I…ugh…"

It is important, Jessica told herself sternly, *not to cry.* Crying was going to be absolutely no help in the matter, so it was crucial that she did not cry.

She could cry later. In privacy. Once she had managed to escape to her bedchamber and shut the door behind her, keeping out the world but not the roaring-red-hot embarrassment that she had made such an utter fool of herself.

The trouble was, none of this made sense.

Oh, the awkwardness, the shifting look in his eyes, that was to be expected in any other situation. Jessica could no longer count on her two hands the number of times that a gentleman had found himself accidentally standing beside her at a ball, desperately trying to find an excuse not to dance with her.

That look, that was almost normal for her. After all, was she not attempting to make him fall in love with her?

But the uncertainty on Reginald's face? Had he not just said, minutes ago, that he was in love with her? All of this time, she had been working hard to make the dolt fall in love with her and somehow, she had managed it—but he did not want to bed her?

Heat, and shame, and worry rippled across Jessica's face in burning waves. He loved her, but he was not attracted to her?

"You do not need to explain. I quite understand," Jessica said softly as she rose from the sofa.

That was, as she attempted to rise from the sofa. Reginald's hand had reached out, preventing her from properly standing, and when he pulled her back down to sit beside him, there was a serious expression on his face.

"You do not know what you are asking," he said quietly.

Jessica almost laughed, and there was just a hint of bitterness within it. "You think I do not know? Reginald, we are to be married and I know enough about the—well, about the theory to know what that entails. I hear things, and my boldest cousins are not exactly discreet when their parents are not within earshot." Why, oh, why did her face have to blossom with burning crimson now? "But if you do not want to—"

"'Do not want to'?" There was a strange tone in his voice, one she did not understand. "What do you mean, 'do not want to'?"

Swallowing did not appear to make her mind move any swifter, though Jessica supposed she should not have been surprised at that, sitting so close to a man with such animal heat, she could almost see it radiating from him.

Reginald's gaze was flickering over her, as though he were attempting to see right through her. He bit his lip, an unusually hesitant moment from a man who had always been so self-possessed.

Was it possible... Was it even conceivable that he was as nervous as she was?

"It's not a case of not wanting to," he said carefully.

"Then what is it?" Jessica leaned forward, taking his hands in hers and trying not to gasp at the sudden influx of passionate heat. "Because I want you, Reginald. I-I want you, and I want you to want me in return."

"It's not a case of not wanting you—dear God, I would have taken you the day I met you if I could justify—but this is a huge step for you, Jessica," Reginald said fiercely, more than a touch of defiance in his words. "As a gentleman in Society, I give up nothing by taking you to bed, but you? You would be ruined if anyone found out."

"You are going to marry me, and I will be your wife." Saying the words aloud shot a flicker of heat through her, but she tried to ignore it, tried to keep her mind on what mattered.

On Reginald.

"Yes. Yes, you are," he said, and there was something different in his voice now.

Jessica swallowed. There was a look of...of covetousness, of dominance in Reginald's eyes that she had never seen there before. Of hunger. Of need.

Of desire.

"You are going to marry me, and you will be my wife," Reginald said slowly, moving forward inch by inch until he was pressing her against the back of the sofa. "You will be mine, Jessica, and I don't need a piece of paper for that. I am going to take you, right here, right now."

And then he was kissing her—and though he had kissed her before, and she had enjoyed every single one, there was something new about this kiss. Something in the way his lips possessed her own, how his fingers sparked heat across her arms...

Jessica closed her eyes and lost herself to the kiss, to him, to Reginald. She had lost herself to him days ago, weeks ago, though she had not known it at the time.

The tendrils of heat sparked by his kisses were pouring through her and Jessica whimpered with pleasure as Reginald brushed a loose curl away from her forehead with a hand that swiftly moved to her breast.

She arched into him.

Oh, it was wanton, but she couldn't stop herself. The gentlest brush of his thumb over her skin was enough to inflame her and she wanted more—more than she could get with all these darn clothes on.

It was a scandalous thought, but it was hers, and she knew what she wanted.

"Jessica," Reginald moaned, his lips releasing her for a moment, but only long enough to utter her name.

She did not permit him to waste any more time. Jessica's fingers scraped the nape of his neck as she pulled him back down, finding herself almost lying on the sofa now as Reginald pressed over her.

It was thrilling, to be so enclosed by the feel of him, the strength and the determination of him. Sensual delight was rippling through her and Jessica could only gasp as Reginald's hand—

Reginald's hand!

Jessica broke the kiss. "What are you doing?"

"I'll stop, if you want me to," murmured Reginald, pressing a kiss just under her ear before starting to trail down her neck. "But I don't think you'll want to."

She squirmed underneath his touch. It was hard to deny that the gentle caresses just inside her thigh felt...wonderful. As though the hot ache between her thighs were leading somewhere delightful. As though the pleasure promised would indeed be worth the risk.

Glancing at the door, Jessica looked back at the man she loved. "Touch me, then."

It appeared the man did not need an additional invitation. Before she could say another word, Jessica yelped, her cry of surprise swallowed by another passionate kiss, as Reginald's fingers traveled upward and stroked her curls.

Oh, dear God.

It was more than sensuality. There wasn't a word for this: this intensity as one of his fingers slowly caressed down the slit of her secret place. She was wet, dripping, even, but Reginald did not appear to mind.

If anything, he was pleased.

His murmurs continued. "God, you feel so good, so ready—you want me, don't you?"

"Y-Yes." It was extravagant to admit it, but how could she lie when the evidence was quite literally at his fingertips? "I—oh!"

Jessica's back arched, pressing herself forward, impaling herself onto Reginald's fingers—but she wanted it, she wanted him deeper, for the merest hint of his digits within her sparked such a wave of bliss that stars appeared in the corners of her eyes.

Oh, how her cousins had boasted, but no one had ever told her that it could be like *this*!

Reginald was still kissing her, his mouth not ceasing its tender ministrations as his fingers stroked bliss into her very core, and Jessica could do nothing but cling on to the man who was giving her such hedonism, such sensations.

"Let go," whispered the man she loved, bringing his mouth to hers. "I love you, Jessica, I love you—take it all, take it all from me…"

Jessica whimpered, kissing him back furiously as her fingers dug into Reginald's shoulders just as his thumb entered her, gently circling that delicate nub inside her and—

She exploded. Every single inch of her burst into frantic ecstasy, her whole body shaking, her mind utterly lost in the wash of unadulterated bliss that rippled through her and ripped a cry from her that Reginald quickly stifled with a passionate kiss.

On and on it went, and Jessica thought she would surely suffocate, it was so impossible to draw a breath, until the waves started to subside and her body twitched with the remembrance of utter decadence.

When Jessica managed to open her eyes, it was to see Reginald looking down with a delighted smile.

"I've wanted to do that to you," he whispered, eyes aglow,

"since I kissed you against the wall in the portrait gallery."

Trying not to think about just how many paintings she would have accidentally knocked over if he had done such a thing, Jessica said the first thing that came into her mind. "I will never be able to sit on this sofa again without thinking of you."

Which apparently had been the right thing to say.

Reginald's eyes darkened, just for a moment. The passion they clearly shared blossomed in his face, then he said gruffly, "Good. Ready for more?"

There surely could not be more—he was jesting with her, wasn't he? Oh, Jessica knew that what they had just shared wasn't the typical encounter for a man and wife... But then, if that was just *one* of the ways that two people could enjoy each other...

"'More'?" she echoed.

Reginald did not reply but merely grinned a wicked expression and rose to his feet. He held out a hand. "Come with me."

It was dashed difficult to walk, something that Jessica had not expected. Her legs appeared to be made of jelly, her knees in particular struggling to hold her weight.

Reginald grinned as she reached out swiftly and grabbed his arm to steady her. "That is the highest praise you could offer me."

Jessica shot him a look. "Is this going to last a while?"

"You know, I honestly have no idea," he said cheerfully, evidently thrilled that his amorous ministrations had had such an effect. "But you'll never make the stairs like that. Here."

"*Reginald!*"

Her sudden gasp did nothing to dissuade him, for he had swept her up in his arms and was now carrying her to the door to the great hall.

"Reginald, put me down!" Jessica hissed as he opened the door, her legs over his arm. "Reginald—"

"You would rather walk?" he teased.

There was nothing she could do but huff—not only because he was right, her legs still felt impressively weak, but because now that they were in the great hall. The last thing she wanted to do was make a noise and bring half the household to their notice.

That would not be a good idea.

And so all she could do was rest against Reginald's chest and watch his face as he carried her slowly yet steadily up the stairs.

Jessica had to admit. It was intoxicating, to be carried like a princess up a tower, waiting for her prince.

Thank goodness the guest bedchambers were in an entirely different wing to the rest of the family. By the time Reginald had stepped along the South Wing corridor and turned the corner, Jessica was able to push the door shut.

"There," she said in a normal voice. "No one will be able to hear us from here."

"You are certain?" Reginald's voice was still in a whisper.

Jessica grinned. "Very certain, for two reasons. Firstly, because my ancestors built this place with thick walls, and secondly, because when we were young, we Chance cousins were all stabled here, as my Uncle William put it. The theory was that no amount of screams could ever reach the adults."

She felt as well as heard his chuckle reverberating through her body.

"And did it work?"

"They didn't hear us when Frank and Samuel tied up Lilianna and left her here for six hours," Jessica said with a shrug that brushed her arm up against Reginald's chest with a spark of heat.

Their laughter filled the corridor, but when Reginald stepped through a bedchamber door and gently lowered her to the floor, Jessica's merriment died in her throat.

Well, she was here. A gentleman's bedchamber.

No matter that it happened to be the one that she and Irene had shared as children, whenever they had come to visit Stanphrey Lacey. It had been redecorated in the intervening years and was now a resplendent blue with heavy, damask curtains and a velvet armchair set either side of the now-marble fireplace. And the bed—

Jessica swallowed. *The bed.* It was large, not like the set of beds that had once been here. No, this was a large, four-poster bed with magnificent hangings of blue velvet. The bedsheets were blue too, with a pattern that swirled and quite distracted one from the fact that she was about to lie on it and enjoy amorous congress for the first time.

She attempted to clear her throat. Not *completely* distracted, that was.

"You don't have to do this, you know."

Jessica spun around. Reginald was standing by the door that he had just closed, and there was a shadow of something she did not recognize in his eyes. "'This'?"

"If you have changed your mind—if you have had your fill, if I have hurt you—"

"Do not do this," Jessica said firmly, striding as quickly as she could over to him and splaying her hands against his chest, her eyes fixed on his. "Do not do this, Reginald."

"Do what?"

"Retreat as soon as we are open with each other," she said, her gaze flickering from one eye to another as her spirits leapt. "Yes, this is frightening. It is frightening, to be so exposed, to be so vulnerable with another, but I choose it, Reginald. I choose you. I will embrace any chance I can take to be with you, like this, and...and when we're married, I want to be by your side whenever I can."

Perhaps she had said too much. Reginald stood there, staring, his hands hanging by his sides, his lips parted.

Heat flushed through Jessica. "Reginald?"

"Close your eyes."

For a moment, she was certain she had misheard. "Close my—"

"Eyes," he exhaled, taking her hands in his and walking her to the center of the bedchamber. "Close your eyes."

There was not a moment's hesitation. Jessica closed her eyes, finding it strange indeed to be standing in such a manner but utterly convinced that he had asked her to do so for a reason.

And then she gasped. Fingertips had brushed across her neck, the hem of her gown, and her whole body crackled with expectation.

"You are so beautiful," came Reginald's voice from behind her. He continued to speak as his fingers moved down her back, slowly undoing one button after another. "Your shapely form has transfixed me from the first moment I saw you."

Jessica tried to breathe, but it was difficult; her whole body was quivering from the sensation of strong, warm hands slowly peeling away her gown. The fabric fell in a swoop to the carpet and she stood there in her chemise and underclothes.

Her eyes were still shut.

Another gasp as Reginald pressed a kiss to her now-bare shoulder. "But it isn't just your gorgeous breasts, or the curves of your hips, or the way your eyes sparkle. Those aren't the only reasons I love you."

Jessica willed her knees to strengthen as the sound of Reginald stepping around her filled her ears, and eager lips pressed another kiss, this time on her décolletage.

This... This is...

"It's because of your softness. Your kindness."

Another kiss, this time on her other shoulder, as confident fingers slowly drew her chemise down and allowed it to drop to the floor.

"Because of the goodness you see in the world, an expression of the goodness within you."

She whimpered ever so slightly, clenching her eyes shut as Reginald's fingers moved to her stays. It did not take him long to remove them, the fabric falling, the soft *thump* following.

"You simply cannot believe in anything less than the best because you are the very best of us, Jessica."

She cried out this time, and who could blame her? Reginald's lips had enclosed on one of her nipples, sucking and twisting it around with his tongue, and Jessica arched her back into him as his hands held her hips.

There were only her undergarments to be removed now. Goodness knew what he would do then.

"And so I fell in love with you, Jessica, and now… Now I get to show you just how much."

Jessica gave a sigh of almost relief as her undergarments were removed. It felt right, somehow, to stand here in Reginald's presence entirely denuded, knowing that he could see all of her, everything she was.

"Open your eyes."

Slowly flickering her lashes upward, Jessica looked into the adoring eyes of a man who was very much her own.

"Lie on the bed," Reginald said, his voice ragged.

It took Jessica but three steps to make her way to the large four-poster, and though he had uttered no further instruction, she did not need to be told what to do. Turning around, she sat on the edge of the bed and moved onto the covers, lying on her back as she stared at her future husband.

He was doing a rather wonderful job of taking off his clothes. Reginald's fingers did not stumble, he did not rush, yet there was a steady fall of fabric onto the carpet as one by one, he removed garments. Cravat. Jacket. Waistcoat. Shirt—

Jessica inhaled hard as she saw the hard planes and rough, wiry hair revealed as he removed the last of his upper garments. Dear Lord, she had thought the man attractive with all the accoutrements upon him.

He was an absolute marvel without them.

There was a glint of knowing in his eyes. "Like what you see?"

Jessica swallowed. "Yes."

It felt wrong to admit to such a thing, and yet there was surely nothing more natural in the world. This was to be her husband. Why should she not admire?

There was a great deal more admiring to do as Reginald slowly removed his boots then languidly unbuttoned his trousers.

Jessica discovered that her lungs had decided not to operate, for she could not inhale as he allowed the fabric to drop and—

"Oh my," she whimpered.

His manhood, tall and proud, was jutting out and was evidently very pleased to see her.

The idea of him—of that part of him—and her... *How, precisely, is it supposed to work?*

Reginald said not a word as he stalked toward the bed. Jessica found herself shifting backward unconsciously, but it was a welcome relief when he mounted the bed and covered her body with his own.

Oh, this was everything: the hot, hard planes of his body seemed to perfectly fit her own and when he lowered his head and kissed her, the kiss deepening with an eager need that Jessica felt thrumming through her own limbs, she gave herself completely to him.

His hand stroked down her neck to her breasts, tweaking and teasing her nipples while his mouth lavished kisses on her before his hand continued down, caressing her hips, eking out flurries of gasps as she tried to breathe and accept his loving touches, and Jessica knew that nothing would ever compare to this.

She would never be able to share this with another. Never.

Only when the aching need was building once again between her legs and Jessica instinctively pulled him against her, her legs somehow around his hips, tugging his manhood closer, did Reginald break off his kisses.

"Ready?"

Jessica looked up, her eyes lust hazed, but her decision determined. "Yes."

She had expected pain. Well, the basic geometry of the situation would suggest that it would be most uncomfortable indeed to have such a man as him—such a manhood as *that*—enter her.

And yet while there was pressure, there was also pleasure. A sharp jolt at first, then Jessica moaned as her body welcomed him, drew him in, made room for him, eagerly accepting more and more as Reginald groaned, sinking himself into her.

"Christ alive, Jessica," he muttered, leaning on his elbow and seeming to grit his teeth. "You... You feel..."

Jessica arched her back, tilting her hips as her body took over, knowing precisely what it wanted.

Reginald muttered a curse.

"Are you quite well?" she asked.

His laughter was not mocking, but genial. "You have—you have no idea what you do to me."

She grazed his cheek with her knuckles, smiling with the enthusiastic expectation of another climax. "Oh, I think I have a relatively recent idea. Ravish me, Reginald. Love me."

He did not need much more of an invitation. The rhythm he built, pulling almost completely out of her then sheathing himself inside her with growing intensity and speed, was not unlike that of his fingers, downstairs in the drawing room—but it was so much more.

Oh, the intimacy of welcoming another into her body, the spirals of bliss roaring through her, the pants and groans of a man working to please her yet working to hold back his own release— it was intoxicating, and soon all Jessica could do was cling on to his wide shoulders and throw back her head, welcoming the building, hot ache between her thighs.

"Al-Almost there," she panted, moaning a little as Reginald plunged deeper within her than ever before. "Yes—yes, there— yes—"

And it was a good thing indeed that they were in this part of the house, because the scream of agonized ecstasy that was ripped from her mouth as Jessica was pumped to her peak was astounding.

Clinging on for dear life, Jessica lost herself in the ecstasy, unaware of anything but Reginald's muttered moans and eventual groan of climax as the ripples of satisfaction washed through her body, carrying her up on a tidal wave of sensual carnality.

Reginald cried her name and jerked once, twice, three, four, five times before collapsing into her welcoming arms.

Silence fell, save for their heavy breathing and the whispered sweet nothings that he poured into her ears.

"…beautiful… so precious… mine, my own…"

Jessica was not sure what was best: the climax itself or the knowledge, as she held Reginald in her embrace and warmed at the lover's words that flowed through her, that they would soon be able to share these moments every day.

Every day, for the rest of their lives.

Chapter Sixteen

September 18, 1840

REGINALD HAD NEVER understood the strange, misty-eyed expression that so often clouded a man's face—and judgment—after they had trotted down the aisle.

It was foolishness. It was a fallacy.

It was now his reality.

The whole of Stanphrey Lacey looked glorious in the dying afternoon sun as he sat with Jessica in his arms in the library's sofa. Her soft breath was slow as her eyes meandered over the lines of the book in her hands. She was reading *Nicholas Nickleby*. He was reading her.

And what a fantastic book she was. Reginald could hardly stop looking at her, seeing new meaning in every facet of her expression.

The more he looked, the more he understood, the more he wanted to read. She was a truly epic tale, one that he would spend the rest of his life attempting to understand. It was an honor, indeed, to be even allowed to open the pages.

Reginald swallowed. And opened the pages of the book he had in his hands.

"Ravish me, Reginald. Love me."

Shifting on the sofa and hoping to goodness he was not disturbing the woman he loved, Reginald tried not to think too closely about the incredible evening that they had shared. An evening that had revealed so much, and not just the stupendous curves those long gowns had been hiding.

No, they had opened up to each other that evening, and it had been perfect. Now all they had to do was wait for the last of the banns to be read this Sunday and they could get married.

Jessica pressed a silent kiss onto his shoulder as she turned a page. His stomach twisted pleasantly.

Who could have predicted that there was such joy to be had in these small moments?

When Reginald had thought about love, and it was not something he had done overly often, it had usually been the dramatic, loud, energetic kind. Star-crossed lovers, weeks of wooing, of hiding their relationship from the world—all of that. And there was nothing wrong with that. Of course there was not.

But it was only now that he realized that it was not the only flavor. No, there was also this: a quiet, gentle love. The love of a wallflower. The love that whispered in comfort and settled happily without words, and communicated silently that here was the place where two people had found true happiness.

Reginald's smile, he was sure, looked utterly foolish. But as it was only the two of them in the library, he did not have to worry. The only person who could see him was Jessica herself, and he was more than happy to be a fool for her.

"You know," Jessica said softly, turning another page, "when you suggested that we read in the library, I thought you meant something quite different."

Parts of Reginald that had absolutely no business getting involved in the conversation stiffened. "You did?"

Gracious, that hadn't even occurred to him. *The delicious minx.*

"Yes," said Jessica quietly, glancing up with mischief in her eyes. "But now I am reading *Nicholas Nickleby*, I am afraid you will have to wait."

Reginald groaned. "Now you've put the damned idea in my head."

"Letter for you, Lord Llyne," came a breezy voice as Lucy entered in a swish of skirts. "I snatched it from Nicholl's tray on my way past him in the hall just now. Good lord, I hope I'm not interrupting something I shouldn't be seeing! Is there no chaperone in here with you? I suppose you *are* engaged."

"I'm reading, Lucy," Jessica pointed out primly, as though nothing else of the sort had ever or could ever enter her mind. "Really."

Reginald stifled a grin. It was a damned good thing that the younger Chance cousin had not heard their previous few sentences, or there would have been a much more awkward conversation.

As it was, the woman grinned. "Oh, you can't blame me for wondering. After all, the two of you will soon be married. It is not as though, by their own accounts, any of our parents waited for—"

"Yes, thank you," Jessica interrupted with a stern look.

His beautiful future bride had been direct and blunt, something that did not come easily to her. It was time to rescue her, if the wince of her shoulders was anything to go by.

"Did you say that a letter has arrived for me?" he asked into the awkward silence. "I am surprised. I would have thought my butler would keep correspondence waiting for me at Llyne Hall."

That was what he had written and requested of his servant after receiving Peter's last letter, after all. One more letter from his brother, and he would be forced to step up as head of the house and do something about it—leave Stanphrey Lacey, to be more precise. And that was not something Reginald wanted to do.

"It has urgent marked on the envelope," said Lucy, her curiosity so tangible, it was almost radiating from her. "Which is why I suppose it was sent on. What do you think—"

"I'll take that, if you don't mind," said Reginald quickly, hoping to goodness his tone was not too stiff.

His shoulders certainly were. Any letter marked 'urgent' had to be about his treacherous brother. Had a date been set for his trial—could a treason trial occur with the accusant absent?

Had someone finally tracked him down in France?

The envelope was handed over and Lucy appeared to realize that her presence was no longer required.

"My papa says we'll have predinner drinks at around seven," she said with a sniff. "I suppose I shall see you then?"

"Yes," said Jessica, to the sound of another page turning.

Despite his racing heartbeat, Reginald grinned. The book must have been good.

"Well, until then," said Lucy with a shrug, sauntering out of the library and disappearing around the corner.

With a great deal of regret, Reginald disentangled himself from the ardent and comfortable embrace that he and Jessica had settled themselves in, and looked down at the letter.

It was a hefty one. More accurately, it appeared to be a package of letters that had been covered in brown paper and tied with string. What could it be? A set of evidence against his brother that he had been asked to verify? A long list of crimes that his brother was going to be publicly accused of?

Had he waited too long to wed Miss Jessica Chance? He ought to have insisted on a special license instead of waiting for the banns.

"I tend to find," came the gentle voice of his companion, "that it is a lot easier to read letters when the envelopes have been removed."

He had to chuckle at that. "I suppose so. You don't mind?"

Jessica waved a hand vaguely, her eyes not stirring from the page. "Can't talk. Heroine about to enter the dungeon."

"In—In *Nicholas Nickleby?*"

"Just checking you were paying attention."

Reginald's chuckles continued as he carefully pulled the string off the package and started to unfold the brown paper. That was something else that he could not have predicted about the young woman who was soon to be his wife. Her fascination with danger—at least of the fictional kind—had been completely unexpected.

A number of sheets of paper fell out of the brown paper,

scattering across not only his own lap, but that of Jessica, not to mention the few pieces that slipped to the floor.

"Damn."

"Don't mind me," said Jessica quietly, a smile lilting the corners of her mouth. "Just use me as a desk."

"Why, thank you, that is most generous of you," Reginald quipped, picking up a piece of paper and examining it.

It was a note from his steward.

My lord—

As your absence continues, I am sorry to say that there are a number of things requiring your attention. As your precise return date is unfixed, I took it upon myself to gather up a number of important things from your desk and send them on to you, in the hope that you will review my decisions for the autumn and new year. If you are happy with the decisions enclosed, please countersign and return in the next post.

I remain your humble servant,
Evans

Reginald sighed. At least it was not the terrible news he'd feared for a moment. He supposed he had ignored the requirements of management—but then, he had not himself planned to stay at Stanphrey Lacey this long. It was all Jessica's fault; she was the reason he had not bothered to yet return.

If he had his way, he would marry her immediately, then take her down to Kent and show her the country idyll that would now be her home.

Days, weeks, months—years ahead of them to explore the woodland together, to sit on the chalky downs and picnic, to sit on the cliffs and watch the tides come.

"What is this?"

That should have been his first warning. Not the shortness of the statement, for Jessica rarely utilized seventeen words when seven would do. No, it was the clipped nature of those tones.

But Reginald did not look up. He had just picked up a long list of what appeared to be focused on cattle, columns indicating which should be sold at the harvest and which should be kept for breeding over the winter. "Hmm?"

"This. What is this?"

Reginald looked up, his mind mostly engaged with the decision over the three bulls in the top field herd. "What?"

And that was when his thoughts stopped.

Jessica was looking at him. She had looked at him several times a day over the last few weeks, but this look was one he had not seen before. Her brows drew together, her lips in a thin line. She had never given him *this* sort of look.

A cold, distant look. A fearful, confused look. One that said they were so far apart from each other, despite the fact they were seated on the same sofa, that she hardly knew him.

"What is it?" Reginald asked quietly, dropping the cattle paper onto his lap.

That was when his attention fell onto the paper that Jessica was holding in her hand.

It was nothing to look at, as far as paper went. The quality was average, and the size was about that of a sheet of paper. There was nothing remarkable like a border, or any color—just rows and rows of his handwriting.

A few of the lines caught his eye.

Miss Irene Chance—far too beautiful, likely to have many other suit

His hand darted out. "That's nothing, don't look at it."

"You… You have written about me. About all of us," Jessica whispered, rising to her feet and taking the piece of paper with her just as Reginald tried to snatch it from her hands.

"It's not—"

Not what it looks like. That was what Reginald was going to say, but how on earth could he say such a thing when the evidence was right there in her hands?

His heart was ice, his whole chest frozen as he stared at Jessica, watching her gaze rake down the paper, knowing how it ended.

> *Miss _Jessica Chance_—by all accounts, dull as ditchwater and very shy. Should be easy enough to win over, as a wallflower, as she's had no attention. Poor thing.*

He had hardly given a second thought to the ranking he had created for the seven Chance cousins who were eligible and unattached. What did it matter, now that he had fallen in love with Miss Jessica Chance?

The trouble was, it clearly did matter now.

"Jessica," Reginald said, rising hastily to his feet. "You must understand—"

"I do understand. I understand perfectly," said Jessica in a dull voice that contained absolutely no joy within it. "'Miss Gwendoline Chance—not officially out, might be too young.' Oh, you think so, my *younger* sister? 'Described by the few who know her as a wallflower just like her older sister, which of course is a downside.' That older sister is me, I suppose."

Reginald swallowed, but there wasn't enough moisture in his mouth. "Please, Jessica, don't—don't read that."

"Why not? Do I not deserve to know how I was ranked alongside my cousins and sisters—how you came to determine that I was the best wife for you?" she shot back, lips flattening into a curl and her shaking voice rising in volume. "I suppose you know this by heart."

Jessica thrust the paper at him and Reginald, despite his better judgment, looked down and saw with regret pooling in him just how callous he had been before he had met a single member of this gracious, hospitable, loving family. In addition to the youngest, Miss Gwendoline, a thought that made him shudder now, he had written:

Lady Maude Chance—too old, though she is part of the most senior branch and so may therefore have more sway when it comes to influencing Society.

Lady Francesca Chance—rumors conflict about this one. Perhaps there is also a cousin Frank Chance with whom people confuse her? Far too dominant—I need a wife I can control.

Miss Theodora Chance—almost no dowry, as far as I can tell, and therefore doesn't have much social standing. Could she be enough to help with Peter? Probably not.

Miss Irene Chance—far too beautiful, likely to have many other suitors. No point in attempting to win her over; probably far too stuck-up for her own good.

Lady Lucy Chance—passionate prisoner reformer, perhaps far too close to comfort to the problem. Though on the bright side, might be able to help Peter if he got into a real pickle?

And then the words about his Jessica.

Jessica Chance—by all accounts, dull as ditchwater and very shy. Should be easy enough to win over, as a wallflower, as she's had no attention. Poor thing.

Somehow, he had to find the words. Somehow, he had to explain himself. Precisely how he was going to manage it, Reginald did not know, but the idea of losing Jessica over something that he himself was ashamed of...

"And there's this," she said coldly, thrusting another sheet of paper at him.

Reginald could not help but wince again as he beheld it. The marriage license, for Reginald, Lord Llyne and...

There was a gap for the bride's name. The only element already filled in...was Chance.

He had told the viscount he would take care of the license. Because he'd already taken care of it when he'd asked.

"How can you stand there so silent?" Jessica's voice was ice and it sliced through him just as easily as a knife could have. "I should have known you'd put some thought into this, considering we had not even met when you rode up to this house and asked for my hand. The cheek! Now that I think of it—the very *cheek* of your actions! I was so foolish."

"Jessica, *please!*"

"No! No. But I never imagined you sat there and wrote it all out. I never imagined your thoughts to be so callous, so calculating. How can you stand in judgment of us all—"

"I did not know any of you when I wrote this—and I was wrong to do that, I know that now," Reginald began.

He was not permitted to continue. God knew, he hardly deserved it.

"My sister is *too beautiful* for you, is she?" Jessica asked coldly.

Reginald winced. *Damn.* "I did not—I was going off rumor. I had no other information to go on."

"Other than taking the time to actually meet us, and get to know us, and form your own opinions, I presume," shot back Jessica, her voice warming now but not toward him—*against* him. "I mean, I-I knew this was a marriage of convenience, but…"

"It's not. Not anymore." Reginald stepped forward, desperate to take her hand and show her, not tell her just how much she meant to him. "It's so much more than that—Jessica."

Jessica stepped back, almost tripping on her skirts but managing to retreat from him at great speed, crossing the entire library as she stared in almost disbelief. As though she could not believe he had done such a thing. As though she could not believe anyone could be so heartless.

Damn, but he had been. And now it was too late.

"As I said, this is—this was a marriage of convenience," Jessica continued, her voice breaking, "but I did not know that I had been roundly compared to all my sisters, my cousins, in order to win the prize. The prize is you, I suppose."

The guilt was eating away at him and Reginald did not know how to make it stop. "I-It was not the best way of doing things, but—"

"I have spent my life compared to others, always coming out ill, and to know that...that you..." Jessica did not appear to be able to continue. There was a sparkling in her eyes that Reginald hated to see, but he did not know how he could stop it.

He had hurt her. The woman he cared about the most in the world, and he had hurt her.

"I can explain," he said foolishly.

All too late did he realize his mistake.

"You can?" Jessica crossed her arms and appeared to swallow back her tears. "Go on, then. Explain."

Reginald opened his mouth, realized that there was no possible explanation for what he had done that any rational person would accept, and closed it again as pain tightened around his temples.

What had he done—other than preemptively utterly ruin the happiness he had found? Other than destroy the confidence of a woman who had not had much to begin with? Other than end all possibility of joy with the woman he loved?

"I wish I had burned the whole thing," he found himself muttering.

Jessica's dark laughter was enough to turn his stomach. "Yes, that way, you never would have been found out, and I would have married you and been trapped forever!"

Trapped. It was a harsh word, and it scratched across Reginald's already bruised heart, causing him to wince. "You would not have been... I love you."

"*That* is not what love looks like," Jessica snapped, pointing at the piece of paper. "I know I said a husband and wife should be allowed some secrets from one another, but you had me convinced that you and I would be different. That there would be no secrets between us."

Reginald threw it to the ground, trying to keep his temper. "That was all before I met you—before I knew you, before I fell in love with you!"

"How can I believe that? How can I believe anything you say?"

"Because it's the truth!" Surely, there had to be a way to explain this. "My steward sent this from Llyne Hall. I haven't been back there since I met you. Look, people—gentlemen, even ladies, matchmakers—do this all the time—"

It was the wrong thing to say. Reginald could sense that the moment the first few words of his sentence had left his mouth.

Jessica's laugh was pained now, almost mocking. "You think that every gentleman in Society has a list of myself and my sisters and cousins, ranking us, discussing whether we would make them good wives?"

"Damnit, woman, you know what I mean!" Reginald could no longer hold back the panic, the fear that he was going to lose her—had she not said she *would have* married him—and he hated that it came out merely in shouts and frustration. "Every match made in the *ton* balances the positives and negatives of both parties."

"But I had no opportunity to balance out *your* positives and negatives, did I?" Jessica pointed out, her cheeks still red but determinedly dry. "Were you concerned that I would discount you based on some idiosyncrasy—on your birth? Again, how little you know me!"

"I did not know you then, but I love you now." Reginald tried to take a steady breath, knowing that he had to make her see, make her understand just how much he loved her. "I love you, Jessica, and I—"

"And who is Peter?"

Four words. That was all it took to halt Reginald in his tracks, to make his words fade in his mouth, to force his pulse to skip a beat.

Peter.

Well, he should have known that in the end, it would be his brother who would be his undoing. That was where this had all started, had it not? With Reginald attempting to prevent his brother from ruining everything, to protect their sister and their good name from Peter.

In a way, he supposed dully, he should have known that just as it had started with Peter, it would end with Peter.

"Peter," Reginald said heavily, "is my brother."

Jessica narrowed her eyes. "And… And he is in some sort of trouble with the law, I suppose? You might have needed Lucy's help. Is he in prison?"

No, Reginald wanted to say. *But I wish he were.*

He could lie. It would be easy enough to lie, and she would never know, until perhaps, she read about the scandal in the papers. He could lie, spin her some tale of mistaken identity and how it would all blow over, and he could leave. He could walk out of Stanphrey Lacey and act as if all of this had never happened. Send the viscount enough funds to cover the wedding preparations to date and walk out of Jessica's life.

The mere thought was so distasteful, so impossible, that he almost laughed.

"My brother, Peter," Reginald said quietly, "is in trouble with the law, but not as you might think."

Jessica raised an eyebrow. "He is innocent, is he?"

"No." It cost him a great deal to admit it, but he was never going to lie to this woman again. "No, he is not. He is a traitor."

Her lips parted, but no sound came out.

"He betrayed secrets of ours to the French. He is on the run," Reginald said quietly, surprised that he was able to speak on the topic so levelly. "He is a wanted man by the Crown, and when the news gets out, my family name will be ruined. That… That is why I wanted to marry a Chance. And when I wrote that list, I would have any Chance I could take. And now I know you and I love you and I want *you*, Jessica. Only you. No other Chance. No other woman. For all my life."

The last few words had come out in a rush and Reginald had not intended to plead, but he would if it meant he could have his Jessica.

Who was standing in complete silence, merely staring.

After a few minutes, Reginald could bear it no longer. "Jessica?"

"I...I think you should leave," she said faintly.

His shoulders slumped, all the hope to which he had been clinging on was extinguished by the coldness of her words.

"'Leave'?" Reginald repeated faintly, hardly able to believe it.

"Yes, I want you to leave. Leave this room, leave Stanphrey Lacey, leave my life," Jessica said, turning away on the last word. "I never want to see you again."

He stared at her back, her dark curls, the curve of her neck. "But—"

"I think I made myself quite clear, Lord Llyne," came the quiet voice.

Reginald had never known it was possible for a heart to actually break. He had presumed that was the poetic license that such creatives were permitted to use in times of great trouble. He had not actually known that it was possible for this agony to weigh so heavily on one.

"This was why I did not tell you," he said listlessly, taking a step forward but stopping as Jessica did not turn around.

She did not love him enough to forgive him. She did not love him enough to stand with him against disgrace.

He loved her. She might even, in a small way, love him. But she did not love him enough.

"Very well," Reginald said aloofly, trying to cut off all the pain, trying to tell himself that he no longer cared. "I shall be gone within the hour. Good day, Jessica—Miss Chance."

It was only when he stepped outside the library and began making his way up the stairs that he allowed the tears to fall.

Chapter Seventeen

September 21, 1840

"THERE YOU ARE! And about time too."

It was not the most welcoming of greetings, but Jessica had to admit that it was far more than she had expected. A small part of her had wondered, as she had sat in her Uncle William's carriage, rattling along with her cousin Maude chattering away about all the excitement she was looking forward to in London, whether her family would have even noticed that she had been gone.

"And why the glum face, after staying longer at Stanphrey Lacey, that's what I want to know," asked Gwen curiously as Jessica stepped through the wide doorway into the hall. "I would have thought you'd be delighted to be back home."

Home.

Jessica had never really given it much thought. Pernrith House had been home for so long that she had stopped noticing the walls, the floor, the rugs and the carpets, the paintings on the walls.

The place had become, somehow, a part of the backdrop of her life, becoming so vague, she could hardly picture it.

It would be her home forever now. She would never marry. She hadn't the heart to tell her uncles, as her guardians at Stanphrey Lacey, that she had called off the wedding. She had simply agreed to their presumption that Reginald—*Baron Llyne* had been called back home on barony business. That meant the vicar would have read the banns one last time the day before at the local church, and assuredly back home in London, too. But she had not been at the church to hear them this time. She'd feigned another headache—though it had hardly been necessary to *feign* feeling unwell.

All the banns were read, but she would never marry. No one would ever ask her, she was certain, but even if a small miracle were to occur and someone did, someone who—mistakenly—did not doubt her chastity, she would have to decline.

She could never marry anyone else, not now. Not after sharing what she had shared with Reginald.

"...beautiful... so precious... mine, my own..."

"Leave this room, leave Stanphrey Lacey, leave my life."

"Jessica?"

Jessica blinked. Her sister was staring with great confusion. "Wh-What?"

"I beg your pardon," murmured their mother, drifting in wearing the most impeccable pelisse and shawl that Jessica had ever seen. Trust her mother to always be the best dressed of the family. "I'm going out to have afternoon tea with Lady Romeril— she wants to hear all about the wedding, Jessica, and truth be told, I am not certain what to tell her."

Jessica's stomach roiled.

Yes, it was an excellent question. How to tell the whole of Society that she had broken off her engagement?

It was a scandalous thing to do at the best of times. A broken engagement was not something one considered lightly, and she had read the torrid stories about broken trust and outraged fathers.

But that was usually when a gentleman had experienced second thoughts. Society rarely castigated a lady for withdrawing her consent to a match.

The trouble was, it was a match made outside of London, far too swiftly, between two people who hardly knew each other, and it had ended just as swiftly as it had begun. Jessica was certain that Lady Romeril would be greatly intrigued to hear all about the sordid details.

Not that her mother knew any of the sordid details.

"Your cheeks look awfully red, dear," her mother said conversationally as she pulled on her gloves. "Is it something I said?"

"No, I... I..."

Jessica swallowed, wishing to goodness she could think of the words—that they did not scatter the moment her mind attempted to grab hold of them.

She had not been able to face her uncles, or even the vicar at Stanphrey Lacey, but she had written a letter to her parents, explaining. Well, a letter. That was, more of a note. She wasn't sure such a short missive counted as a letter.

Mama and Papa,

Engagement ended. Do not ask me about it. Please cancel all wedding plans.

Your – Jessica

Jessica had told herself at the time that she had no wish to waste paper. Only now, faced with her mother's expectant face, could she admit to herself that it was because she had no idea how to explain the treachery that she had suffered.

That list! Any Chance he could take, using them for their name, using them for their reputation—and her most of all.

And she had loved him.

She had to have known this deep down from the start—why else would a total stranger ask for her hand? It was not *her* he'd wished to marry, but the idea of her. She had told herself she'd been all right with that, that she would make him fall in love with her for real.

But faced with written evidence of the whole scheme, presented with the truth about his brother...she'd found she had not been all right with that at all.

"Jessica, can you hear me?"

Jessica blinked. Her mother was waving an elegantly gloved

hand before her eyes and Gwen had disappeared, though goodness knew where. Jessica had not been paying attention.

"Yes. Hello," she said a little lamely.

Her mother bit her lip. "I do not have to take tea with Lady Romeril, you know. If it is going to be too difficult for you, the topic being spoken of."

"No, no, you go," Jessica said hastily. What she did not say was, *If we all retreat from Society, it will be talked of. The small whispers will become a shout, a roar, and suddenly, the whole of London will not be able to move without talking about it.*

And she couldn't bear that. She just couldn't bear it.

"Hmm," said her mother, evidently not convinced. "Well, Reeny is in the drawing room, deciding on invitations."

All the warmth drained from Jessica's cheeks. "Mama— Mama, I told you in my letter, the wedding preparations had to be canceled!"

Surely, they had understood? Perhaps she should not have been so circumspect, perhaps she should have given greater detail...but that would have betrayed herself as a fool and Reginald as a cad, a rogue of the worst order, and...

And somehow Jessica could not do that. To accept that Reginald was that sort of man was to accept not only that she had not spotted it, but that she had been entirely taken in. That she had fallen in love with a man who could treat her so ill.

That was not something she could accept.

"Invitations we have received, dear," said her mother patiently. "Invitations to dinners, and card parties, and a late picnic that I think Hyde Park will be far too damp for, if you ask me. I do not know what the Duchess of Axwick is thinking."

Jessica blinked. "Oh. Oh, I see."

Obviously, there was more than one type of invitation. She had to remember that. There would be a great deal of invitations to stave off, she supposed, now that she was no longer going to become Lady Llyne.

"Though I did have word from the vicar at Stanphrey Lacey.

He read the last of the banns yesterday? And he wanted to know if our plans included a wedding there or if we would be staying in London for it."

Jessica swallowed.

"But I suppose it was more a matter of you not relaying your change of heart to the man before you left?" her mother asked. "I have not received word of any changes in expectations from your aunts, either."

Reginald's face flashed before Jessica's eyes and she hastily pulled off her bonnet and traveling cloak as she said, "It…. I wasn't feeling well. I'm better now. The drawing room. I will go and assist Reeny."

Her mother said something, though precisely what, Jessica did not know. She had stepped with indecent haste, not even bothering to change her shoes for her town slippers, across the hall and down the west corridor toward the drawing room.

This is home. With every footstep, she could feel the tension in her shoulder blades starting to dissipate. Every echo was familiar, every inch of the walls intimate.

And this was where she would spend the rest of her life, wasn't it? Jessica knew that now; her choice to never marry—not that it was much of a choice, as the door was hardly being battered down by suitors—meant that unless one of her sisters married and asked for her Jessica's help with her children, she would live out her time as a spinster here with her parents, and then when her father died, here in Pernrith House with her brother, who would become the new viscount.

That was a disarming thought. Michael, a viscount. It did not bear thinking about.

At least I like the old place, she thought as she entered the drawing room and saw her sister poring over a plethora of cards and papers laid out on top of the pianoforte, the lid closed. At least she could reconcile herself to the future before her.

"There you are. We thought you'd never get here," Irene said without turning around.

Jessica smiled, despite herself. "And you knew it was me because…?"

"Because no one else walks that quietly, not even the servants," her sister said brightly, glancing over her shoulder with a laugh. "And—dear God, what has happened?"

Jessica froze. Surely, her parents had—she had presumed they would tell her siblings what had happened. The idea that they did not know…

"Other than the blasted man being an absolute rogue, of course," Irene said lightly, turning back to the pianoforte and moving a few cards around. "I was saying to Wilfred only yesterday, it is deplorable, the way men gad about. I suppose he broke your heart?"

How precisely Jessica was able to move farther into the room without bursting into tears, she did not know. She did reach the pianoforte to see so many cards of invitation that she could now understand why it was the instrument, and not a small console table, that was being used to sort them.

The Baroness Grasemere invites you to…

The Duke and Duchess of Sharnwick are hosting…

Viscount and Viscountess Walden would appreciate your company at…

The Earl and Countess of Dalmerlington hope you are available for light drinks…

The Duchess of Axwick is welcoming a select group of friends…

"We are popular," Jessica said weakly.

All these invitations. They crowded her mind, making it impossible for a brief moment to think of Lord Llyne at all. It came as a welcome relief, but the moment she noticed it, the relief was gone, flittering away like a butterfly that never quite came down to roost.

"You are popular," said Reeny darkly. "The news of your engagement—"

"I don't want to talk about it."

The statement had been made automatically, without a great deal of involvement from her brain. Jessica was not surprised, though, to hear the words uttered by her own lips.

The last thing she wanted to do was discuss the pain, the heartbreak of knowing that she had been directly compared to her sisters, her cousins, and had been found not the most beautiful, or the most interesting, or even the most useful. No, Irene or Frank or Lucy could claim those prizes.

No, she was the most desperate, according to Reginald—to Lord Llyne's perspective, and that was why she had been chosen.

Was there anything in the world more mortifying?

"I did not ask you to talk about it," said her sister mildly. "I merely pointed out that it is your engagement that was greatly increased the number of invitations we have received. Look."

Jessica did so, examining the cards and letters of invitation more closely. Then she winced.

The Baroness Grasemere invites you to her afternoon tea. Miss Jessica Chance, the Baron Llyne, and her family…

The Duke and Duchess of Sharnwick are hosting a private ball and request the company of Miss Jessica Chance and family…

Viscount and Viscountess Walden would appreciate your company at dinner on the 9th. Miss Jessica Chance will be the guest of honor…

The Earl and Countess of Dalmerlington hope you are available for light drinks before a musical performance hosted in anticipation of the wedding between Miss Jessica Chance and Lord Llyne…

The Duchess of Axwick is welcoming a select group of friends and is delighted to include Miss Jessica Chance…

"Yes, I get the general idea," Jessica said weakly.

Why she had not expected this, she did not know. It was precisely what had happened to Cousin Evelyn, and Cousin

Lilianna, and undoubtedly to her male cousins too, though she rather doubted the invitations had been this numerous. Why, almost the entirety of the pianoforte lid was covered in them!

All sent to Viscount and Viscountess Pernrith on the occasion of their eldest daughter finally finding a suitor who had actually agreed to marry her.

Jessica's stomach curdled. What on earth would they all say when the news of the broken engagement spread through all good Society? Would the invitations addressed primarily to herself dry up? Would the Pernrith branch of the Chance family find itself ostracized? Even more so than it ever had been before?

It did not sound particularly like a bad idea to Jessica's mind, but she knew her family may not concur.

"I do not know how I will ever go out again in public," she found herself saying.

"Nonsense," said Irene soundly, moving a few cards around in a sorting system known only to herself. "Engagements have been broken before."

But not like this. That was what Jessica wanted to say, but that would necessitate an explanation she was simply not willing to give.

Her sister had not read the piece of paper that ranked all the Chance cousins, Jessica reminded herself. Perhaps Irene would be less blasé about the whole thing if she had done.

Or maybe not. She had come out quite well on it, had she not?

"What did he do, anyway?"

Jessica blinked. Her sister came back into focus, her expression inquisitive. "'Do'?"

"Well, I presume the pest must have done *something* to attract your ire and your eventual rejection of his hand in marriage," Irene said quietly, more softly than before. "You were so obviously in love with him, Jessy."

Jessy. It had been a long, long time since anyone had called her that. It was almost impossible to remember how long, and it awakened in Jessica the softness that she had desperately attempted to stamp down.

She could not allow herself to cry. She had shed enough tears. She had cried the instant that Reginald—that Lord Llyne had left the library, and she had cried from the morning room as she had watched his horse disappear down the drive at a gallop, the man not even waiting to leave by carriage with his valet, who followed after, and she had cried herself to sleep that night.

And she had told herself: *no more tears.*

"I was… I thought… I was in love with the man I thought I knew," Jessica said awkwardly, knowing full well that all the statement was going to do was increase her sister's curiosity. "And that's all."

"'That's all'?" Irene leaned against the pianoforte and narrowed her eyes. "It doesn't seem like *all*. So what, he was a little less well-mannered without Papa looking over his shoulders?"

"No," Jessica said, desperately hoping to change the conversation. "Which of these invitations do you—"

"He didn't… He didn't try to take advantage, did he?" Her sister's eyes were wide. "Men are such pigs!"

Laughter was not the correct reaction to the statement, for it was earnestly said and in full support of her, Jessica knew.

But still. It was an amusing thing to hear coming from the lips of her sister Irene, of all people, whose best friend was one of those pigs. Men.

Besides, he had not taken advantage. She had wanted what they had shared, wanted it desperately. Even now, knowing they were parted forever, Jessica could not find it within herself to regret what had happened. He had been—he still was a very handsome, very charming man.

And that was the trouble, wasn't it? Altogether too charming.

"I don't want to talk about it," Jessica said again aloud, forcing herself to look at the invitations. "Surely, we cannot be expected to attend all of these."

"Papa suggested a *divide and conquer* approach," Irene said softly, not following her sister to look at the invitations. "He and you, Mama and I, and then Michael separately, if he can ever be encouraged to attend anything on the family's behalf. That way, the Pernrith Chances can attend triple the number of events."

Jessica nodded mutely. It was an excellent plan, save for the fact that it still required her to attend social functions. And the topic of her engagement would undoubtedly come up. Would she be forced, then, to tell each acquaintance, one at a time, that the wedding had been called off? Polite society dictated that they be satisfied with that and not pry, but the moment she'd left the room, they would speculate. Rumors would fly throughout Town by day's end. Ideally, she could just remain here and never leave the house again, though she couldn't see her father agreeing to that.

He may have been the quietest of the four brothers, but he knew the family's responsibilities to Society. Apparently, at least one of them was to be present, heaven forbid.

"Jess."

Jessica blinked and saw her sister looking at her with such affection and concern, it rather shocked her. "Reeny."

"You know I hate that name."

"Sorry," said Jessica, remembering all too late.

Her sister sighed. "You know you are going to tell me about it, eventually, don't you? Why not do so now?"

It was difficult not to laugh. She was right. Naturally, Irene was right; Jessica was going to tell her about it, and the longer she held on to this secret, the more she felt as though she were going to burst.

It wore heavily on her, this knowledge that they had all been weighed and measured and had all, in some way, been found wanting.

Her, it seemed, most of all.

Jessica took a deep breath. "You remember when Reginald—when Lord Llyne first arrived at Stanphrey Lacey?"

"He stormed up on a white steed and swept you off your feet, if I recall correctly," said Irene with a smile.

A roll of her eyes was the only appropriate response to such nonsense. "If you're not going to be serious—"

"No, no, I can be serious," her sister said hastily. "He turned up, unannounced and uninvited, and asked for your hand in marriage. Surprising all of us, I must say."

"You were not alone in that," Jessica said quietly, twisting her hands together and wondering how on earth she was going to explain this. "But as it turns out, there is a reason that I was the one who was chosen. I mean, obviously, there was, but I never imagined it would be… that."

Irene tilted her head, awaiting further explanation.

Much to her surprise, it did not actually take that long to explain the whole sorry business to her sister, the longcase clock ticking away the seconds in the corner. Irene was a good listener: appropriately silent, but gasping in all the right places, and even lifting a hand to her bosom when she heard about the list.

"The blaggard!"

"You know Papa doesn't like that sort of language," Jessica reminded her.

"Papa would say far worse if he had heard the story I just did," Irene shot back, two pink dots flaming in her cheeks. "The nerve of the man!"

"And that is, essentially, what I said," came Jessica's reply. "Except…"

Except now that she had explained the whole thing aloud, she could see the sense in it.

Oh, it was nonsensical to the extreme, when viewed from the outside. But when viewed from the inside, knowing Reginald, knowing how greatly he cared for his family and his family name…knowing where he came from, the battles he had already faced in being legitimized…

And he spoke the truth, Jessica thought guiltily as she replayed their argument back in her mind. Matches were made on far more mercenary terms. It was well known that the old Miss

Ashbrooke—the Countess of Lenskeyn, as she now was—had always been sharp but fair in her assessments of potential matches, declining some due to a mismatch in taste, or fortune, or breeding.

No one had criticized her for doing such a thing.

Jessica bit her lip and tried desperately to hold on to the fact that she was angry at Reginald, very angry.

But the heat, the flames circling in her, did not feel like hate. They felt like love.

"I can see why you were so upset," said a voice from a long way off. Jessica blinked.

Irene was staring, clearly troubled. "I suppose you are never going to see him again, after such a revelation. I suppose none of the family is."

"I… I would not wish to dictate to anyone what they should do in their personal lives," Jessica said awkwardly.

Never see Reginald again. That was what she had told him, after demanding that he leave Stanphrey Lacey. It was only now she was back home that she realized just what a lonely prospect that was.

A life without Reginald. A life without the man who made her smile, who had somehow won her heart—who had said that she had won his.

But how could she love a man who was so…so painfully and honestly logical?

"Is it possible that you have made a mistake?" asked Irene quietly. "We all knew there was *some* reason he asked for your hand before he even met you."

Jessica swallowed. "No! No. No, I don't… I don't think so."

"But you don't know," pressed her sister. "You are not absolutely sure."

It was all so confusing. It had hurt, to know that the beginning of their connection had been so intensely cold, had marked her as someone who would be desperate to accept any proposal, any man, merely because she was a wallflower.

Though she had proven him absolutely right in that point.

But no, she would not have accepted *any* man in those circumstances. She was certain of that. There had been something special about the baron that had drawn her to him from the start.

Still, he would not know that. How gratified he must have felt that the *dull-as-ditchwater* wallflower had accepted him without a fuss.

She sighed. Jessica could not deny that though the beginning had perhaps been unfortunate, what had blossomed, what had grown between them…that had been something truly spectacular. Something special.

Something she had never expected to know.

But her own feelings aside, Irene had not mentioned her thoughts on the baron's brother being accused of treachery. Whatever the man had done, whatever information he had leaked, could her family accept that? Her marrying into the family of a traitor?

Could *she* accept that?

She did not know the circumstances, or whether the man's actions had been proven beyond a shadow of a doubt. But she found she did not care. Lord Llyne—Reginald—was not his brother. And she would not punish him for his brother's actions, even if all of London chose to do so.

Just as no one should have punished him—or punished her father—for the choices made by *their* fathers.

"It's a good thing I have not canceled any of the wedding plans, then," came a quiet voice.

Both Jessica and her sister spun around, but it was the former who cried, "Mother!"

"Well, disagreements almost always happen during an engagement. It is a natural part of the courting process, if you ask me," said the Viscountess Pernrith leisurely as she stepped around the door she had clearly been hiding behind as she'd listened to their conversation. "You should have heard the rows your father and I enjoyed in the lead-up to our wedding."

The idea of their parents rowing was quite astonishing. Jessica stared, open-mouthed. "You and Papa?"

"He was in the wrong, mostly, but I was wrong to hold it so against him for so long," her mother said gently, reaching the pianoforte and placing a hand on her shoulder. "If you love him—if there is absolutely any part of you that wishes for reconciliation—then you know what it is you have to do."

Jessica tried to force down the nausea that rose up at the very thought. "Y-Yes. Yes, but…but I can't."

"Jess," Irene began, but she was spoken over by their mother.

"You are a wallflower, Jessica, but that does not mean that you can just let life pass you by."

Jessica laughed bitterly. "Oh, it is so easy for you to say that, Mama. You were the flourishing rose of your Season! You were beloved wherever you went. Grandpapa told me once that you had to fight men off with a stick."

There was just a flicker in her mother's expression. "Well… Well, not quite all of *that*."

"He told me that you declined several proposals before accepting Papa," Irene said—not quite accusatorily, but with a certain amount of direction. "You're not like Jessica."

She was so accustomed to the casual slight that Jessica did not even wince. "I cannot go to Reginald—to Lord Llyne. I cannot find the…the confidence, the bravery to do it."

And she hated that about herself, and she had no idea why she could not bring herself to do it, except that she couldn't.

Jessica tried to grin, but the tears were falling now and there was no point in attempting to stop them. "I'm just not brave enough. What if he rejects me? What if—what if he laughs at me? I love him, I couldn't stand to face that. I'm not brave enough to take that chance."

Chapter Eighteen

October 7, 1840

REGINALD THUMPED HIS head against the wall. Then he did it again, three times, just for good measure.

"Stupid, stupid, stupid."

He should have burned the piece of paper. He should have hidden it. He should never have written it in the first place.

"Stupid."

And his head was hurting—but that was nothing to the pain within him, reminding him with every pulse that he had done the most foolish thing possible.

Not write the list. He stood by it, in a way; it was the only way he could conceive of deciding between the numerous Chance cousins, and it had been the best and only way he could think of to save his family.

No, the foolish thing had been not fighting for the woman he loved. She had asked him to leave, but Reginald should have stayed—should have tried to explain, continued to apologize, tell her that she was right and that he was sorry.

And what had he done instead?

Walked out of the room and walked out of Stanphrey Lacey and rode out of her life.

Reginald thumped his head against the wall in his study one final time. "Stupid."

He'd arrived back in London two weeks ago to discover that his sister had accepted an invitation to stay with a friend for a fortnight. The house was empty, save for a few servants, and there was a particularly miserable tinge to the air with the knowledge that he had hoped to bring Jessica here.

Now he never would.

Miss Jessica Chance—by all accounts, dull as ditchwater and very shy. Should be easy enough to win over, as a wallflower, as she's had no attention. Poor thing.

Reginald sighed heavily as he stepped across his wood-paneled study and threw himself into his green leather armchair. What a fool he had been. He could never have guessed, when he'd written that list, just how little he had understood Miss Jessica Chance from the rumors.

Wallflower, yes. But passionate. Eager. Clever.

Unlike any other woman he had ever met. He had been foolish, and reckless, and much to his own chagrin, Reginald had to accept that he did not deserve her.

Sighing again, he reached out and took the bottle of brandy from his desk, where he had deposited it within ten minutes of arriving home. Drowning his sorrows wasn't a habit he currently had, and he certainly hoped it wouldn't become one—but it seemed like a very good idea now, from where he was sitting.

The top of the bottle opened with a satisfying *thunk*, and Reginald grinned weakly. Well, he had done all he could. He had tried to keep his sister out of it. He had tried to marry into one of the most eligible families to save their name.

He had even been foolish enough to fall in love.

All he had to do now was—

"And I said the damned Baron Llyne will see me now!"

The door flew open and a whirlwind entered.

Reginald blinked. Well, not quite a whirlwind. Whirlwinds didn't wear gowns, for a start, and one of the people now standing in his study was most definitely wearing a gown.

She was also familiar.

"Miss Irene?" he said, hardly able to believe his eyes as he rose to his feet.

Miss Irene—Irene Chance. *Jessica's sister.*

What on earth was she doing here?

"Forgive the abrupt introduction, Lord Llyne. Aynor," said the dark-haired gentleman beside her, who was dressed rather well and spoke as though he had been bred from nobility. Aynor... The title sounded familiar. "Friend of the family. The Pernrith side, at any rate. Not that there's anything wrong with the rest of them, you understand, but—"

"Wilfred," said Miss Chance calmly, "do shut up."

He chuckled. "Shutting up, Reeny."

"And don't call me that. You know I don't like it when people call me that," said Miss Chance without missing a beat, closing the door in the face of Reginald's astonished butler and turning back to her host. "And *you!*"

It was not quite a malediction, but it was spoken as one, and Reginald's feet moved automatically, stepping backward so that he fell backward into his chair.

"Don't be too hard on the man, Reeny," said Aynor nonchalantly, as though the two of them regularly stormed into a man's house to castigate him.

Perhaps they did.

"Oh, excellent, brandy—a tad early, but then it's always six o'clock somewhere," said Aynor cheerfully, plucking the bottle of brandy out of Reginald's unresisting hands before glancing about. "Now, where do you keep your glasses?"

"This is not the time for brandy, Wilfred," Miss Chance snapped as she moved to sit in the chair opposite Reginald. Although she spoke to her companion, her gaze did not leave Reginald for an instant.

Her friend snorted. "I was going to pour you a large glass, Reeny."

"Oh. Well." Miss Chance appeared mollified. "That's all right, then."

Reginald could not help it; he gaped.

There was something about these two. They appeared to

work in complete tandem, not needing to speak to know what the other was going to do next. Was he a cousin? No. Not a Chance. A distant cousin? Who was he to be so casual with an unwed lady, and without a chaperone in sight?

Aynor had managed to find three glasses and had popped them on the desk, pouring a generous measure in the first one.

Miss Chance picked it up. "For you. You cad."

Reginald could hardly argue with her, but it was a most strange encounter, being given brandy in his own study.

The gentleman poured the second glass and Miss Chance glared at her companion. "I'll tell you when to stop."

When the beautifully golden liquid was a mere quarter inch from the top, she nodded almost imperceptivity and Aynor moved to the third glass. Miss Chance took the second, downed it almost in one go, coughed, grinned, then fixed Reginald with a stare made of daggers.

"So. You and your list."

The bottom fell out of Reginald's stomach. "I-I beg your pardon?"

"Do not bother to deny it," said Miss Chance fiercely, leaning back in the chair and folding her arms. "Jessica has told me all about it, and I must say, I am very disappointed."

Reginald opened his mouth, looked at Aynor, who had mimicked the young lady and crossed his arms too, and closed it. The gentleman winked from where he was standing, crucially behind Miss Chance's back.

"I saw that," said the unrelenting Miss Chance.

"Well, every man is permitted at least one mistake, isn't he?" Aynor suggested as he perched on the arm of Miss Chance's chair. "I mean, does a man have to be perfect to be permitted to marry your sister?"

Miss Chance turned in her chair to stare incredulously at him. "Yes!"

Reginald shifted uncomfortably in his own chair.

He had expected something like this. Oh, not something like

this. He had thought Mr. Michael Chance, or perhaps even the Viscount Pernrith himself might appear on his doorstep and demand answers. Not a woman from the family, and certainly not a stranger to the situation—though the way the two of them were carrying on, he wondered whether the two of them... Though he had not uncovered a betrothed during his own research into the family.

The reminder of his *research into the family* made the guilt heavy in his stomach.

"Jessica is a very precious and very delicate flower," Miss Chance was saying hotly to Aynor. "You know that as well as I do, and she deserves—"

"Oh, she deserves the very best, obviously," interrupted the gentleman, "but no one is perfect, Reeny, and—"

"Stop calling me 'Reeny'!"

"—and you cannot blame a man for getting it wrong once. Once," Aynor said magnanimously, "is acceptable."

The two of them turned, slowly, to look at Reginald. Their focus pinned him to the chair.

Reginald swallowed. "It was a mistake—a terrible mistake. One I wish I had never made."

"There you are, then," said Aynor, thrusting his brandy glass at his host and sloshing the expensive liquid onto the rug. Reginald made a mental note to mention it to his butler for cleaning. "The man is sorry. The man won't do it again."

"The man will not have a chance to do it again if he is not careful," Miss Chance said slowly. "And I rather fear that he is not going to give himself the opportunity to do it again. Are you, Lord Llyne?"

At this point, Reginald was utterly lost, and so he did the only thing that made sense. He took a sip of brandy.

The deliciously sweet, heady liquid unfortunately went to his head, exacerbated by the lack of luncheon he had taken while on the road.

Reginald blinked. For a moment, just a moment, he thought

it was Jessica seated on the chair. He blinked again and the mirage cleared, revealed an increasingly irate sister instead.

"And worst of all," Miss Chance said slowly, "is that you do not even realize that the whole thing could be solved in about five minutes."

"Five—Five minutes?" Reginald asked.

"Oh, hang on, Reen—Irene," Aynor amended hastily. "I do not think that five minutes would be sufficient to fix this."

"My point is, you dolt," said Miss Chance, presumably addressing her friend, though Reginald was not quite sure, "that they could be happy."

Happy.

Reginald had not understood the meaning of the word until he had met Jessica. The rest of his life had been good, yes, but not great. The sun had shone and life had continued, one day after another, and then suddenly, he had been faced with a traitor in his family and he had made a decision that had brought him to…

Her. Jessica Chance. The one person in the world with whom he wished to be, right in this moment.

"I can't be happy."

Miss Chance and Aynor looked up at Reginald's words, the former saying sharply, "And why is that? More brandy, Wilfred."

As the gentleman poured another incredibly generous portion of brandy into the young lady's glass, Reginald said quietly, "I'll never be happy again. I… I have lost the affection and trust of the most incredible woman I have ever met. Will ever meet. I… She…"

His words trailed away, his mind unable to explain just how lost he was.

Reginald swallowed, his whole chest tight. He had lost her. He had lost his Jessica.

When he looked up, a little surprised that there was no response to his despair, it was to see the two of them grinning. "What the devil are you smiling at?"

"She is completely in love with you, you fool," Miss Chance

said quietly. "Did you think she could forget you so easily?"

For a moment, the room spun. It was impossible to accept, impossible to believe.

Jessica, still love him? After what he had done?

"She definitely loves you," Aynor said quietly. "I have never seen a woman so in love. Save for the viscount and viscountess, of course."

"And that's just sickening," Miss Chance said matter-of-factly. "Seeing Jessica moping after you all the time, it's just sad. You need to do something about it."

Reginald blinked, not accustomed to such blunt conversation. "'Do something'?"

Miss Chance rolled her eyes. "Honestly! *Men!* It's a wonder anything gets done in this world! Wilfred, more brandy!"

"What my best friend is attempting to say," said Aynor quietly, removing the brandy glass from the young woman's fingers and putting it beside his own on the desk, "is that Miss Jessica Chance loves you, and you run the very real risk of losing her if you do not hurry up and do something about it."

"'Do something about it'?" Reginald echoed blankly.

He probably deserved that eye roll.

"Yes, *do something* about it!" said Miss Chance, rising to her feet and brushing down her skirts. "I would like to think you are worthy of her, and you can do me a favor and prove that you are by going over to our house, declaring your undying love, apologizing profusely—"

"I've done that!"

His protestation was ignored. "Do it again," said Miss Chance darkly, "or accept that you were not worthy of her in the first place."

"You don't understand," said Reginald lamely, staring down at his brandy and watching the liquid slosh in the glass as he stirred it. "There's something she learned that will soon affect my family terribly. It's a miracle it hasn't gotten out yet...but it will.

If I married her, it would affect her, too—affect *you*. All the Chances."

"Oh, *that*. Yes, well, we've talked about it, and we don't care."

Reginald's head whipped up. "You've *talked* about it?" He supposed it only right that Jessica had explained to her family what had led her to end the engagement. Though perhaps he'd hoped she'd stuck to his petty list and kept his brother's secret for now. Still, he could not blame her.

"I think you were right the first time, chap," said Aynor amicably. Reginald wondered if that meant this man, too, this *stranger*, knew what his brother had done. "Marrying into the Chances will save you. Nothing can ruin their reputations."

Miss Chance backhanded him across the chest. "Excuse you! I won't accept that as a reason to marry my sister."

Aynor rubbed his chest, as if the flick of her hand had indeed hurt him. "I wasn't saying *that*. I was saying it'll solve his problem, just like he apparently thought it would."

The sigh Irene let out could have moved a mountain. "Come on, Wilfred. I would imagine Don Saltero's Chelsea Coffee House is still open, and I'm gasping for a hot chocolate. Maybe we'll run into Wharton on the way and I'll get less of an earful from Mama this evening. Shall we?"

Aynor leaned toward Reginald and whispered, though rather loudly still, "We ditched her chaperone to come here."

"*Shall we?*" Irene repeated, louder this time.

The study door shut behind the pair of them, and all Reginald could do was blink into the silence.

Dear God. That was certainly a lot to think about it. If the evidence of the two now-empty glasses on his desk was not most definitely real, he would have been tempted to think that he had dreamed the whole thing.

But he had not. Miss Chance and her friend, Aynor, whoever he was—they had been here. They had told him that that her family did not care about his brother's past, that Jessica still loved him, that there was almost nothing he could do to stop her loving him—and the glare in Miss Chance's eye had dared him to find something.

And that meant that there was still, perhaps, a wedding to plan. Still happiness that could be reached. Still joy to be found.

Well, now all he had to do was—

"I can explain everything later, man, but at this very moment I need to speak to my brother!"

Reginald stiffened. *That isn't... It couldn't be—*

For the second time that day, the door to his study burst open, and the person standing in the doorway was just as unexpected as its previous occupants.

This time, however, Reginald rose to his feet, swore loudly, marched over to the individual, punched him hard in the nose, and then, as the man staggered back and gripped his face, blood dripping on his white glove, hugged him.

"Peter, you idiot," came his muffled words into his brother's shoulder. "What in God's name do you think you're doing here?"

"Being punched by you, apparently," said Peter, their mother's blue eyes watering over the carefully dabbing nose. "Goodness, you have a mean right hook."

"And you have taken an awful risk coming here, you dolt," Reginald said, pulling away from his brother as the panic started to rise. "Who else saw you?"

"That butler of ours."

Well, that was no worry, the loyalty of their servants was beyond reproach. The fact that rumors about his brother had not leaked into Society gossip long before now was proof of that.

"And I saw Lady Romeril on the street and she asked—"

Reginald swore loudly.

"Look, you don't have to like her, but she is one of the doyennes of Society," protested his brother, dabbing at the small trickle of blood descending from one nostril. "You could hardly expect me to give her the cut direct."

It was a disaster.

Reginald had known it would be the moment his traitorous brother had walked into the room. The instant his brother returned, there would be disaster for the whole family, and he found he was still not prepared for it.

Lady Romeril, of all people…

"—mentioned something about a wedding of yours," his brother said lazily, walking around Reginald seemingly without a care in the world and picking up the bottle of brandy. "Oh, good, an excellent year. You don't mind, do you?"

Reginald blinked. This was all too much: the revelation that Jessica still cared for him, still loved him, and now this?

"'Mind'?" he echoed weakly.

"Excellent," his brother said happily.

It was only when Peter poured himself a large measure and gulped it down in one go with the phrase, "Far better than anything that you can actually find in France, would you believe it," that Reginald regained his focus.

"In France."

"You absolute fool," he said heavily. "What on earth are you doing here? You do know you'll be caught?"

Peter grinned as he threw himself down into Reginald's armchair. "Going to give me in?"

"You know full well that I have no choice in the matter. You're a traitor to the Crown, for God's sake!" Reginald could hardly understand why his brother was so calm.

There he sat, brandy in hand and boots—boots on his desk?

Peter saw the direction his brother was looking and slowly removed his boots from Reginald's desk. "Look—"

"And to think, I had almost had it all sorted," Reginald muttered, pulling his hand through his hair and dropping into the second chair in the study—a far less comfortable chair. "And here you swan about, without a care in the world—"

"Well, actually," began Peter.

"—as if it hasn't been a strain on all of us—"

"I have some news in that quarter," said his brother quietly.

Reginald was not listening. "Thankfully, our sister has no comprehension of what is going on, but I have had to make some hard decisions. It is no joke having a traitor for a brother, and—"

"Reg," said Peter firmly, "I am not a traitor."

Reginald snorted, pulled the bottle of brandy out of his brother's hands, and dispensed entirely without the thought of a glass, drinking it directly from the neck of the bottle.

"*Reginald!*"

"You don't know what I have been through," he said ominously, glaring at his younger brother through a heady haze of brandy. "You don't know what I have done, what I have tried to do to keep this family respectable."

For some reason, all the color drained from Peter's face. "What—What have you done?"

"Well… Well, it didn't work, if it comes to that," Reginald had to admit gruffly. "But—"

"If you would but listen to me for five minutes, you would know that you don't have to do anything," Peter said, far more patiently than Reginald could ever remember his sibling being. "I am not a traitor."

The scoff was loud, but Reginald made no apologies for it. "Oh, of course not!"

"No, really, I'm not." His brother shook his head, holding back a smirk all the while. "I am glad the subterfuge fooled even you, though I admit myself to being a tad offended. You would believe me capable of treachery that easily?"

Reginald opened his mouth, hesitated, tried to replay the words he had just heard, then closed them again.

It wasn't possible, was it? After all these weeks of trying to figure out the best way to keep the family safe, to maintain their reputation…surely, it wasn't possible that he had gotten the wrong end of the stick?

His brother grinned. "Voila!"

"Explain." Reginald took another swig of the brandy, swallowed a large gulp, and grimaced. "Now."

"It's all very simple, really," said his brother airily. "The government needed to discover an actual spy, and so they put about the word that I was the traitor. I holed up in France for a few weeks, spent my time eating a vast amount of cheese and getting to know one of the local ladies very—"

"*Peter!*"

"I'm just saying, it was not much of a hardship." Peter chuckled, crossing his legs and winking for good measure. "The real culprit was apprehended, having gotten too lazy, thinking that the heat was off him, and so here I am. Exoneration to be published the day after tomorrow, once the details are ironed out. Great service to Queen and Country, great thanks from government, small pension, etcetera, etcetera. You look surprised."

He felt perplexed.

Reginald could hardly understand what he was hearing. His… His brother was not a traitor. It had all a lie. A trick. A ruse.

"A ruse," he said weakly.

Peter nodded. "It was only going to last a few weeks, a few months at the most, and it was crucial that no one knew, so I'm afraid I wasn't permitted to tell you, old chap. But now I am back." He shrugged, as if it were all no great concern to him.

"You… You have no idea," said Reginald weakly, "the stress I have been under."

His brother cleared his throat. "I am sure it was a rum situation, but it's over now, and no harm done."

"*No harm done.*"

Reginald tried to smile, but he couldn't. His brother was not a traitor. He did not need to save the family name. He had no need to marry anyone, let alone convince Miss Jessica Chance that he was worthy of her.

So why was he filled with such…such disappointment?

In the silence, his brother's jovial expression was starting to fade, and as he spoke, it was with a concern that grew with every syllable. "Oh… Oh, dear Lord. You did not do anything rash, did you? While I was away, I mean, thinking that I was indeed a traitor to the Crown, you... You didn't do anything impulsive, did you?"

Without letting go of the brandy bottle, Reginald slowly lowered his head into his hands, and started to laugh.

Chapter Nineteen

October 8, 1840

T HERE WAS SOMETHING so miserable about rain.

"When is it going to stop?" asked Irene, apparently to herself, as she peered out of the drawing room window. "It's been like this all morning!"

Jessica nodded and hummed her agreement as she turned a page of her book. It was the very least that she could do in response and keep her sister happy, though it earned her a scowl from her sibling.

"You know how rain bores me," Irene said.

It took all Jessica's self-control not to nod and hum again. What was she supposed to say? *I'm sorry that the rain is dampening your mood. Why don't you try a little heartbreak instead to lighten your spirits?*

"Wilfred and I were planning on going for a walk across Green Park." Irene sighed, dropping into an armchair and plucking at the arm. "I was going to invite you so Mama wouldn't feel the need to send a chaperone along, though I know you'd rather not."

"Not in the rain, no," Jessica said vaguely as she turned a page.

"Well, obviously not in the rain!"

There is something about rain that makes tempers fray, Jessica thought darkly as she wondered if there were any way to make her sister less irritable. Something in the dampness in the air, perhaps. Something that made it impossible to fully understand another's point of view.

Not that it mattered. The only person whose point of view she wanted to understand was entirely incomprehensible to her.

A doorbell clanged and Jessica saw out of the corner of her eye that her sister immediately brightened.

"Maybe it's Wilfred, after all?" Irene said, her voice lively. "Perhaps he wants to go for a carriage ride."

"You know, I am here," Jessica said somberly, trying not to allow the pain in her voice to be too obvious. "You don't always have to wait around for that friend of yours to turn up before you—"

She cut herself off abruptly as the door to the drawing room opened and the stern looking Mrs. Kinley, daughter-in-law of their previous housekeeper, appeared, kneading her hands together at the front of her dress.

"Yes, Mrs. Kinley?" Jessica said eventually.

"It's a gentleman, Miss Chance," said the housekeeper uneasily.

"Send him in. The blighter is late," Irene said with a grin. "Honestly, Wilfred knows he doesn't have to go through this rigmarole."

"It is not His Grace to whom I am referring," said the woman, glancing at Jessica. "It is a young man who calls himself Baron Llyne."

Jessica's book slipped to the floor.

"No!" Irene gasped with what appeared far too dramatic a tone, then turned immediately to her sister. "You must see him!"

"No," Jessica repeated, though her meaning was quite different.

Reginald, here? Lord Llyne that is. What is he doing here? What was he thinking? Why did he—

"You have to see him, Jessica," her sister hissed, rising and crossing the room in mere seconds. "You simply must! He is clearly here to apologize!"

"We cannot know what he wants and most of all, I do not

care," Jessica lied, her pulse hammering and hands somehow clamming at the mere thought of Lord Llyne in this house.

This was her safe place. Not just her safe place against the world, a place where she never had to worry about what she said or how she looked, a vital component of a wallflower's existence—but it was a place where she had been that Reginald...that Lord Llyne had not.

There were no shared memories here. No pained reflections that may attack her as she stepped into the dining room. No pangs that would confront her as she quietly ate breakfast. No recollections could assault her as she lay in her bed, attempting to find sleep.

Reginald had not stepped foot here, and so it was safe from any suggestion that he may return.

She would not end that safety.

"Tell Lord Llyne that we are not at home," Jessica said in what she hoped was a clear voice.

"Jess!"

"Now, please, Mrs. Kinley," Jessica continued, not looking at her sister. "Thank you."

For a moment, she wondered whether the family housekeeper would question her order—Jessica was unaccustomed to giving them, in the main, and she knew the head servant's curiosity would be piqued. After all, the woman had cared for her father for decades.

But the old woman nodded, curtseying as she left the room. Jessica attempted not to listen to the woman's footsteps, tried to prevent her ears listening out for the muffled tones at the front door. The quiet close of the door was not the slam she would have given it, but then, she had not been the one to answer the door.

It was her sister's sigh that alerted her attention. "I cannot believe you have done that."

"Done what?" Jessica knew her voice was too defensive, knew that she was being ridiculous—but she could not help it.

Irene had gone back to sitting in the armchair by the window that was being heartily washed by the rain. "You don't even want to see him?"

She had. Weeks ago. She had resolved to forgive him—she *had* forgiven him. But he had seemed so unbothered. He had not come. Had not written.

Now, it was simply too late. For all she knew, he'd felt compelled to tell her he was sorry for what he had done, but he was moving on. He'd found some other match to save him.

"He was surely not here to beseech me to marry him, not after all this time," Jessica said decisively, her stomach twisting painfully as she spoke the words, "so there is absolutely no point in seeing him. And besides, I... I am sure I would not accept him if he did ask again. Not after he did not fight for me."

The words sounded certain as she spoke them, which was a relief, because she certainly did not feel certain. There was an edge to her voice because there was an edge to her soul.

She did not trust herself.

That was the truth, though Jessica was loath to admit it, even to herself.

The trouble was Reginald was that he was so...so captivating. So alluring. She could be convinced by him, she knew, in a way that no one else could. She could not risk seeing him—allowing him to talk to her could only make things worse.

Jessica picked up the book that had fallen to the floor. Her page was lost, but that hardly mattered. She had merely been turning the pages at regular intervals to give the impression she had been reading, after all.

"Well, the rain isn't going to let up all day, I don't think," Irene mused as she gazed out of the window. "There's hardly anyone about."

"I do not suppose there would be many people out and about in this weather," Jessica said, almost grateful for the neutral topic.

Is this what my life has descended to? Gratitude for conversations about weather?

"Except… What on earth is he doing?" Irene tilted her head.

Jessica remembered to turn a page. "Who?"

"There's a man out there, standing on the opposite side of the street."

It did not sound the most remarkable thing that had ever happened. Jessica turned another page, the words flickering in and out of her focus as she stared down at the page, unseeing.

"Yes, he's standing there under an umbrella, just…just staring. At this house."

"What house?" Jessica asked idly, turning another page.

Irene snorted. "Why, *this* house, obviously!"

And that was when Jessica froze. "This house?"

Book forgotten, she allowed it to fall to her seat on the sofa as she rose and moved across the room, taking care to do so as far from the window as she could possibly be. When Jessica reached her sister's armchair, she crouched behind it.

"What on earth are you doing, Jess?"

"Who is it?" Jessica hissed. "Is it him?"

"Who?" Her sister appeared genuinely perplexed.

Jessica's fingers tightened on the back of the armchair as she attempted to slow her breathing. *This is ridiculous.* It was surely a sheer coincidence that there was a man standing outside the house. The pavement was not owned by anyone. It was perfectly permissible for anyone to stand anywhere. If they wished to do so in the rain, well, so be it.

Still. A part of her knew, even before she lifted herself over the edge of the armchair to look. She knew who it would be.

Slowly, inch by inch, Jessica rose to look over the back of the armchair.

"What are you doing?" Irene whispered, seemingly drawn into Jessica's attempts at secrecy, even without noticing.

It was him.

Jessica could tell. Though the window itself was several feet away and the gentleman was standing on the other side of the road, even through the rain, she could tell it was him.

Reginald, Lord Llyne. He was standing outside her house and just…staring.

"It's *him*, isn't it?"

Jessica swallowed as her sister's quiet voice intruded in her thoughts. "Yes."

When she looked down, it was to see Irene biting her lip. "What are you going to do? I can make him go away, if…if you want."

If only she knew what she wanted, it might be easier to know what to do. If her parents were here and not out lunching with friends—though Jessica was not certain she could articulate precisely what it was that she wished them to assist with.

Her attention was dragged inexorably back to the dark figure holding a black umbrella under sheets of rain on the other side of the road.

Reginald. What does he want with me?

Jessica stood up quickly, her head spinning at the sudden elevation.

"Jessica?"

"He'll never leave me alone unless I speak to him," she said tightly. "One more conversation, then this can all be over with."

Irene frowned. "And do you *want* it to be over with?"

Firmly ignoring her sister's question and marching deter-minedly out of the room, Jessica strode down the hall and hoped that her courage would not fail her.

She had to do this. End this properly, once and for all.

"Miss Chance?" said Mrs. Kinley from the hallway. "Where are you going, unaccompanied? It's pouring out there, you'll be drenched—"

There was no time to talk, no time for a pelisse, not even time to find the errant family umbrella that seemed to have a mind of its own and wander about the place, only coming out from hiding when it was lovely and sunny. Jessica grabbed the door handle, wrenched the door open, and stepped outside.

She was drenched within a moment. The rain, which had

looked pretty and sparkling as it had slid down the panes from the drawing room, was torrential. It splattered her skirts, poured down her sleeves, and quickly pasted her curls to her forehead.

Jessica ignored it.

There were few carriages about and even fewer pedestrians in this weather, so she did not need to hesitate before she crossed the road. Holding her arms stiffly by her sides, she approached the man she had hoped never to see again and spoke coldly.

"Well?"

Reginald, Lord Llyne, looked at her with wide eyes. "You shouldn't be out here!"

"You were staring at my home. There was talk," Jessica said woodenly. Well, it was technically true. Irene had said something. "Well?"

"But you're going to get wet!" Reginald said, clearly alarmed.

Going to get was not quite the right way to phrase it. Based on the chilly trickles down her shoulder blades, Jessica would hazard that she was already wet through.

"I *am* wet," she said blandly, trying not to notice the rugged line of his jaw and his intensely kissable lips. It was so unfair. *Why does the man have to be so…so handsome?* "Please, say what you came to say, then go."

Reginald hesitated. His umbrella had prevented the worst of the rain, but his feet had to be soaked and the bottoms of his trousers were sodden.

"At least come closer so you can gain protection from my umbrella," he said quietly.

Jessica tried not to think about the temptation. "No, thank you," she said curtly. Even an inch closer to the man who made her want to throw herself into his arms would be too close. "What did you want to say?"

Until now, she had managed to avoid looking directly into the man's eyes, but as the silence elongated out between them, Jessica found that she could no longer resist.

She looked up, into Reginald's stormy eyes, and wished

things could have been different.

She wasn't sure quite how different. Just not...this. Not mis-understandings, and anger, and lies. Not desperation from him to be part of her family, in any way he could. Not realizing that she was considered low-hanging fruit, so desperate that she would accept any offer of marriage.

Perhaps if they had met across a ballroom, or seated next to each other at a dinner, things could have been different.

She had to trust that he would have loved her even in those circumstances. But a voice inside her mocked her, telling he never would have looked her way without that desperation to seek a suitable Chance wife. And that voice's whispers hurt.

Jessica swallowed, hardening her heart. They had not met under beautiful beginnings. Their circumstances had been this. He might have believed that she would grasp at any chance she could take to be married, but she wanted more than that.

Better than that.

"I... I had a whole speech prepared."

Jessica watched as Reginald swallowed, his throat bobbing and reminding her of illicit kisses. She knew precisely what that part of him tasted like—

She blinked. *Concentrate!*

"I had a whole speech prepared that was designed to make you forgive me," Reginald said, his grin nervous and lopsided. "I was going to convince you that...that I was the man that you should want. That I was the right sort of gentleman for you to marry. That you should marry me."

The rain continued to pour down, falling into Jessica's eyes, but she did not look away.

She braced herself. He had not come to tell her he was moving on with another. "Go on, then."

"No."

Jessica's lips parted in astonishment. He had come all this way, stood outside her home staring at her through the rain, made her come out in this downpour...and he still wasn't even going to fight for her?

"No," repeated Reginald, smiling ruefully as he lowered his umbrella, closing it up and leaning it against the house they were standing outside as the rain now beat down on him. "No, I won't. A speech designed to convince you to marry me isn't fair on you."

It was difficult not to gape. "I... I don't understand."

"I don't want to *convince* you to love me," he said simply, rain now dripping into his hair. "I don't want to use words to trick you into forgiving me. I could say any number of things that would manipulate you, Miss Jessica Chance, and I won't do that. I admire you, I respect you too much for that."

Jessica blinked, partly to rid her eyes from the rain and partly because she was struggling to comprehend just what this man was saying.

"You see, I have made so many mistakes already. I think it's about time I stopped making mistakes and started making the right decisions," Reginald said, with almost a laugh. "Jessica, I have made so many mistakes! Not telling you how this all came to be. Pretending to myself that I did not care for you, that all I sought was the security of a respected family's connection. Rushing into a marriage to fix a problem that did not even exist."

"'Did not exist'?" Jessica found herself taking a step forward through the sheet of falling rain, hardly able to hear the man standing before her. "You're speaking of your brother?"

"My brother—I thought he was a traitor to the Crown, but now it appears I was wrong about that," Reginald said heavily. "And I was wrong about you."

Jessica stiffened. *So he is only here to offend me!*

"I was wrong in thinking that I could get to know you and not fall desperately, head over heels in love with you." Reginald's gaze raked her face. "I was wrong in thinking that I could withhold my own feelings and make this a true marriage of convenience, not caring if my bride was hurt by my family's scandal. I was wrong thinking that I could live a day without you,

Jessica, because I-I can't. I can't do it. Not anymore. Not ever again."

Emotions churned within Jessica and she tried to blink away what could have been tears or could have been rain. She did not know.

"You hurt me," she said quietly.

"And that is something for which I will never be able to forgive myself," Reginald said hastily, stepping forward.

Jessica took an instinctive step back and she saw the pain flash across the man's eyes, heard the hitch in his breath.

"I…" She swallowed. "I knew from the start it was a marriage of convenience, but to read that list—"

"I should never have written that list," Reginald said hastily.

"But you did." Jessica looked up at him, searching his expression for she knew not what. Repentance? That was there in abundance. Was it enough? "To be compared, my whole life, to always know there were others in my own family more beautiful, more intellectual, more entertaining…"

Her voice trailed away as thunder rolled above them. The rain did not cease. Her gown was sticking to her now, the damp reaching all the way through her chemise to her skin.

When Jessica looked back at the man opposite her, it was to see that his woolen coat was just as wet, and his eyes were just as soft.

"I wanted to be someone's first choice," she said simply. "I thought, when you first arrived at Stanphrey Lacey, that I was. That you had chosen me because you wanted me."

"I did not know what a fool I was then," Reginald said delicately, and when he stepped forward this time, Jessica found she did not want to step back. "I would be even more of a fool if I were to lose you for a second time."

"You lost me because of your own actions," Jessica reminded him, her lungs shortening as his intoxicating presence took another step toward her.

Reginald pushed a damp curl of hair away from her face and

her skin burned where his fingertips brushed it. "I know. What I want to know is, can I win you back because of my own actions?"

And then she was kissing him. Jessica knew she would not be able to stand it, stand him for much longer, and it was a relief to step into his embrace and lift her lips to be worshipped.

Reginald evidently did not need any further convincing. He captured her lips with a low groan of need that crushed her mouth, but Jessica accepted it, accepted the fervor and the need, his hands swiftly cupping her face as though he had been hungering for her for days.

The pleasure that rippled through her teased to a higher peak as his tongue swept across her lips and parted them, delving deeper as one of Reginald's hands left her face but swiftly grabbed her waist, pulling her close. The rain poured down and Jessica could hardly tell anymore where she stopped and where Reginald began.

Then the kiss was over.

The kiss was, but the embrace was not. Jessica pulled back just enough to look into Reginald's eyes and prepared herself to say what she must.

"No more secrets," she said sternly.

"Never," Reginald said, leaning forward for another kiss.

Jessica held back, trying not to smile. "No more rankings."

"Never again," he murmured, trying with a laugh to capture her lips. "Unless it is to say you stand above all others. Far above. Kiss me, Jessica."

"Only when you agree to marry me."

The words had been those she had dreamed of these last few days, words she had hoped she would one day say, but she could hardly believe that in this downpour, they had fallen from her lips.

Reginald stared. "You—You want to marry me?"

"You are not perfect," Jessica said quietly, "but—"

"Tad of an understatement."

"But neither am I. I don't want perfection, Reginald, that was never what I hoped for." Jessica grabbed his lapels to pull him closer. *Oh, this man.* "But I want honesty. I want truth, and I want devotion, and I want… I want *you.*"

It cost her a great deal to say such things, laying her heart bare and making it possible for the man to injure her.

But as she looked up at Reginald's open expression, she knew he would not. Not on purpose, at any rate—and was that not what trust was? Knowing that a person's intentions were good and even if—even *when* they failed to be the best they could possibly be, to love them, anyway?

Reginald lowered his forehead to hers and their breath mingled, both of his hands now around her waist as a passerby tutted. "Jessica, I do not deserve you."

"No, perhaps not," she murmured, joy singing so sweetly in her that she was rather surprised that he couldn't hear it. "But I want you. We can learn together, grow together. I just want to be together."

"Always," said the man she loved, kissing her forehead before capturing her mouth once again to lavish another kiss as the rain poured down. "Always."

Chapter Twenty

October 13, 1840

T O REGINALD'S GREAT delight, Jessica's mouth had fallen open. "When you said 'hall,' I thought—"

"Oh, you didn't expect this?" he said with a grin, helping her descend from the carriage.

It was not exactly cruel of him—*cruel* would have been to lie, and he had not lied. He would never lie again to his beautiful woman, even if it meant telling the truth beyond what perhaps other couples would expect.

But he had never lied about this.

"Llyne 'Hall,' you called it," Jessica said, whirling around with a look of accusation in her eyes. "Llyne *Hall!*"

"And that's the name of my home," Reginald said innocently, though he couldn't completely remove the grin from his face. "You don't like it?"

"'Like it'?" repeated Jessica in a sort of daze as she turned back to the house.

Reginald looked over her shoulder at the home where he had, eventually, been raised. It was splendid, even he had to admit. The high windows let in a great deal of light, which was perfect because the thick, stone walls rather prevented it. The terrace along the front was designed to catch the sun, as was the solar at the top of one of the towers. There were three.

"The fourth tower was destroyed in the Civil Wars," Reginald said conversationally, stepping away from the carriage that he had asked to stop at the top of the drive. "One of my ancestors considered rebuilding it, but there were other things to worry about."

Jessica was still staring, her mouth open. "It… It's a castle."

"Oh, I suppose it is, by the general and vague definition of a castle," Reginald said casually. "Ouch!"

His future wife glared, though there was a twitch to her mouth that told him she wasn't exactly angry. "Reginald, it has a moat!"

"Yes, it does," he said with a grin. "Though once you have seen one moat, they all look—now *that* hurt!"

"And you deserved it," Jessica shot back with pink cheeks and wide eyes as she looked back at their future home. "I said, *no secrets*—Reginald, you live in a castle!"

It *was* a castle, and it had a moat. Reginald had relished swimming in there as a boy, learning to row, fishing when he'd been permitted to. Aside from a slightly dangerous run in with a pike that had grown to a stupendous length, he had always had a wonderful time there. It was nice to be back and to be showing it to someone who would, he was sure, learn to love it much like he did.

"It's been in the family for generations. I think it was Empress Matilda who gave a Blakley the permission to build here, and the Llyne title," he said bracingly. "The moat was added on early, I have been told, but precisely where the trebuchet was left—"

"*Reginald!*"

"Fine, fine, we didn't have a trebuchet. Probably." Reginald grinned. "You'd be astonished what we've found in the attics, though. And there are cannons along the ramparts."

"'Cannons'—'ramparts'?" Jessica stared in almost disbelief. "You're pulling my leg."

"Wouldn't dare," he said cheerfully. Seeing her here, it awakened something in him. Something he had not expected. "And it'll be ours, all ours, Jessica."

Theirs. A place where they could be themselves, far away from the crowds and expectations of Society. Here, they could just be, wandering through the fields, the gardens, down to the sea. Bathing in the moat. Picnics under the wide sycamores.

Reginald's pulse jolted. It was everything he had not known he had wanted.

"I thought you'd want to see it from here, at the end of the drive, which is why I sent the carriage ahead with your mother and our things. Most accommodating of her, to allow us these few moments together," he said quietly. Jessica giggled. The viscountess had seemed quite aware of what her daughter had been up to since the previous night, but she'd feigned the need to get inside quickly and encouraged the young ones to take their walk without her. "We can walk to it from here. It's not half a mile."

The woman he loved turned to him with an astonished expression, but delight dancing in her eyes. "And I am really going to live here? With you?"

The eagerness in her tone shot fire through Reginald. Her delight in his company, her eagerness to be with him... There was nothing more intoxicating. Nothing more warming.

Well. Except perhaps last night, when she had crept into his room in the inn, wearing nothing but a chemise and a hungry expression.

That had been particularly warming.

"I did not think that you would be this surprised," Reginald said conversationally as they started to walk down the gravel drive lined with reddening oaks. "I mean, I am a baron. I am *Lord Llyne*."

"Yes, but there are plenty of gentlemen with titles with absolutely no money and no house to speak of," Jessica pointed out, her cheeks becoming as red as the leaves cascading down around them in the gentle breeze.

He stared, and when she would not meet his eyes he barked a laugh. "You thought I was penniless!"

"I thought you had little in the way of funds," she retorted, her cheeks still pink, though she did at least meet his eye. Her smile was a little rueful. "Well, you marched into Stanphrey Lacey and asked for my hand without knowing a thing about me!"

"That is true."

"And my dowry is not too poor, for all that I am the daughter of a viscount and not a duke," Jessica continued with a giggle. "It was the only thing I could think of at first that would have tempted you to ask a stranger to be your bride. I may not have Lilianna's deep pockets, but I am a suitable match for anyone."

"Particularly a rogue baron like myself," Reginald teased.

Just for a moment, he thought he had gone too far. Jessica's smile faltered and she did not laugh with him, and he felt pain— the worst pain as he worried that he had hurt her.

Nothing would ever hurt him like the pain of losing Jessica. Thinking that she'd been out of his life… The only thing close, he was certain, would have been a bullet wound that refused to heal.

Going back to that… No. He would not do it.

Jessica slipped her hand into the crook of his arm. "Precisely. A rogue baron like yourself."

It was a challenge to restrain his chest so that she did not immediately realize he had been holding his breath, but Reginald managed it.

He loved her. This woman, this complex woman, and though he knew she had forgiven him for the wretched way they had first found each other, Reginald also knew there was a bruise against her soul. He would not be the one to press against it.

He would not hurt his Jessica.

"I suppose," she said quietly as they crossed the drawbridge and she peered down into the moat, "you have swum in that?"

"Many times. Peter was always a stronger swimmer than I was, but I can hold my breath for longer," Reginald said, the tension around his ribcage slowly dissipating. "My sister—"

"Don't tell me," Jessica teased, "she was better than both of you."

"How on earth did you know?" Reginald stared, genuinely

astonished.

His soon-to-be bride giggled. "Just a feeling."

As they stepped up to the great front door, the oak creaked open and a face appeared.

"Ah, my lord, how pleasant to see you again," said Reginald's butler, a short and stiff-backed man, with a deep bow. "Mrs. Tapper is escorting the viscountess to her rooms for her stay. And this must be the future Lady Llyne."

Reginald was not surprised to see Jessica flush, though it did make him smile. Would there ever come a time when she would not color to hear her new title? A part of him rather hoped that it would never come. That she would always glow at the sound of his name attached to hers.

"Jessica, this is Evans. Evans, Miss Jessica Chance. So long as Mrs. Tapper is engaged, I'll be giving the future Lady Llyne the full tour," Reginald said, his pulse skipping a beat as he watched roses appear in the cheeks of his beloved. "Any chance you could see that Mrs. Tapper arranges for tea and scones and cakes and the like in the orangery for about… Oh, I don't know, an hour's time? You may let the viscountess know."

"Of course, my lord." Evans bowed as Jessica stared in astonishment.

Only when the servant had disappeared behind a door did she hiss, "'Orangery'? I did not know medieval castles had orangeries."

"They don't," Reginald said blithely, taking her hand in his and relishing the sense of her fingers against his own. "At least, they didn't. This one does. Shall we start in the drawing room?"

After being the houseguest of the Chance family at Stanphrey Lacey for so long, it was pleasant to be able to show Jessica that, though Stanphrey Lacey was grander, she was not exactly marrying into poverty. There was the drawing room, after all, the large fireplace headed with a tapestry that had been in the family for six generations.

Then there was the dining room, with the suit of armor in the corner standing guard over his drinks cabinet, and the silver, which had been in the family seven generations.

Then there was the long gallery, which featured the seven generations themselves.

"My father and his fathers and all their fathers," quipped Reginald as they stepped along it, the rushes beneath their feet giving a potent yet delightful scent to the air. "I come and walk here sometimes with my sister—I have no idea where she is, though. She must be somewhere about."

"And your brother?"

He hesitated, and though it was only for a heartbeat, it was enough.

"I should not have asked. Father showed me the story in the paper, but I know it's a sensitive topic for you."

"No, I knew we'd have to talk about it sooner or later," said Reginald heavily, though he squeezed Jessica's fingers to show her that there was no topic barred, not for them. "He is a scoundrel, though perhaps not in the direction I had thought."

There had been… Well, not precisely an argument. An argument required someone to be in the wrong, and Reginald was gentlemanly enough to admit that there had technically been no one in the wrong in this situation.

It had not ended half badly, with him marching off the next morning to find his future wife and remedy the disaster he had created with his rash actions, but that was also not Peter's fault. Mostly.

"You said that you would explain what had led to all of this— your brother a hero, but you were so sure he was a traitor—in time," Jessica said quietly, her voice not exactly nervous, but she was clearly uncertain. "Is this the right time?"

Reginald turned to her and marveled that he had ever managed to find a woman who would be so patient with him.

He was not an aggravating man, on the whole. At least, he did not think he was.

But he made mistakes, and when he made them he was not

very good at recognizing that. All too often, he would refuse to accept that he could have made a mistake at all, and only when he was neck-deep in trouble did he finally admit that perhaps his chosen direction was not the best.

Having done so in such an obvious way when it came to Peter, and Jessica, and the whole Chance family…

Well. It had rather done a number on his ego, which his brother would undoubtedly say was not a bad thing.

But having Jessica here, here, in his family's long gallery, knowing she loved him and forgave him and loved that he wanted to right his mistakes—that was more than enough motivation to do better. To be better.

Reginald sighed. "It all started a year ago, when my brother started disappearing off. I knew he was probably doing something for the government. Our father had done something similar. It… It was an awkward time. I had inherited the barony. My brother felt, for a time, as though he should have done so."

That was the sanitized way of expressing it, anyway.

Jessica nodded as they started to walk slowly down the long gallery. "Legitimacy is a complicated business, but at least my father was not the eldest of his brothers. That would have created—complications, I suppose."

"*Complications* is the right word for it. But we managed to get along well—we like each other, and that helps," said Reginald with a laugh.

"My sisters are much of the same mind."

"And your brother?"

"You know," Jessica said seriously, "sometimes I forget I have a brother. That's terrible, isn't it? But he was sent away to school while we were kept home, and he really does keep to himself. I suppose it would take a great woman to make him her hero. But you were telling me about your brother. The scandal."

"The scandal that wasn't," Reginald said darkly as they stepped out of the long gallery and into a corridor that led to a wide, sweeping staircase. "To cut a very long story short, I received a letter saying that he had been accused, with plenty of evidence, of treason."

Just saying the word aloud raised bile to his mouth. Reginald swallowed it down—*it was not true, it had not happened*—but the pain of that moment, the dread that something so truly awful had happened to his family…it would take a long time to forget.

"I could not tell anyone, I could confide in no one—Society would censure us and my sister did not deserve to bear such a burden," Reginald continued, his lungs still tight with the memory. "I knew that I had to do something, and the only thing I could think of was—"

"Marrying me."

When he glanced at her, he saw with relief that Jessica was grinning. "Something like that," he said wryly. "I needed any Chance I could take to become my wife, then I would be free—free from the censure of Society. At least, that is what I thought. It all seems like a dream now."

Like a fever dream, Reginald thought privately as they ascended the staircase and meandered along the corridor. *Like a sickness got hold of me.*

What on earth had he been thinking?

"And I cannot apologize enough for—"

"I'm going to stop you right there," Jessica said sternly, halting in her steps.

Reginald blinked. "You are?"

"You have already apologized for that list, which is what I presume you were going to apologize for," his future wife said sternly. "You have apologized, and I have forgiven you. Why do you apologize again? Is my forgiveness insufficient?"

It was impossible not to wince. "It's not that."

"Then what is it?" Jessica looked up at him with brilliantly clear eyes, her focus on him absolute. "Because I-I love you, Reginald. I love you. Forgiveness only has to happen once. You don't—You don't have to earn my forgiveness every new day."

When she phrased it like that…

Reginald had not even noticed that he had slipped into that way of thinking, but that was precisely what had happened.

How, his mind appeared to be asking him on a daily basis, *could she have forgiven me?*

And so he woke up day after day with this knot of tension in him, unsure precisely how he had managed to trick this wonderful woman into accepting him, and he felt obliged to apologize again and again and—

Jessica kissed him, briefly but passionately, then flushed as she continued to walk along the corridor. "There. Forgiven, once and for all. Now, you are certain that your brother has been pardoned, or let off, or whatever it is? Papa showed me the article in the paper, but the details. I found, were quite vague."

Reginald blinked, slightly dazed by the fiery passion they had shared, then caught up with her. "Oh, yes, official writing and a seal and even a signature from the queen."

"From *Victoria*?"

"The very one," he said with a grin. "And that means I can stop worrying about my brother and start worrying about something completely different."

Jessica raised an eyebrow. "Oh?"

"Just how much I am going to love you and take care of you," Reginald said, fire spreading through his limbs, a flame he never wanted to put out. "Like how I can bring sunshine into every day of your life. Like how I need you to know just how precious you are."

Somehow—Reginald was not quite sure how—he had managed to pin the woman he adored to the wall.

A recurring issue, being around this woman.

Jessica was smiling. "I thought I was about to receive the full tour."

Reginald groaned, lowering his head to her neck and pressing a hot kiss under her ear. "I did promise that."

"And what would a full tour be like without a trip to your...bedchamber?"

Jolting upright and hoping to goodness that she couldn't see just how delighted that suggestion had made certain parts of him, he tried to say calmly and oh-so-suavely, *"Oh, my darling, I think there is plenty of time for that later."*

Instead, he garbled, "Wh—now?"

Jessica grinned, her eyes alight with both mischief and desire—a heady combination—and took his hand. "Is it down here?"

"Any bedchamber will do," Reginald growled, throwing open a guest bedchamber door and pulling her through it. "Oh, Jessica—"

"No words," she said with a wicked look, shutting the door and pushing him against it with such force that Reginald could have melted inside.

Dear God, this woman—she knew what she wanted, and it was him. She was wonderful.

Still… "'No words'?" Reginald rumbled, tugging at her gown and relishing the skin that it revealed.

"Just show me," Jessica whispered. "Show me how much you love me."

Reginald did not need any further encouragement. Just keeping his hands away from Jessica had been a constant torment in the carriage, and though they had engaged in slow, muffled amorous congress in the inn last night, just being in her presence was enough to arouse him.

There would be time for slow. There would be time for languid, and soft, and delicate. There would be time for reverential and worshipful.

This was not that time.

Growling under his breath, Reginald pushed himself away from the door and caught at Jessica's hand before she tipped backward, pulling her to the bed, which was not made.

It did not need to be.

Ardor roaring through his veins, Reginald pushed Jessica onto the bed and she immediately reached up for him, needing his touch. Who was he to deny her?

"Oh, Reginald," she moaned as he quickly rid himself of his trousers, allowing them to fall around his ankles as he found the hem of her skirts.

His manhood lengthened, thickening with every inch of her legs that he revealed. Christ, it was almost impossible to keep his mind as he swelled at the sight of her.

She was beautiful. Far more beautiful than he deserved, far more beautiful than he could have dreamed. Each time that Reginald uncovered her, he was surprised at how his imagination could not compete with the reality of Jessica's attractive body, her welcoming curves, her beckoning softness.

When Reginald had covered her body with his own, strength meeting softness, she whimpered and shifted underneath him— but Jessica was not attempting to escape him, only position her secret place closer to his manhood.

The friction caused his hardness to twitch and Reginald distracted himself momentarily by kissing her, his mouth eagerly brushing kisses across Jessica's lips, down her neck, to her heaving breasts, which were so close to escaping their stays, but he could not wait for that.

He could not wait for anything. The aching need between his legs would no longer brook any delay, and Reginald grinned wickedly as he slid his length into her soft folds.

Jessica moaned. "More—more, I need more—"

Stopping her mouth with another kiss, just in case a servant was meandering down the corridor, Reginald tilted her hips and groaned as he sank deeper into her wet and quivering center.

Was there anything like this? Could anything in the world ever compare?

Jessica fixed her eyes upon him and spoke directly, the directness something she only revealed with him. The knowledge that it was theirs, that only he saw this side of her, almost made Reginald explode. "Take me, Reginald. Now."

Obedience was its own reward, but Reginald shuddered with heaving pleasure as he almost completely withdrew himself then plunged himself deeper still into the woman he loved, triggering a shaking bliss that overtook his body, just for a moment.

The moments became more frequent, his gentle plunging becoming rapid pounding as Jessica's moans heightened and the sensations threatened to overwhelm Reginald's sense.

So close—so close, but he had to make sure first that she—

"Oh, yes—"

Swallowing her screams of ecstasy, Reginald concentrated, head spinning, bliss almost overwhelming, as he thrust her further and further into ecstasy. Only when Jessica's limbs ceased to shake and she fell back, eyes wide and smile languid, did Reginald permit himself to lose control.

"Jessica," he groaned as his own climax came, claiming him just as surely as this woman had.

Reginald managed to withdraw before collapsing next to Jessica on the unmade bed.

Their breathing was the only sound, and it was harsh, ragged, proof of the suddenness of their coupling.

Reginald tried to blow out slowly, regain his equilibrium. *Dear God.* He was going to spend the rest of his life trying to keep up with this woman.

Jessica sat up, leaning over him with a wide grin and pink cheeks. "Right, then. Did you say that your housekeeper will have tea and cake waiting for us?"

Epilogue

November 1, 1840

TAKING A LONG, deep breath, Jessica carefully placed the heavy, gold earbobs into her lobes and sighed.

Well, this is it. The day that every wallflower dreamed of, and dreaded, in equal measure.

"You look lovely," came her sister's voice from behind her.

Jessica smiled at her reflection in the looking glass. There sat a woman with perhaps not the features that fashion would consider the most beautiful. There was too much of her father in her nose, and her mouth didn't quite fit her face.

And yet it was on days like this that she could look her reflection in the eye and know precisely how Reginald would see her.

He would see her—and know she was beautiful.

"You don't think the dress is too much?" Jessica asked, tugging at the lace around the cuffs of her sleeves.

"If anything, it's not enough," said Irene with a snort. She was lying on Jessica's bed and playing with a pearl bracelet around her wrist. "I told you, you could always add lace to—"

"No more lace," Jessica said confidently. It had been more than her life was worth to prevent their mother from adding lace to the hem of her many skirts.

Irene's delight was visible, even from her reflection. "Is it possible to have too much lace on your wedding day?"

Jessica's stomach twisted, but it was a flip of happiness rather than one of fear.

Her wedding day.

She had thought it would never happen. Then she had been surprised by a proposal from a man she had never met, and who seemed entirely untrustworthy. Then she had discovered he was untrustworthy, and yet she had learned to trust him. Now she was going to begin the day as Miss Chance, and end the day as Lady Llyne.

She had thought she would embrace any chance she could take to be a bride. Then she had thought that the last thing in the world that could make her happy was being a wife.

Now all she wanted to do was be with Reginald again.

The door burst open and though Jessica expected to see their mother step in, it was the Duke of Aynor who grinned.

"And here's the blushing bride—yes, there it is. Don't you think it's a remarkable trait, Reeny, that she can blush on command?"

"It's not that impressive." Irene snorted, getting up from the bed and shoving her friend's shoulder. "Besides, you fool, men ought not to barge into a woman's dressing area, even if he's like a brother to the family. As Mama loves to remind me, you are not *actually* my brother. And Jessica needs to be alone."

Jessica threw a grateful look at her sister. Perhaps she did know her well, after all.

The duke blinked. "How on earth can you tell?"

"If Jessica has been in company for more than an hour, she needs to be alone," Irene said darkly, though she grinned at her older sister as she started to push her friend toward the door. "We'll be downstairs, Jess. You come down when you're ready."

When she was ready.

Jessica's smile faded as the door shut behind the two best friends and their bickering crept around the frame. When she was ready?

It was difficult to imagine a time when she would be ready. Oh, she wanted to marry Reginald. In a way, she could hardly believe that they had waited this long. But in a very real sense, today was going to present a certain number of challenges to a wallflower.

All that staring, for one thing.

Jessica gave her reflection just one more glance. She looked back at herself: bright eyed, her hair elegantly pinned, and her hands clasped before her.

Hands that would, in a few hours, have an additional ring adorning them.

When Jessica descended the staircase, it was to find her two youngest sisters in high dudgeon, her brother missing, and Irene snorting with laughter at something the duke said.

"There you are!" Their mother hurried toward them with a brilliant smile. "I was worried I'd lost you!"

"No, it's Michael who's gone walkabout," muttered Jessica's father, pulling on his gloves. "You put him down for five minutes—"

"He's not a baby anymore, Frederick," fussed his wife as she brushed off what could only be imaginary dust from Jessica's shoulder. "None of them are."

Much to Jessica's surprise, her mother's eyes filled with tears.

"Oh blast—come on, Edie, pull yourself together," muttered her father, dashing toward the pair of them and thrusting a handkerchief under her nose. "She's only getting married."

"She won't be a Chance anymore!" The Viscountess Pernrith sniffed.

Jessica's eyes itched at the corners as she did her best to keep sudden tears from falling. Taking her mother's hands in hers, handkerchief and all, she squeezed.

"I will always be a Chance," she said fiercely in an undertone as her mother gave a bubbly laugh. "Always. But I have to take this opportunity to be happy. You do know that, don't you?"

Her mother nodded, eyes watering, and pulled her eldest daughter toward her in a crushing hug.

"Put the bride down and don't drip on her," came a teasing laugh from the other side of the room.

"Michael!"

"Oh, good, you're here," muttered Jessica's father, wiping his brow with another handkerchief and looking unexpectedly harassed. "Right—everyone, in the carriages!"

It had been decided that attempting to fit all eight of them into two carriages, considering this was a bridal party, was too much. Three carriages therefore waited outside Pernrith House, and Jessica could hardly believe that they were here for her.

For her, and Reginald.

Her aching need to see him was growing with every passing moment. As the carriage rattled along the streets, snow threatening to fall, Jessica pressed her hands together and reminded herself that it would not be long.

Just a short walk and a few sentences. Just a short walk before hundreds, and a few sentences that would bind her together with the man she loved.

When the carriages pulled up outside the church, Jessica could not help her legs from shaking. What did she think she was doing, attempting to get married? This was ridiculous; she couldn't have all those people looking at her. Looking—at her!

"Jessica?" It was Irene's voice, and she seemed concerned.

Jessica looked up, lips parted, unable to say anything, unable to do anything, trapped in a panic of—

"Everyone, inside," Irene said smartly, pushing her now-sobbing mother into the church, having to pull her handkerchief from her reticule and offering it to the viscountess. "Come on, Mama, you can cry with Uncle George. See? He's already onto his second handkerchief."

The panic was still swirling and Jessica could do nothing but reach out for the wall, but it was too far and she was sure to fall.

A strong hand grasped hers. When she looked up, it was to gaze into the eyes of—

"Reginald."

The man she loved gave her an earnest smile. "I had a feeling you might be a tad overcome."

"Llyne! This is most irregular," muttered her father in a low tone. "It's not customary to—"

"I don't care," said Reginald quietly, still staring into Jessica's eyes and holding her hand. "She needed me. And so I'm here."

And that was when she knew, beyond a shadow of a doubt, that she was doing the right thing. How could she do anything else when this man, this wonderful man, was standing by her side?

She grinned, the panic subsiding. "You."

"Me," Reginald said quietly. "Us."

If her father had not been there, she would have undoubtedly thrown herself into his arms. Goodness, she loved Reginald Blakley, Baron Llyne, more than anything in the world. More than being stared at, more than discomfort, more than half-truths that took a while to emerge.

More than anything.

"Now," Reginald said quietly, his eyes burning with clear affection, "I am going to give you to your father for the last time. I hope that in a few minutes, he'll give you back to me."

Jessica half-expected her father to snort at the ridiculously romantic statement, but—

"Oh, not you as well," she said with a smile as her father blinked away tears. "And Mama has my spare handkerchief. Where has yours gotten to?" Her father held up the sodden material.

"Never fear, my lord," said Reginald jovially, offering one that had appeared from his pocket. "I brought several. I'll see you at the altar, Jessica."

"*At the altar.*"

All of a sudden, that moment could not come soon enough. Jessica longed to be back with him as Reginald slipped into the church and her father gave a hearty sniff. Back to the man she loved.

Not that she didn't love this one, too.

"Come on, Papa," Jessica said softly, slipping her hand into the crook of her father's arm. "Let's get me married."

The wedding service itself was a blur. That was mostly because of the numerous faces, Jessica was certain, all staring as her father led her down the aisle.

She said vows. She was almost certain of that, but she was more certain that Reginald had said them. His gaze had never left her face as he'd promised to love her, to care for her in sickness and in health, through all the troubles that life would inevitably throw at them.

Jessica knew that whatever they were, she could overcome them all—as long as Reginald was with her.

Precisely how they had managed to leave the church and return to Pernrith House for the wedding luncheon, she was not sure. There had been a carriage, and a great amount of passionate kissing, which had almost led to a climax if they'd had just a few more minutes.

"Damn," Reginald breathed, slumping against the carriage seat.

Jessica was already slumped against it, her pulse roaring, her body tingling as he removed his hand from her skirts. "Damn, indeed."

She caught his eye, and they collapsed into laughter as the carriage drew to a halt and the door was opened.

"Lord Llyne, Lady Llyne," said the footman formally, bowing as he extended the steps.

Jessica's lungs tightened. Jessica Blakley. *Lady Llyne.* It was the first time she had heard herself addressed in such a way. The buzz that tingled between her shoulder blades was most enjoyable...though that might have had something to do with what Reginald had been doing with his fingers moments ago, in fairness.

The house was almost empty.

"We thought, the church ceremony was for everyone else," Reginald explained as Jessica stared in wonder as they entered the drawing room. "This is for us."

He had thought of everything. Her family was there, all the

Chances, which in truth was more than enough of a crowd. There was the Duke of Aynor, and a few of the wallflowers Jessica had spent many a ball standing beside. A lady who looked remarkably like Reginald was chatting away to her mother—that was Felicity, Reginald's sister, and she was standing with their brother, Peter, who looked like Reginald but not nearly so handsome. There was the vicar, his cheeks pink as Michael pressed another glass of wine into his hands. And…that was it.

"A small party," Reginald said quietly, as though able to read her thoughts. "Just the people who matter."

Jessica was about to attempt to express just how much it meant to her, that he had considered this for her, but she was interrupted by her sister before she could utter a single syllable.

"Well, who would have thought it!" Irene said with a laugh, pressing a kiss on her cheek. "I am delighted for you, my darling."

"And so am I," said the duke, warmly shaking Reginald's hand. "It's hard to believe, isn't it! A Pernrith Chance, getting married!"

"It is certainly not something that I think will happen again soon," said Jessica's sister with a grin.

For some reason, her friend's face fell. "You—You don't?"

"Well, Teddy and Gwen aren't out, not properly, and Michael is too much a rakehell to be tied down," Irene said with a shrug.

Jessica glanced at Reginald, then back at the duke. Something odd was happening here.

"And… Well, and what about you?" asked her sister's friend, his voice somehow strange.

Irene snorted. "You don't see me surrounded by admirers, do you? After all, I spend too much time with you!"

"And for that, I must thank you both," Reginald said smartly, giving her sister a look that Jessica could not interpret. "Thank you. Both of you. Your Grace."

"You owe me one," said the duke with a slap on his shoulder. "And please, I hate being called 'Your Grace.' By friends, anyway.

Aynor will do."

Jessica stared. *"Friends"? "Owed him one"? One what?*

"Yes, I expect jewels of my own as recompense, now we know you have a fortune." Irene laughed. "Come on, Wilfred. I think the punch is about to be served."

"You hate punch!"

"And I have a duty to attempt to like it. Almost every Society affair has it."

The two friends bickered quite happily as they wandered away, but Jessica could not help but feel that she had missed something quite important. Two somethings, maybe.

"Reginald," she began slowly.

"Don't ask me and I won't have to lie," her husband said quickly.

Jessica could not help but laugh at that. "You don't even know what I was going to say!"

"You were going to ask me why I thanked your sister and her best friend," he said promptly, smiling in that way that made her want to take all her clothes off.

She opened her mouth, hesitated, then said, "Well. Yes."

Reginald pressed a kiss to her forehead. "See, I know you."

"I should think so," Jessica retorted, warmth spreading throughout her body as Reginald took her hand and intertwined his fingers with hers. "I am your wife, after all."

Your wife.

It was a wonderful thing. Too wonderful. Sometimes, she wondered how she could have been this fortunate.

"So, what do we do now?" Jessica asked, girding her loins for an afternoon of socializing and small talk.

Reginald's look was potent.

"Other than that!"

"I only want to do that," he said with a grin that faded into a look that was far more serious. "That, and love you, and look after you, and be by your side for the rest of your life. Or as long as you'll have me."

Affection mingled with desire rolled through Jessica as she stepped closer to her husband and lifted her mouth for a kiss, despite all the others in the drawing room who would see them.

"Good," she said quietly. "Let's start with forever."

A Short Letter From the Author

Hello! Thank you so much for reading *Any Chance You Can Take*, the ninth novel in my The Chances series. I truly hoped you enjoyed it and fell in love with Jessica and Reginald just as much as I did.

If you've read the first eight books of this series (which I strongly recommend!), then you'll have seen the four uncles fall in love, and four of the cousins. I had always wanted to write a series of brothers, but I could never 'meet' the characters who were quite right. After waiting years to meet them myself, I have had a lot of fun writing the four Chance brothers—and now we're diving into their children. Make sure you go back and read them!

If you're desperate to read the happily ever afters of Jessica's siblings, then you'll want to look out for Book 10 *Chance Would Be a Fine Thing* (Irene's story), Book 14 *A Chance of a Lifetime* (Michael's story), Book 15 *In With a Chance* (Gwendoline's story), and Book 20 *Leave it All to Chance* (Theodora's story). As you can tell, our next Chance adventure is going to stay with this branch of the Chance family, and you'll meet Irene's happily ever after...

Being an author can be a lonely business, but knowing that there are readers from all over the world who are going to adore my stories makes it all worthwhile. Thank you for support, and I hope you love reading more of my books!

Happy reading,
Emily

About Emily E K Murdoch

If you love falling in love, then you've come to the right place.

I am a historian and writer and have a varied career to date: from examining medieval manuscripts to designing museum exhibitions, to working as a researcher for the BBC to working for the National Trust.

My books range from England 1050 to Texas 1848, and I can't wait for you to fall in love with my heroes and heroines!

Follow me on twitter and instagram @emilyekmurdoch, find me on facebook at facebook.com/theemilyekmurdoch, and read my blog at www.emilyekmurdoch.com.